ON THE HUNT

ON THE HUNT

V.J. FITZ-HOWARD

Published by Bloodwilde Press

Published in the United States of America

ISBN (Paperback): 978-1-7342234-1-5
ISBN (Hardcover): 978-1-955039-02-4
ISBN (E-Book): 978-0-9974657-9-2

During the fifteen hours I was in the air, I lay in the silence, eyes wide open, hands folded across my chest, against which was pressed my World War II-era munitions box, as though its contents was a live human heart I was tasked with delivering to a surgeon for transplant—which, in a way, I reckon, it was.

I was no crier, but I wept as I had never wept on the flight back to the States as I thought about the fallen comrades beside me in the cargo compartment of the C-5 military transport plane—especially Command Sergeant Major Moellering, who was in the coffin next to mine. He had been hit in the leg when we got Mehdi Hashmi. In the convoy on the way back from Karz, the doctors said he'd be fine. And he was—for a few days. But a week later, after they sent him to the Uzbin Valley, nobody knew—least of all Command Sergeant Major Moellering—that his blood was infected. It could have been me—and probably *should have been me* in his place. It was a numbers game, war was. Plain and simple. When a soldier's tour was done, he couldn't believe his luck that he had got out in one piece. When he signed up for a second tour, and come out alive a second time, he felt tough as nails. But when he went back and touched the hot stove a third time, that's when the edgies started. He's been too lucky for too long, he rightly reckoned. He knew there was a bullet out there with his name on it. He wouldn't dare show his buddies fear—*ever*—but it was there alright. And by the fourth tour, he turned into a walking bag of jangled glass.

I thought about all my tours—and all the men who shot back at me. And the men who had my back. I hoped they knew somewhere in their hearts that I did not intend to let them down. I hope they knew that a mother is a mother. And a mother has to put her duty to her baby first.

The plane landed in Fort Bragg at zero-one-forty-two hours. Out of respect, nobody on the ground crew talked when they rolled the caskets into the hangar. The one I was hiding in came to a halt. The brake was engaged. I heard footsteps as the men walked away. Then the "whoomp, whoomp, whoomp, whoomp" as what must be four banks of lights were turned off, followed by the slam of the sliding doors.

I counted silent to thirty, then turned on my flashlight and cracked open the casket in the darkness. There were nine others lined up beside me, the flag draped over each.

When I saw them, I started crying all over again.

That time, not for the men inside, but for the end of my military career. I hadn't wanted to go out like this, going A.W.O.L. If they had let me stay, I would have fought till I was sixty. Desertion was dishonorable. That I could not deny. And even if I killed more terrorists than the Army's got medals for, even if I had infiltrated more cells than any soldier in the history of the United States military past or present, even if my actions saved thousands of lives, both military and civilian, none of that made up for being absent without leave. I would have never believed I was capable of deserting my post until I looked at that bright pink line on that plastic strip telling me I was with child. I wasn't making excuses to myself—or anyone else. I reckoned I'd wind up in the United States Penitentiary at Leavenworth—and was prepared for that. If they sent me there, I deserved it. I would have served my time and I wouldn't have complained about it.

But there was no way I was not going to try and get me a daddy for my child first.

Before I exited the hangar, I walked up to each casket and kissed the flag. I said farewell and Godspeed to my fallen comrades . . . and to the United States Army. I loved them, both. Truly, I did. I would have died for them and on many occasions almost did. All I could hope was that both my comrades and the United States Army would forgive me.

I was gazing out my window, just north of Beckley, West Virginia, when I observed the effects of the flood. I saw the pictures in *Stars and Stripes*, of course, but had no idea it was so bad. The corrugated-tin storage-rental place where we used to go in high school was underwater. Only two-thirds of the Payday Loans store was above water.

I got out at Thurmond and hoofed it over to River Road Bancshares, through the water and muck. I walked in the bank lobby, mud caked on my uniform up to my knees. I handed my driver's license and ATM card to the clerk. "I want to close my account. Big bills, please."

The girl inspected the cards. She handed the cards back to me. "These are both expired."

"I've been overseas for a long time." I retrieved from my

munitions box the passport and military I.D., which were current. "I don't touch this account—ever! It's all savings. Ninety percent of my income is direct-deposited here, the other ten gets carved off to my U.S. Army Federal Credit Union account, which I use for petty cash when I'm deployed."

She cracked her gum and punched the buttons on her computer. She looked up at me and squinted her eyes: "This account's got no money in it."

"Not true."

"It's overdrawn."

"No, it ain't."

She spun the terminal around for me to look at. "Minus $373.23. Under $103.23 in cash, plus $270 in returned check fees."

"The United States Army's been direct-depositing money in my account since I enlisted. I've served four tours!"

"Minus $373.23. It says it right here."

I told her I wanted to see the manager. She shrugged. "Suit yourself."

"Give me my money," I warned the manager, "or I'll report you to federal authorities."

He told me to wait and went to see the branch manager. The two men sat in the branch manager's office for thirty minutes as the branch manager banged away at the computer keyboard. A man in a gray security uniform came to fetch me. "The branch manager wants to see you."

"He'd better," I told him.

The branch manager told me to come over to his computer and look at the screen.

"These are your bank statements. It clearly indicates withdrawals."

"Not by me."

"But surely you saw the statements."

"I did not; they were sent to my permanent address here in Thurmond. For the last time, I've been away—on four military tours."

"And you never came home and read your mail between tours?"

I was not keen to return to Thurmond between tours, which now made me ashamed. But my family life was none of his business. "I re-upped as fast as I could so I could continue serving."

"We have video," he said.

"Show me."

He showed me videos. One after another. Always on the first Friday of the month. On the day my U.S. Army paycheck cleared, a woman in a US Army master sergeant's uniform was shown in the lobby withdrawing the money from my account.

"Is that you, Miss Vaduva?"

"No."

"It sure looks like you. Same height, build. Army fatigues. Black hair tucked under a beret."

"I was in Iraq and Afghanistan."

The printer started grinding out documents. "These are copies of the withdrawal slips. Is that your signature?"

"No."

The two men looked at each other. They put the photo copies on the desk, laid them side by side with my passport and military I.D. They compared each Luludja Vaduva signature. "They're a perfect match," the branch manager said.

"I didn't sign those documents. Like I said, I was away at war. And I can prove it."

The men looked at each other but said nothing. Finally, the manager said, "Ma'am, that's you in those videos."

"No it ain't."

"It's unmistakably you."

"Show me the videos again."

The branch manager swiveled the computer screen around. In the first two, I could not see the hands of the person signing for the cash. But in the third, I saw what I was looking for. "Pause it."

The branch manager paused the video.

"Look at the woman's right hand."

"I don't see anything," the manager said.

"Count the digits."

The branch manager studied the image and looked up. "Four, including the thumb."

"That's right. Her index finger is missing." I waved my hand in front of the gentlemen's faces. "How many you count here?"

"Five," the branch manager said sheepishly.

"I told you that's not me."

"Miss Vaduva! Miss Vaduva!" the branch manager shouted as I blasted through the lobby doors and headed head straight towards the banks of the New River. I ran up and down the dock until I saw a johnboat with a Johnson 90 outboard moored to a post. I hotwired it and headed downriver.

I settled my mind on the journey, doing the breathing exercises I was taught in sniper school. The objective of the mission was to get my money back, not get in a fight. Confrontation was the last resort. I needed to woo the enemy with charm, the way I did in the deserts of Iraq and the mountains of Afghanistan, the way I did as a girl when I had to influence that malicious woman better known as my mama.

At the shoreline in front of her place, I stepped out of the boat into the mud. It should have been deathly quiet—it always is after flooding—but her dog, Bitch, who I reckoned would have been long been dead by now, went into a barking fit when she saw me. Her pen—four mismatched panels of chain-linked fence fastened at the corners with bungee cords—was mostly underwater. But Bitch was safe. Somebody put a big slab of plywood up on top. There was no fencing surrounding it, but none was required: a five-foot chain was fastened at one end to her neck, the other to a railroad spike driven into the plywood. She was hopping around like mad, her chain bangling against the plywood as she leapt up on her hind legs. Even if she had broken free, she'd have had nowhere to run as she was surrounded on four sides by water, atop which floated tree branches, slabs of aluminum home siding, empty buckets, empty motor oil cans, loaded diapers, beer cans, milk jugs, plastic tarps, and wadded-up sheets.

I waded through the muck, past Bitch's pen, to the entrance to Mama's place. I had to hand it to Mama, who had always been an industrial woman—or more accurate, always got her gentlemen friends to be industrial *for* her. After the third time the New River flooded, she had a gentleman friend lift her trailer up on stilts.

I climbed up to her front door and pushed it open. Her sandpapery voice greeted me in the manner to which I had since my childhood grown accustomed: "What the fuck *you* doing here?"

"I come home early, Mama," I said all nice and sweet, despite her cursing, which she knew full well I objected to.

She pulled a long toke off the bong. "You bring me my cigarettes?"

Mama smoked a brand she could no longer find in West Virginia. It was my job since high school to locate and deliver her cigarettes. I tried to hand her the smokes, but her hands were occupied with the bong. She pointed to the table, where I set the pack of cigarettes down. She exhaled a big puff of pot-smoke. After she waved the smoke away, she looked down and scowled. "These is *regular* Eve Ultra Lights 120s. I smoke Eve *Menthol* Ultra Lights 120s."

"I'm sorry, Mama. It's all I could find."

Mama was sitting on a grimy plaid sofa somebody got for her when I was a child. A gentleman friend was next to her. "This is my baby," she said to her gentleman friend. He looked to be about my age. "Let me show you something," she said to her gentleman friend. She got up and walked to the wall. Her gentleman friend followed like a baby duckling. He didn't look too healthy, that one, even though he was at least fifteen years younger than Mama. Way too skinny. Shaved head, big scabs on his forehead and next to his goatee. Not much to look at, that fella.

Mama pointed at all the pictures, lined up side by side, thirteen generations of Luludja Vaduvas, dating all the way back to the first one, who arrived in America in 1823. "Tami's the latest—but she ain't gonna be the last, I can guarantee that—in a long line of Vaduva women."

All the Luludja Vaduvas of each particular era were depicted—either in a drawing, a painting, or in a photograph. And each picture was rendered the same: The Luludja Vaduva of her moment was standing beside her "company car"—the vehicle she used to crisscross the state telling fortunes, staging cockfights, or entertaining gentlemen callers. The first series of pictures were nineteenth century Luludja Vaduvas in front of donkey-pulled carts and vardos, fancy Gypsy wagons painted in bright gold and red with tubular-shaped roofs. Then mama moved on to the twentieth century Vaduva women: Luludja Vaduvas in front of modified hearses, de-commissioned ambulances, and one of Mama standing next to a pest-exterminator's van, the vardo of her time.

Mama's gentleman friend moved in closer to inspect her likeness. "You holding what I think you're holding?" asked her gentleman friend.

She unwrapped her pack of Eve Ultra Lights 120s and tapped the filter of one of its cigarettes on her wrist. "It's a rattler alright. Before we moved up here to Thurmond, we was downstate. Got tied up with a snake-handler at the Pentecostal Tabernacle of the Holy Ghost's Testimony church."

"You don't strike me as a churchgoer," said Mama's gentleman friend.

Mama lit the cigarette, inhaled deeply, and shrugged. "You go where the money is. We fared good in the snake trades. You get five or six snakes wrapped around your forearm and people open wallets. Even taught Tami how to handle them. She was a natural: never bit her once."

"But not you, Velvet," he said through grinning brown teeth.

"No. Not me." Mama nodded all matter-of-fact and waved her index-finger-free right hand. "Should have gone to the hospital right away but figured I'd be fine if I rubbed coconut oil and turmeric on it. That's what the pastor told me to do. It was his fix when they took a swipe at him but didn't get their fangs in deep, which the one that struck me did not. By next morning, the finger was as black and thick as a Ho-Ho."

With the finger she usually displayed at stop signs to strangers who had offended her, mama pointed at the picture of me, when I was sixteen, after I got my El Camino. "Fine looking girl, wasn't she?"

Mama's young gentleman friend purred. "Still is."

I chose to ignore his comment, not to mention the skeevy look in his eyes. "I come home to get my money and my car, Mama. I got to leave double quick and get to Charlottesville."

"Charlottesville?" She said the name of the town like she just sucked a lemon. "What business you got with all them snooty-tooties up there?"

"Personal affairs to settle, Mama. I can stay for fifteen minutes, then I've got to run."

"Jesus, girl, I ain't seen you in God-knows-how-many years. You ain't even got enough respect for to drop in on your grandmama and great-grandmama to say hello?"

"I'll go see them now, Mama."

"I'll go see them now, Mama," she snorted, mimicking me. *"Git!"*

I loved my grandmama and great-grandmama more than pepperoni rolls or the sight of a G.I.'s boot heel on an Arab's neck, but I hated going to their room since I was a little girl. Between them, they smoked four hundred cigarettes a day. And they never opened the windows, regardless the season.

I knocked on the door but nobody heard me above the racket inside, screeching tires and cop sirens. I let myself in. Great-grandmama Charlene was sleeping. Grandmama Marlene was sitting next to her bed, her wide bottom spread across that same brown pillow she'd set on for twenty years. On the TV tray before her was the computer. She didn't notice my arrival as she was playing GRAND THEFT AUTO. I snuck up on Grandmama Marlene and planted a kiss on her cheeks. She jerked in surprise. "What you doing here, child!" She gave me a hard squeeze. "I ain't seen you in how many years?"

"Too many, Grandmama Marlene." I looked over at the bed. "What's wrong with Great-grandmama Charlene's mouth?" I shouted above the racket.

Grand-mama Marlene scowled. "She's been a lip-licker her whole life. Now she's paying the price, even though I warned her. Them chapped lips of hers is hard and cracked as hundred-year-old leather."

"What's that thick ring of white stuff around her mouth?"

"All she eats is them powered doughnuts."

I dunked the cuff of my sleeve into Grandmama Marlene's coffee mug full of Sprite, which she would only drink at room temperature, and walked over to where Great-grandmama Charlene lay asleep. I gently scraped the powder out of the folds, careful not to wake her.

"So what's new, Grandmama Marlene?" I asked, knowing full well nothing had been new for many years. She set down the handset. "Bitch killed Chickadoo."

I never much like Grandmama Marlene's bird and, truth be told, wasn't too sad to hear the news he expired. Generally, he flew free around their room and splattered everywhere. But I felt bad for Grandmama Marlene. Chickadoo was her special companion, the only person in the house she wasn't always in a fight with.

"Did Bitch eat him?"

Grandmama Marlene lit up a Pall Mall. "Worse. Bitch tortured him to death. Every morning when Chickadoo ate his breakfast, Bitch would jump up on the table and bark at him, making him all hysterical. He'd get all nervous and fluttery and fly round in circles. Two months back, Chickadoo did a head-first collision into the wall. Dead on impact."

"That's sad," I said as I climbed up on a chair and popped the ceiling panel that offered access to the cross rafters. My actions provoked neither comment nor curiosity from Grandmama Marlene as I told her that what Bitch did to Chickadoo was in the military called PSYOPs—short for Psychological Operations—and that I'd won two different medals for my work tormenting the enemy.

"You was always a good tormentor, girl. You got your mama to thank for that."

"Um huh," I replied, half listening, as I waved my flashlight back and forth, breaking up the spider webs.

When the reunion talk in Grandmama Marlene's room was complete, I returned to Mama and inquired about my car. I'd cover that territory first, I reckoned, then get to the issue of my money. Mama said the car was safe, up on high ground at Ricky Ray Jeeter's place. She cracked open a Budweiser. "But you ain't going nowhere in that car, girl," mama said. "It ain't been driven for years."

I told mama I took the transmission apart and put it back together when I was 17 and had won Army medals for my work in motor pool: the El Camino would start. "By the way," I added, all casual, "I'm going to be closing my bank account while I'm here, too." I made a confused-looking face, though I was not in the least bit confused. "I had a metal lock-box with all my important documents in it. Tucked away in a little nook above Grandmama Marlene's bed. I just went to fetch it, but it wasn't there. Any chance you seen it, Mama?"

"Just you slow down, girl. Tell me what you're doing here, and why you're in the biggest hurry I ever seen you in."

Mama's gentleman friend got up and said he had to go meet somebody behind the Jiffy Lube. "Get over here and give Velvet a kiss," she told her young admirer. He obeyed, then tipped his baseball hat to me as he collected all his marijuana-smoking paraphernalia from the table.

The instant the screen door slammed shut I turned to Mama. Wherever she hid my money, I had to convince her to give it back. So instead of accusing her outright, I thought maybe I could persuade her to hand it over willfully. "In Afghanistan, I read the fortune of a man named Colonel Bland."

"There's still money to be made in that?"

"I read him for free."

"Fool."

"My reading showed we're destined to be together forever, to be true lovers inseparable."

"If you say so, darlin'."

"I'm relocating to Charlottesville, to be with him."

"You didn't see nothing."

"My visions was real, Mama."

"You know what your destiny is? It ain't moving to Charlottesville, that's for damned sure. It's to empty men's pockets and move on to the next town and the next man—before the man whose pockets you just emptied gets wise."

"No, that's not going to be my destiny, Mama. No disrespect to you and all the Luludja Vaduvas before me, but I'm going to get me a man and a house and babies and live me a normal life. I'm pregnant, Mama. I'm getting married to Cleet. We're gonna have a family."

"Cleet!" she snorted. "What kind of pussy name is that?"

"It's short for Cletus."

"That's even worse. Now listen to me, girl, and you listen

good. You'll do what every Vaduva woman's done since 1823: you ain't marrying no man. Yes, you gonna have that baby. If it's a girl, you keep her and train her in our arts and she'll take care of her mama—that's you!—when you're old and all dried out. The same way you're gonna take care of *your* mama—that's me! And if it's a boy . . ." Mama paused to inspect her chipped fingernail. ". . . Well, we ain't got much use for them in this family. Never did. Never will."

"That ain't my destiny, Mama."

Mama snarled as she looked me up and down. "Look at you in your fancy uniform. You think you're too good for this work, is that it?"

"That ain't what I said."

"I put them tattoos on you to make you alluring to men. I bought you that El Camino so you'd have a place to work when it was time for you to start earning."

"You didn't buy it, mama. I paid the hundred dollars for the car and the tow from the junkyard with money I earned at Baskin-Robbins."

"No store-bought plain vanilla ice cream was ever good enough for the little princess. Always the fancy stuff for you. Snickers fuckin' cheesecake or whatever. Just remember who bought you that set of Craftsman tools."

I should have stopped talking then and there. I should not have taken the bait. But her perpetual dishonesty—she'd lie about what she ate for breakfast, even though you were setting next to her the whole time—had a way of riling me up. "Not you, Mama. You got the tools when they 'fell off' the Sear's delivery truck one of your gentlemen friends at the time was driving—along with the microwave oven and the Mr. Coffee. You never spent a penny on me."

Mama slapped me. "You ungrateful little *bitch*."

"I'm grateful to you for doing your best. I really mean it, Mama. But it's time for me to move on. To become a wife and mother."

"You was always a Gypsy and you'll always *be* a Gypsy. And ain't nothing you can do about it!"

"It's Romani, Mama. That's what we're called now."

"I ain't no Italian. Besides, I'm only part-Gypsy. We've been mixing with other groups in America for two hundred years!" I stepped towards her. She knew I was a soldier who had neutralized enemies far stronger than her. She stepped back. "I'm leaving now, Mama," I said. "Just give me my money and my strongbox with my paperwork. I know you took it."

"I didn't take *shit*."

"Mama, it's okay. I am not mad at you. But I need that money to get set up in Charlottesville."

Mama twitched her lips.

"What?"

She talked so low it came out as a whisper: "The money's lost."

"What you mean it's 'lost?' The Army direct-deposited seventy-eight thousand dollars in my account over the duration of my tours. After deducting the one hundred and fifty dollars a month I sent to your account for cigarettes and beer and supporting Grandmama Marlene and Great-grandmama Charlene, that's fifty-six thousand and four hundred dollars remaining in my account!"

"You ain't never been good at math, girl. Ain't nearly that much."

"I need my money, Mama. And I need it now! I went A.W.O.L. from the Army to find the colonel. There's no more paychecks!"

Mama squeegeed something off the roof of her mouth with her tongue.

"GIVE. ME. MY. MONEY!" I shouted at her.

She scratched behind her neck, which she always did when lying. "It's lost, girl. I told you."

"She means she blew it, girl," Grandmama Marlene said. She was standing beside the sofa, arms folded across her chest. "Every last cent. Fancy dinners at the Bob Evans . . . hundred dollars a month on lottery tickets . . . fifteen thousand dollars for that off-road vehicle—which you ain't seen because one of Velvet's gentlemen friends drove it in the river when he was drunk."

"You shut up," Mama barked at Grandmama Marlene.

"Where's the rest of it?"

"The IRS come for all them back taxes your mama never paid, and took what was left," Grandmama Marlene continued, answering on my mother's behalf, though she had not been invited to. "That's the curse of all of us being named the same. Walk down to the bank, show them an I.D., copy a signature, and you can clear out any account in the name 'Luludja Vaduva.'"

"Like you done to me," Velvet hissed at Grand-mama Marlene—in the 1990s."

It was quiet as three generations of Vaduva women seethed.

Mama looked at me all defiant. She shook her head. Her braids twirled like a cheerleader's skirt. "You owe me, girl. I done a lot for you."

"You stole my money!"

"Don't you *dare* speak to your mama that way!" She picked up the bong and tried to strike me, but I caught the tube in my hand. Her face, which had reddened badly as a result of the rosacea she now suffered from, was scarlet. Her breathing was crazy. When finally she got her anger under control, she collapsed onto the sofa and squashed out her cigarette, albeit with a shaking hand. "There's some money in my room, inside the porcelain Bambi. Take it and get out."

I went to her room and found the money: $138.16.

I took it all, grabbed my gear, and climbed the hill up to Ricky Ray Jeeter's place to get my El Camino.

2.

My blood was boiling on the drive out of West Virginia. My mama had been pulling stunts like that my whole life. When I was in the tenth grade, she claimed my pumpkin earrings was accidentally thrown out by Great-grandmama Charlene; a week later, they dangled from her ears on Halloween night, when she left with a gentleman friend for a party in Minden. In eleventh grade, when Mama was in her early thirties and still alluring, she stole my boyfriend. Now she absconded with my life savings.

I climbed the mountains east of Beckley. The El Camino glided over long stretches of bridge above the gorges, where five hundred feet below the trees were dense and thick and I began to cool off. That stretch of highways between West Virginia and Virginia, mostly uninhabited, always calmed me. By the time I crossed the border into Virginia, my mind was off my economic misfortunes. My disposition brightened as I contemplated my new life . . . with Colonel Bland and our child on the way.

Traffic being light, I got a chance to exercise the El Camino, which ran fine—just like I knew it would, though it had developed a big patch of rust on the hood. There was only one cassette tape that wasn't all unraveled or chewed up by the player: Dolly Parton's "White Limozeen." At Covington, I pushed it in the deck and turned up the volume all the way. The tape did its automatic turnover three times between Covington and Charlottesville. The drivers on Interstate 64 must have thought I was crazy when they looked over and saw me singing my lungs out, pointing at the invisible man beside me all sassy and shouting: *"Why'd you come in here lookin' like that in your cowboy boots and your painted-on jeans, all decked out like a cowgirl's dream?"*

It was drizzling when I arrived in Charlottesville. I followed the signs to the HISTORIC DOWNTOWN district. The cobblestone streets were rough on my feet, to be perfectly honest. But after what I endured in Basra and elsewhere, I was not inclined to complain about aching feet in my quest to locate and reunite with the father of our baby.

Outside the courthouse there was a statue of Emmett Bland, a Confederate general. I wondered if he was a relative of the colonel.

I was pulled off to the side and interviewed after the security men ran my munitions box through the metal detector. "Those ain't weapons," I said as the men held the brass butt-lock and crystal ball up to the light and inspected them, "they're for romantic and fortune-telling purposes. I know better than to bring firearms into a federal facility."

The guard rummaged through the box. "And these?" he said, holding up a few surveillance equipment items.

"Standard military gear, non-lethal. Any civilian could purchase these items at an Army surplus store."

The men rolled their eyes at each other, but said nothing. The fat one clamped the box shut and handed it back to me. "Go ahead."

I asked at the front desk how to find Colonel Bland. The clerk said she didn't know. Nor did any of the tellers at the half dozen Bland Bank of Virginia branches I visited over the next two hours. Nor did the people at the University of Virginia, where the colonel had gone to school. Nor at the pediatric cancer wing at the hospital, which was named after a Bland family member.

I went to the main post office next, but when I asked the man behind the counter about the Bland family, he said they didn't come into town much—except to go to court and fight over inheritances. The Bland clan all live outside of town, he said, on big horse farms.

I went to the outskirts of town.

The country post office was a little shed about the size of a toenail-painting salon. Parked outside were fancy cars: Range Rovers and Jaguars and Mercedes-Benzes, plus historic cars, among them a bronze Cadillac convertible from the 1950s with whitewalls.

Everybody inside the post office was either old or acted old. Fancy people—women with poufy hair and men with pink sportscoats, all of them chattering like cousins—put keys in their boxes and collected mail. They looked at me curious, though not in an unfriendly way. A few of them even thanked me for my service.

I got in line at the counter, where people were purchasing stamps or shipping boxes or being given boxes by the postmaster, a heavyset gal who'd let her face and hair go. Still, she was too young to be so ornery. Every time someone came up to the counter they were nice to her, but she was nasty to them. "Another certified letter from that law firm, Mr. Deal," she said to a white-haired gentleman in a green sports coat. "Lawsuits are expensive." She smiled malicious at him. Maybe she was just in a bad mood from the poison ivy all over the right side of her face and neck, which was all bubbled up red and crusty. She got it while camping, I heard her say to the customer before poor Mr. Deal.

When it was my turn, I smiled real nice and asked the gal where I could find Cletus Bland.

"He's right here," she said. She bent down, reached under the counter, and pulled out a copy of the local newspaper, tapping her index finger on the front page. I just about busted a button on my blouse. There before me was a picture of Colonel Bland, up in Washington, D.C., looking as handsome and official as I ever saw him. The Secretary of Defense was pinning a MSM—Meritorious Service Medal—to his chest for "capturing"—which in the military is a code word for killing—Mehdi Hashmi.

I told the gal I'd come all the way from Afghanistan on urgent business and needed the colonel's home address to deliver classified news direct. She smiled and said, "I can't give that information out."

But something inside told me she wanted to. I started to tell her all about our work in Iraq, but nearly every time I got a sentence out she'd turn her back to talk to her daughter, who was stacking and unstacking boxes just to have something to do. The girl couldn't have been more than ten, though she was as heavy as an adult woman. In need of P.T., that one. "It's important I find him," I told both mother and daughter.

"Who's Barney?" asked the girl.

"Barneys is a store in New York," the postmaster replied, ignoring me. "You won't be buying anything from them in this lifetime, Misti."

The postmaster turned back around and faced me.

"Like I was saying . . . Colonel Bland was my C.O.—"

"—Cordwainers custom-makes ladies' alligator cowboy boots, Misti," huffed the postmaster, who was growing as exasperated as me with her child's constant interruptions. "You won't be buying anything from them in this lifetime, either."

The postmaster's stony face was in front of me again.

"Your girl is adorable."

The postmaster shrugged.

"Do you think she might like to see a souvenir from Iraq?"

She shrugged again.

"You take care of your other customers, ma'am," I said to the postmaster. I stepped aside and reached into my munitions box, fishing out a coin purse. It was peacock-colored fabric, green and blue and gold and orange, embroidered fancy, with plastic gemstones sewn on. "Misti, Come here and take a look at this." The girl unsnapped the coin purse and took out the wad of bills. She studied them. "Who's he?" she said, pointing at Saddam Hussein.

"The president of Iraq."

"Is he alive?"

"No."

"How did you get his wallet?"

"It's not his. It belonged to the one of the girlfriends of his son, Qusay."

The girl tossed the bills up in the air life confetti. "Mommy, Mommy. I'm rich!"

But the postmaster paid no mind to Misti. "Declined," she grinned, handing an American Express card back to a white-haired lady trying to mail a package.

"Bless your heart," the smiling lady said to the postmaster

as she walked away from the window with an air of dignity I had to admire.

The postmaster announced it was closing time and people would have to come back tomorrow. Just as she began to yank down the screen, I put my elbow on the counter and block it. "Would it be okay with you if I gave Misti this little purse as a gift?"

The postmaster said it was against regulations for her to accept it, but finally relented after I told her that the 1,500 Iraqi dinar were all but worthless, probably not enough to buy a candy bar. "I won't miss it, ma'am, honest."

The postmaster warmed up, as best as she was able. That's when I made my fiercest appeal. "You're a mama. I'm about to become a mama, too. And Cletus Bland is the papa of my baby. I've got to find him," I said.

This news pleased her immensely.

"Can you help me, ma'am?"

She frowned. "Like I said before, it's against federal law for me to give out his address."

"Then can you at least tell me when he comes for his mail?"

She looked both ways to make sure all the customers were gone. "He doesn't get his mail." She leaned across the counter and talked in a confidential whisper. "The Blands' caretaker is an old man named Harlan. He arrives daily, at six p.m. sharp, to get their mail. Drives an old International Harvester pickup with FARM USE license plates. I'll leave it to you to find the Blands from there."

Then the screen came crashing down and I heard it lock from behind.

3.

The Blands' caretaker arrived at six to fetch the mail. Hastily, I climbed into the bed of his truck and buried both myself and my munitions box beneath a half ton of horse manure. With two fingers I scraped out a little hole to breathe through.

Twenty minutes later, after driving down the windiest road I had ever been on, we turned off the main road into a long driveway; it must have taken forty-five seconds to get up it. After Harlan killed the engine and I heard the door slam, I popped my head all the way up. Outside the house he entered was a hand-painted sign, scrubbed white, on which were displayed big green words: CARETAKER'S HOUSE. I stood up in the bed of the truck and shook off the manure, wiggling my hips and belly sideways. After excavating my munitions box, I climbed out of the truck bed and did my best to get the rest of the muck off of me but discovered no amount of dusting would get the smell of manure off me.

It was dusk, but I could still see. I was on at least a couple hundred acres, because every direction I looked I saw either clusters of gigantic trees or open fields leading to mountains. I walked the gravel road in the direction of the mountains. Above them was a cluster of blue-pink clouds.

On both sides of the driveway horse-jumping obstacles were stationed. I kept walking, not knowing even if I was headed towards the main house. The stables were located in a big white building with more green trim around it. Covered horses—a dozen or more of them—were munching hay. On the same side of the road, about five minutes' walk later, I saw a small hangar. The nose of an antique WWII British Spitfire peeked out. Nice bird. I walked some more. This was no three-hundred-acre spread, I surmised; it was more like three thousand acres.

Then I saw the house—behind the big lake, where a half-dozen deer were foraging around its banks. The house lights were on, a pale gold color.

I walked up to the door, took a deep breath and banged the knocker: It was brass, a woman's hand hanging downward, with a ring carved on its finger. I didn't much care for its design; I saw too many dead hands while in service.

I heard footsteps on the tile inside—squeaking rubber—and the door opened. I was hoping to be greeted by the colonel, but it was an African-American woman instead. "May I help you?"

"Is this Colonel Bland's house?"

"It is."

"I'm here to see the colonel. I come from Afghanistan to speak with him."

She surveyed my muck-coated military uniform.

"Your name?"

"Master Sargent Tami Vaduva."

"Just a moment." Her nose wrinkled. I reckoned she smelled me.

"Who's at the door, Peaches?" said a female voice from upstairs.

"Cleet's got a visitor."

"He's not expecting anybody."

Peaches showed me in. The floor was covered in the shiniest black and white tiles I ever seen, arranged in zigzag patterns. "Begging your pardon, ma'am," I said to the black woman when I saw the manure I tracked in. I pulled off my boots and held them in front of my belly.

"Don't you worry, sugar," she said, then disappeared behind the stairway.

I stood in the entry alone, looking around. I had never been in any house like that. I had an eerie sensation though, as if I had been there before. The fancy blue wallpaper in the hallway, with flying birds painted on it, was familiar. When the grandfather clock chimed, I recognized the two big cows resting in a green meadow painted above twelve o'clock. Then I remembered: this was the house that was in that fancy picture book I perused in Colonel Bland's tent.

A woman came down the steps. She looked a lot like the colonel, with pale hair, skin, and eyes. "I'm Ginny Bland," she said. She stuck out her hand. Bony, that hand was.

I shook it. "You must be the colonel's sister."

The woman laughed. "That's the first time anyone has said that. No, I'm Cleet's wife. How can we help you?"

"Wife?" I felt a big knot ball up in my stomach. "The colonel said he had no kin."

Her voice got stiff. "Well, he most assuredly does—at least the last time I checked." She looked down at the big blue gemstone on her finger. There were diamonds all around it.

I felt my face running hot. I fixed my breathing to even out my heart rate. What I was hearing could not be true. "I got important news for the colonel."

She leaned over and said, "Why don't you share it with me, honey, and I'll relay it to him. The colonel is busy at the moment."

"It's private, ma'am."

Her lips sealed shut into a thin line. "The colonel just returned from a trip to Washington. He's quite tired. Really, you can just tell me."

I looked her in the eye. "Sorry, ma'am."

"Peaches?" she called out, exasperated.

Peaches came back, wiping her bands on a dishtowel. "There's shell in the crab. Bad batch. I can send Harlan out for more."

"Make tuna tartare instead. There's a packet of rice crackers in the pantry. Don't forget the dill sprigs. And use the good Japanese stuff in the Whole Foods wrapper, not the junk from Kroger's, which is for *salade niçoise.* Before you start dinner, may I trouble you to find Cleet? He has a visitor."

She turned back and gave me a long, not-so-pleasant look-over. "Come this way." She walked a few steps ahead of me, and I noticed she was as skinny as some of them ISIS boys who sustained themselves on tea and crushed beetles. I followed her to the library room. I recognized the big red chairs where gentlemen cigar-smoked from the picture book. There was also a giant birdcage by the bay window that was built to resemble the colonel's house. Took up half the wall. Inside it was a bright macaw with wings as blue as Superman's tights and a chest as yellow as the sun, sizing everybody up, like it owned the place. I did not recall seeing the bird in the picture book.

"*Braaa,* she's not from here," the bird squawked. "*Braaa,* she's not from here," the bird repeated.

"Quiet, Lady Astor!" scolded Ginny Bland.

The bird obeyed, saying nothing after that.

When Colonel Bland walked in, I snapped to attention and saluted.

The colonel's face was frozen. He did not return my salute. After recovering from the shock of seeing me, the colonel said, "Those days are over, master sergeant. I'm a civilian now." He chuckled. Sort of. "I'd be lying if I said it wasn't a surprise to see you—a pleasant surprise, to be sure—but a surprise nonetheless."

"I got news, colonel."

The colonel looked over at that Ginny. "Maybe I should speak privately with the master sergeant, Gin. Probably something classified. She's one of General Loehr's messengers."

"What's your name again, sweetie?" Ginny asked me.

"Master Sergeant Tami Vaduva, ma'am."

"Ooh. So shiny!" Lady Astor squawked. *"Ooh. So shiny!"*

Ginny Bland looked over at the colonel. "Your friend here mistook me for your sister."

The colonel twitched. "She must have seen some of the family photos on my desk. I had one on display, from Easter brunch at Worthington about a decade ago. Sippy was in it. Master Sargent Vaduva must have mistook you for each other. Not surprising, you and Sippy could be sisters: both blonde, gorgeous, close in age."

"I remember you telling me about the Captain, Wand and Sippy in the back of the FOOD AND MEDICAL RELIEF convoy, on the way back from Karz."

"You two rode in a convoy together?"

"Master Sergeant Vaduva was under my command."

"Hmmm." Ginny plopped down on the sofa. She picked up a horse-picture book off the coffee table and pretended to be interested in it, but really wasn't.

"Gin, why don't I find out what the master sergeant is here to discuss and you and I can catch up at dinner?"

"I think it might be better if I stay." She turned a page in the book without looking at it. "If Master Sergeant Vaduva has other topics she's confused about—in addition to whether you have a wife—I can help clarify."

The colonel was wearing the same expression I saw on his face before we entered combat situations: the half-smile, the darting eyes, the body hunched forward. Though his hair was now longer. He kept pushing back his bangs, even though they were pushed back as far as they could go. He walked over to a table where there was big crystal jug filled with whiskey. I admired the way he moved. It was the first time I'd ever seen him outside of his uniform, except of course for when he was nude. He was wearing an old dress shirt frayed at the neck and cuffs, which surprised me. Given that he lived on a fancy historic plantation and all, it's not like he couldn't have afforded a new shirt. His blue jeans were held up by an embroidered belt with cavalier swords on it.

"Drink, master sergeant?"

"No, sir. Even if I was a drinker—which I ain't—it wouldn't be right for me to drink alcohol right now, sir."

"You don't have to call me 'sir' anymore." He poured a drink for himself and offered one to Ginny. "You know I don't touch that stuff, Cleet," she said.

The colonel took a sip of whiskey, then a big deep breath. "So what's your news, master sergeant?" He should have been looking at me, but out of the corner of his eye he kept watching Ginny.

"I'm fixing to have our baby, colonel."

"What?" Ginny Bland screamed.

The colonel swallowed, quickly took a second swallow, only much bigger this time, and refilled his glass. "Take it easy, Gin. If Tami—Master Sergeant Vaduva—is pregnant, which is entirely possible, as she was the most promiscuous member of my regiment, I can assure you it's not my baby."

"That ain't true, colonel," I told him.

"Cleet?"

"You was there with me, in the tent and later in the FOOD AND MEDICAL RELIEF convoy, when I predicted a dark-haired prince would come out of the desert. Now he's here. There's no pictures yet, but I know in my heart it's a boy."

"Cleet?" pressed Ginny, her voice slicing through gritted, pearly-white teeth.

The colonel turned to her. "Standing before us is a great soldier, Gin. Less than two percent of female members of the Army ever see combat. The master sergeant here is the most highly decorated female in U.S. Army history. More than 1,500 official kills and God-knows-how-many unofficial ones. She's seen more than her share of combat. Endured torture, been under extraordinary stress, all in the service of her country and defense of our ideals." The colonel paused and downshifted the tone of his voice, like a Camaro preparing to climb a steep hill ahead. "But all that killing takes a toll on a soldier," he said, shaking his head. "After all that action, the master sergeant became rather"—the colonel paused—"unhinged. I'm sorry, truly sorry, to have to say it that way. But it's true. Who wouldn't be? We all agreed she'd benefit from some counseling. As her C.O., the task fell on me to—"

"—I ain't unhinged, sir. I read your gear, and you know exactly what I saw. You and me are supposed to be together. Forever. It is in the cards."

That Ginny woman made a face like she had just stepped into a Phillips 66 gas station bathroom that hadn't been serviced in 20 years. "Gear?"

"Have you ever noticed his left ball, ma'am?"

"I beg your pardon?"

The colonel leaned over and attempted to take the picture-book out of Ginny's hand. "I heard you saying something to Peaches about dinner. I'll be there in five. Let me handle this, Gin. I'll brief you fully."

Ginny swatted the book at the colonel's hand. "His *ball*?"

"Testicle, ma'am. The colonel's left—"

"*—Testicle?*"

"Yes, ma'am. It hangs lower than his right."

She looked up at the colonel. "And that matters *because* . . . ?"

"If it is indeed true that you are his wife—which I do not believe, no disrespect—it means you are not meant to be together. I reckon this is hard news to hear, ma'am, and I'm sorry. Truly. But when we was together in the tent, the night before we took out Mehdi Hashmi, they hung even—"

"—Hung . . . *even*?"

"I didn't believe what I was seeing when I saw it, so I kept the news to myself, as a pair of even-hangers is a rare sighting. But then that next day in the convoy, they hung even again. That's when I knew—"

"—I think that's quite enough, master sergeant," the colonel interjected. When Ginny looked at him, he twirled his finger at his temple. "Not stable. I told you, Gin."

"True love only happens once in a lifetime, sir."

The colonel sat down beside Ginny. He placed his hand on her knee, which she removed. He let out a big sigh and looked at me directly, like he was about to give an order.

"I'm very sorry for you, master sergeant," he said. "I honor you for your service—more than you know—but we need to get you some help. I'm going to put in a call to Walter Reed Hospital. It's only a few hours away. Harlan, our caretaker, he can drive you up."

"My mind is sound, colonel."

"Harlan!" The colonel called out.

I opened my munitions box and slid out a Ziploc bag. Unzipping it, I dumped all three plastic EPC pregnancy test sticks on the table. "Look," I said, holding up the first stick, directing attention to the "+" sign shown in the window. "That one I took five days ago." Then I picked up the next one and showed the colonel the "+" sign. "That one I took the night before I left the base." Then the next one. "This one I took this morning, in the ladies room at the Walgreen's on Robert E. Lee Highway. I'm pregnant, sir. It's your baby boy inside me."

Ginny looked at me with contempt as Harlan entered the library.

"This doesn't have to be difficult, master sergeant," the colonel said in his giving-orders voice. "Harlan, kindly drive Master Sergeant Vaduva up to Walter Reed."

Old Harlan tried to put his hand on my shoulder and I swatted him away. "I ain't going nowhere."

"Please, master sergeant. It's time to go," the colonel pleaded. "Let's not make a scene."

Harlan grabbed me hard at the wrist. In a split second I twisted the inside of my forearm sideways, at the weakest part of his grip, and snapped my arm upwards, breaking free.

"Don't waste your time, Harlan. She can kill you with two fingers."

Harlan backed up.

The colonel walked leisurely over to the cabinet behind the desk, removed a Winchester 30-30 lever-action rifle, cocked it, and said, "I'm sorry it's had to come to this, master sergeant. If you back up slowly and find your way out of here, I won't have to shoot you in the foot."

"Get this woman out of my house!" Ginny shouted. Even though it was the colonel's house, not hers.

I evaluated the situation. If there's one thing I'd learned from my years in service, you don't stick around fighting a battle already decided. You regroup, go back to camp, get some shut-eye and prepare for the next one. "I didn't come here to cause trouble," I mumbled. "I come to share good news."

"*Braaa,* she's not from here," squawked Lady Astor. "*Braaa,* she's not from here."

On the way to the car, the colonel walked about ten steps behind me and Harlan. That Ginny walked about ten steps behind the colonel. Peaches watched from the doorway, her arms wrapped around a blonde-haired girl's shoulders. "You can put the rifle down, colonel," I said after I climbed inside the front seat and rested the munitions box on my knees. "You never needed it. Besides, I could have taken it off you. You know that."

The colonel lowered the rifle.

"Goodbye, colonel," I said.

He looked down at the ground and said nothing.

We drove down the driveway, past Harlan's house, then turned on to a winding country road. Harlan said nothing as we drove. Neither did I. We just listened to the sounds of bugs outside. When we were rounding what must have been the twentieth curve on the road leading away from the colonel's estate, I gripped the handle of my munitions box with my left hand, flung open the door with my right, and threw myself out, landing in a pile of muck and leaves, praying that I had not just killed our baby.

Five Weeks

EARLIER

(Kandahar Province, Afghanistan)

Colonel Bland was standing in front of me, way deep in my personal space. He pointed at my chest candy. "I suppose it's only fair that since I pinned all these medals and ribbons on you, I should be the guy who gets to take them off."

"Yes, sir." I smelled a Middle East spice on his breath, though I was unsure which one.

"This one I recognize," he said. "For infiltrating that group of seamstresses in the Ghazni Province garment factory." He unhitched the ribbon and tossed it on the table. "You got us some great intel."

"Thank you, sir."

He unhitched the next ribbon, the one I got for motor pool, which I could've got blindfolded, and set it down.

"What have we got here?" He traced his thumb over the next medal, squishing it against my breast.

My knees knocked.

"Your commanding officer is asking you a question, master sergeant."

I regulated my breathing. "For surveillance work. In Al-Karkh."

After tossing it on the pile, he unfastened my Soldier's

Medal. "This was for hacking into the phone of that guy in Abbottabad, wasn't it?"

"Yes, sir. That fella pretending to sell goat kebabs who was really a point man for Al Qaeda."

"This one you got in Fallujah, if I remember correctly," the colonel said as he unhitched my Distinguished Service Cross.

"That's right, sir."

"If you hadn't waterboarded those scumbags at the tea shop, the Empire State Building would be a pile of rubble right now."

"Yes, sir."

After he dropped the Cross on the pile of ribbons and medals, he cupped my breasts with his hands and massaged them, swirling them around in circles. "How's that feel?"

"Good, sir."

Colonel Bland laughed as he removed my Good Conduct Medal. "I think it's time we get rid of this one, master sergeant, because you're about to become a very, very bad girl."

"I'm fixin' to, sir."

As the colonel rubbed his hands along my ribs, outside the tent I heard a M4's rapid-fire pop-pop-pop-pop-pop-pop-pop-pop.

"We got hostilities, sir!"

"Ignore it."

"Yes, sir."

He removed my beret. Then unhitched the brass buttons on my coat, one by one. After that, he flipped up my collar and unfastened the neck tab, running his fingers through the hair above the base of my neck. The blouse was next. He pulled it down slow over my shoulders. Then he undid my bra.

"Those nipples of yours are as pink as a little white bunny rabbit's eyes."

"Yes, sir."

With the palm of his hand he rubbed my bare belly. "You're perspiring, master sergeant."

"I reckon it's 115 degrees in here, sir."

He looked me up and down. "My God, I wondered from the first day I laid eyes on you and every day since what was beneath that uniform."

"I wondered what was under yours too, sir." A flash of heat surged across my chest.

Outside the tent, a fella shouted, "Secure the perimeter and wait for the Humvees!"

"Sir, I think we better stop."

He unzipped my skirt. "Take that off," he commanded.

I shook the skirt off my hips. I was twitching something fierce.

"How do you say 'goodbye' in Persian?"

"*Khodahafez*, sir."

"Well, I think it's time to say *khodahafez* to those panties, too, master sergeant."

The colonel hooked his thumbs at my hips and slid the panties down. At mid-thigh, the colonel let go of the panties and stood back. "Well, would you take a look at that?" He traced his fingers over my shaved pelvis. "A zipper tattoo."

"Yes, sir."

"Does that slider go up and down?"

"It don't move, sir; it's permanent."

He studied my tattoo like a general studies satellite photos of a terrorist training camp he's about to bomb. "Usually you unzip a zipper from top to bottom, master sergeant. That way, when the fly opens up and reveals what's beneath it, you're treated to a big surprise. But your zipper opens from bottom to top. And it's already open at the bottom. All of your mysteries revealed." He pinched his forefinger and thumb together, tracing them up and down my pelvis, pretending to zip and unzip. The colonel grinned. "For the man who doesn't like surprises?"

"Yes, sir," I gasped.

He peeled my panties all the way down. They were all bunched up at my ankles.

"Permission to remove my pumps, sir?"

"Permission denied, master sergeant."

"Yes, sir."

As he unfastened his belt I heard choppers overhead. "Sir, it sounds like there's a real hot mess outside."

"Relax, master sergeant. It's just a drill. I set this up before the Valor Award ceremony. Major Psotka knows that if he interrupts me for any reason whatsoever, up to and including the detonation of a nuclear weapon, he'll be court-martialed." The colonel's trousers and boxers were bunched up at his knees. "Now turn around for me, darlin'."

"Yes, sir."

From behind me I heard the colonel groan. "Oh, dear Lord, I think I've died and gone to heaven."

"Yes, sir."

"When did you get that one?"

"I was about fifteen, sir."

"Fifteen? How'd you get someone to put that on you when you were fifteen?"

"Long story, sir." I wasn't about to tell the colonel it was Mama put them tattoos on me.

He kneaded my right butt cheek like it was bread dough. Then he put his other hand on the other cheek, where the second

"W" was inked on. "The letters appear to have smeared—albeit ever so slightly—as you grew."

"Yes, sir."

He didn't say anything for a second or two, then added, "Not that I'm complaining."

"No, sir."

"I suppose there's a tiny little letter 'o' hiding somewhere between those big W's, master sergeant. Am I right?"

"Yes, sir."

"I'll have to take your word on that, darlin.' No need for further inspection from this end." Then, from behind me, the colonel made a big exhale noise and said, "WoW indeed, master sergeant!" Then he said it again, this time slow: "WoW indeed!"

5.

It was dead quiet when I woke up. No more choppers. The gunfire was done. The stink of burning rubber I smelled earlier was gone, too, blowed away by the night breeze. The drill was over. I checked my watch: 12:38 a.m.

Colonel Bland was stretched out next to me on the bunk, naked and asleep. His legs were crisscrossed at the ankles, his arms flopping over the side, his head drooping over his shoulder. He looked like the crucified Christ on His cross—but in a happy way.

I looked around the tent for the first time. His gear was piled up everywhere: blankets, rolls of duct tape, a big spool of cord, a drop leg holster, weapons lube, winter desert boots, foot powder, a tactical flashlight, a big pile of socks and skivvies, running shoes, sunblock, spare rolls of TP, barbells and weights, bottled waters.

It was weird: he'd been my C.O. for seven months, but I knew pretty much nothing about him. He didn't like to talk about himself, he told people. He said more to me in that tent than in the whole seven months before that. Not that grunts and moans and him constantly shouting "Holy shit! Holy shit! Holy shit!" as he discharged his rounds like a MGL-140 repeat-action grenade launcher counted as "conversation."

I limped over to the pile of books stacked against the tent wall. Glossy picture books, stacked up high. They were all about Virginia, those books: *Tally Ho: An Illustrated History of Fox-Hunting in Virginia, Remarkable Trees of Virginia, Virginia Plantation Homes, The Corner: A History of Student Life at the University of Virginia, Worthington Country Club: Tales from the 19th Hole, Our Cadets' Journey: The Virginia Military Institute and the Making of Men.*

I opened the tree book first. Pictures of mighty oaks, weeping willows, and so forth. I got bored because we got bigger, older trees where I grew up. So I looked at the book about big Virginia houses. Plantation houses, with fancy grandfather clocks in the entry. Strong and sturdy clocks. Always on time. Always there. Like a daddy.

Not that I ever had one of them.

I flipped through the pages and saw the most beautiful clock of all: thick-carved wood, polished-up shiny, with big Roman numbers on its face. Two big cows in a meadow were painted above twelve o'clock. The house in which the grandfather clock stood proud was the most beautiful I ever seen: rooms with fancy blue wallpaper, flying birds painted on them. Sofas yellow as ripe lemons. Men's cigar-smoking chairs in the library, red as a freshly-shot deer's blood.

A few minutes later, while I was flipping through the book about being a student at the University of Virginia, Colonel Bland growled, "Who'd have guessed you were a Hoos fan?"

"Who?" I ask.

He laughed. "Hoos. H-o-o-s. It's Virginia's football team. They're better known as at the Cavaliers, but we call ourselves Hoos."

"That sword leaned up against the side of the tent, it's

the same one as they got pictured on the football players' helmets."

"Yes. And it's not a replica either; it's the real thing. British Cavaliers, defenders of the crown in what was then the Royal Colony of Virginia, brought them to America."

"It's antique?"

The colonel laughed again. "By golly, it is! That sword's pushing 400 years old."

I reached over and grabbed the country club book. "You been on that golf course, too?"

"Worthington is the third oldest country club in the U.S. Built in 1886. Members of my family joined that inaugural year."

"You've got fancy gear, colonel."

He nodded his agreement as I pointed at the sticker on the first page of the book. It was a big picture of a medieval knight's helmet. A red and gold family shield below it, with a bunch of arrows and crosses and squiggles. "That's our family crest," the colonel said.

"There's one of them stickers in every book." I read aloud: 'FROM THE LIBRARY OF GINNY BLAND.' Is she your kin?"

"A relative, yes." Then the colonel looked down at his hands. After he scraped something off his fingernail, said, "Long lost."

"So you're all alone in this world?"

"It sure feels that way," the colonel said.

"I got no kin neither, 'cept for my mama—and her mama and her mama."

The colonel reached over and pretended to zip and unzip my tattoo with his thumb. "I think of this battalion as my family. And if I had to pick my favorite family member, it's definitely you, Tami."

"Thank you, sir."

"Considering what we did to each other in this tent tonight, I think it's about time you start calling me by my first name."

"Yes, sir. Cletus, sir."

"My intimate friends call me 'Cleet.' And I can say without fear of contradiction that I've never had so intimate a friend as you."

"Thank you, sir. I mean, Cleet."

"No, thank *you*, Tami." He unwrapped and clipped a cigar. Then he looked me up and down again. "Christ almighty, girl," he said as he lit it.

"Sir?"

He blew a big smoke ring he told me I got the hardest, finest body he'd ever seen. "I had to keep my eyes open just to convince myself I wasn't sleeping with a man. You're pure muscle."

"Yes, sir."

Then the colonel looked at me all dreamy. "Want to have another go, darlin'?"

"I do, sir. A lot," I said. "But we had three goes earlier. No disrespect, sir, but are you sure you got another go in you?"

The colonel winked at me. "I may need some coaxing."

"I got some coaxin' tools, sir."

"Really?"

"Permission requested to go fetch them, sir."

"Beat feet, darlin'."

When I came back to the tent, the colonel was standing up, all six feet four inches of him. He was still nude, drinking bourbon from a fancy whiskey glass with a big "B" carved on the side.

"What do you have there, master sergeant?"

After I was naked, I unhitched the munitions box.

"World War Two vintage, yes?"

"Mama thought it'd make a good cigarette-storage box while I was at war. But I don't smoke," I said.

The colonel told me smoking is bad for me, then asked me to open it up and show him what was inside. "Oh, my," the colonel said when I pulled out the first item. "Tell me about *that*."

"It's made out of—"

—Major Psotka burst into the tent. "Colonel!"

"I thought I made my instructions clear, major, when I—"

"—Corned Beef Hash is alive, sir!"

"Mehdi Hashmi?"

"Affirmative, sir," the major gasped, turning his eyes right, since the colonel was dressed only in his natural.

"He's *dead*, major," the colonel barked as he yanked up his pants. "I watched Master Sergeant Vaduva here take him out in Kandahar City."

Major Psotka looked at me and then, seeing I was naked, looked away as I wrapped myself up in a sheet.

"He was just spotted in Karz, colonel."

"She put a bullet through his *eye,* major," the colonel said as he buckled his belt. "I watched her take the shot." He looked at me. "From what, master sergeant, 1,500 yards?"

"2,200, sir."

Major Psotka showed the Colonel the intel photo. "He's got an eye patch now. And a nasty limp. But Langley facial-recognition software confirms it's him, sir."

"Jesus H. Christ," the colonel said.

"The bird goes up in four minutes, sir."

"Get me Moellering and McKim."

"They're already on the chopper, sir."

"You're coming, too," the colonel said to me. "Grab your gear, master sergeant. All of it."

"Yes, sir."

Aboard the Black Hawk, the colonel said, "If we can manage not to get killed, there'll probably be another medal in this for you."

6.

The chopper landed just before dawn. It took us about an hour to get to the town center. Everyone was in morning prayers. Mehdi Hashmi was behind Shahidan-e-chowk, we were told, where all Karz's jobless men assembled to find work for the day. Holed up in a cinderblock building, the intel boys said.

The sun was creeping upwards. By the time we secured a rooftop across the street, to assess the situation, hawkers were setting up for business, clustered outside the entrance to Mehdi Hashmi's building. They were selling bird cages, metal bowls, teapots, rugs, secondhand clothes—all the usual stuff. Next to the stall where the shoe-fixer sat was a passageway. Hashmi was up on the second floor. Three of his men were outside his quarters, pacing on the balcony, machine guns slung over their shoulders. We saw Hashmi inside, with two more men. God knew how many were downstairs, guarding the entrance.

A deathtrap that place was, plain and simple.

Colonel Bland's plan was to knock out Hashmi's ground floor guards and storm his rooms. My job was to stay on the roof and protect our men's flank when they entered, then pick off the balcony men after that.

Our men—Colonel Bland, Private Second Class McKim,

and Command Sergeant Major Moellering—went in. It wasn't more than two seconds before the shooting started.

The hawkers scattered every which way down the block.

After the shots were fired, a grenade explosion blew the front door of the building clean off. One of Hashmi's men wobbled out into the street. Blood was squirting out of his shoulder socket—where his upper arm was formerly connected—like an unscrewed fire hydrant. Hashmi's guard crawled over towards his arm and picked it up with the one good arm still connected to him. Then he stood up, bobbed, weaved, took a few steps, then fell over.

It was dead quiet again inside the building. This was my cue to pull the trigger on the grenade launcher. I landed it on the glass panel separating the balcony from inside Hashmi's quarters. A shard of glass half the size of a car hood flew across the balcony and sliced off clean the head of one of Hashmi's outside guards. The head fell from the balcony and hit the street with a thud. Everybody inside the apartment dove under tables. I switched to my rifle and picked off the other two guards on the balcony. Clean head shots, both.

It took a half minute or more before the smoke faded. Then I spotted Colonel Bland, Hashmi, and two of Hashmi's men—all of them scattering like cockroaches in the apartment. Private Second Class McKim and Command Sergeant Major Moellering weren't with the Colonel: either dead or wounded down below.

I saw Hashmi. Over his left eye was a black patch. He was weaving and ducking like the armless man. It was impossible to get a clean shot at him. So I took out one more of Hashmi's men who was behind an upturned dining room table.

Suddenly, Colonel Bland disappeared into a bedroom.

Shots kept firing.

Then I saw Colonel Bland enter the living room. He did not hold a weapon. His hands were up.

Hashmi's last man standing approached the colonel with caution. He frisked the colonel. Satisfied he was unarmed, the terrorist jammed the butt of his bolt-action rifle hard into the colonel's gut. The colonel slumped down to his knees before tipping over sideways on the floor.

I was afforded a clean shot. I took my time. The colonel's tormentor was standing over the colonel, hurling insults, when I sighted that patch of real estate between the enemy's upper lip and nose. That little zone Hitler's moustache called home. Best place for a certain kill. I exhaled slowly and gently squeezed the trigger. The innards of the man's head splattered against the wall behind him.

I swept my weapon sideways and tried to scope Hashmi, but he was nowhere to be seen. I had to go in after him.

7.

The street was deserted. Most of Hashmi's guys in the entry passage were dead, except for one. He tried to scream when he saw me, but the scream came out like a wounded dull yelp. I cupped my hand over his mouth and plunged my combat knife into his liver.

Private Second Class McKim and Command Sergeant Major Moellering were both down. McKim was concussed, still groggy from the grenade blast. Moellering had been shot in the leg before the grenade blast, but it went clean through, he said. He tightened the tourniquet on his thigh and pointed to the staircase, where crawling up the stairs was one of Hashmi's men. A boy was more like it. Not more than twelve or thirteen. About a hundred-ten pounder, I reckon. When I got to him he was moaning. He pulled himself up into a seated position and started to reach for his knife, but it was like he was half asleep. He slumped and went still. Dead. I took his dagger.

The boy laid still, eyes wide open. I noticed his eyes. His shiny black hair. Both like mine, which gave me an idea. I dropped my pack and stripped him. Shoes first, a pair of red leather Nike high-top basketball shoes. Lord knows where he got them—or who he took them off of. His vest and ammunition belt came off next. His tunic and trousers, two sizes too big for him, were caked in dust and blood. Finally, I took his turban. It was a dirty yellow-brown, the color of fancy French mustard. I wrapped the turban around my head and neck—and a full three times around my mouth, since I had no moustache or beard, like them Taliban men. I traded my M107 for the boy's Kalashnikov, which was bigger than him. I radioed the driver: "Come and get us in three minutes," I whispered.

At the top of the stairs, outside Hashmi's apartment, I took the biggest, longest breath of my life and shouted, *"Aye-aye-aye-aye-aye-aye-aye!"* as I burst through the door.

Hashmi aimed his rifle at me and was about to shoot. But at the last minute, he hesitated when he saw what he reckoned was one of his guards.

I spun around to where the colonel was sitting on the floor and sprayed the Kalashnikov's magazine, in a perfect horseshoe, around the colonel's head. *"Allahu Akbar! Allahu Akbar! Allahu Akbar! Allahu Akbar!"* I shrieked as I fired. Colonel Bland's eyes were screwed shut in prayer. I stopped firing and cradled the Kalashnikov, pointing the muzzle at the ceiling. Colonel Bland blinked, opening his eyes slowly when the gunfire ceased. Then he looked down at the floor and made a sniffle noise.

Hashmi waved me towards him.

I approached, head bowed. *"Bebakhshid."*

Hashmi sat silent, sizing me up. In Arabic, the phrase *"Mohammad is the messenger of Allah"* was embroidered on his eyepatch. He looked up at me kind and approving with his one good eye, then laid his gun across his lap. He reached over and stroked my cheek with the back of his hand. *"Pesarè xub,"* Hashmi said, meaning "good boy."

I leaned in towards him, still bowing, and put both my hands on his cheeks, gentle as possible, stroking his thick, white beard. Up close, Hashmi smelled like a dead goat. He smiled at me, at which time I grabbed the enemy's mouth and did a quick jerk left with one hand and twisted his skull right with the other. The neck snapped; his head plopped down sideways. Then, for good measure and because I failed to kill him proper the first time, I plunged my combat knife into his neck.

I turned around and roused the colonel. "Let's get out of here, sir! Double quick."

The colonel wiped a tear from his eye with his sleeve, then got up, took a deep breath, and pounded his chest with his fist. Without a word, he followed me downstairs.

The colonel loaded Command Sergeant Major Moellering over his shoulder and I carried Private Second Class McKim on mine. Outside the door, the first of the fifteen-truck FOOD AND MEDICAL RELIEF convoy was passing, a bunch of fifty-year-old Kurzhaube trucks, all of them on life support. Most of them had water pumps, medicine and food inside, like the flags on the outside of the trucks promised, but the fourteenth and fifteenth trucks were reserved for us. We loaded McKim and Moellering into Truck Fourteen, the mobile hospital. The colonel and I climbed into Truck Fifteen, where he collapsed, eyes fluttering, eyeballs rolling backward in his head.

"You okay, Colonel Bland?"

8.

It took a few minutes, but the colonel finally came around. Neither of us said anything for a few minutes. We just listened to the sound of the convoy, all the trucks' metal parts jangling as we bounced along the potholed road leading out of Karz.

"Check on Moellering and McKim," the colonel moaned.

I radioed Truck Fourteen. They were both in stable condition and would recover fine, I reported.

We were flat on our backs, silent for ten minutes or so. Soldiers don't like to talk after combat situations. When we couldn't stand the bouncing no more, the colonel sat upright. I joined him.

We both sat there quiet, staring up at the roof of the truck, water-damaged from years of leaks. Another five minutes of silence. Finally, the colonel said, "Why the PSYOPs in a straight-ahead combat situation, master sergeant, when there was two of us and only one Hashmi?"

"Sir?"

"Dressing up in the enemy's uniform."

"Because you was unarmed, sir. If I'd of barreled in as an American G.I., guns blazing, Hashmi surely would of got one round off—and either you or me wouldn't be setting here, sir."

The colonel was deep in his thinking. "When did you start to ululate, master sergeant?"

"I was twelve, sir."

"Twelve?"

"Yes, sir. While skinny-dipping in Beryl's Hole. The water's clear as a just-washed window. I was underwater. When I come up for air, Ricky Ray Jeeter and Scooter Skinner pointed at me, laughing. I had a big trail of blood following me. Ricky Ray said I was gonna get eaten by a shark."

"I don't think we're talking about the same thing."

"Sir?"

"That high-pitched tongue trill you did before you stormed in to Hashmi's apartment. That Arab battle cry. It's called 'ululation.' Nobody in the West can make that sound—much less at your pace and frequency."

"Oh, that, sir. I learned it from watching YouTube videos of the enemy."

The colonel chuckled. The "old" colonel was slowly coming back to life. "Hashmi was convinced you were the real deal." He appraised me carefully, then leaned in close. His voice was low. "You made history today, master sergeant." He blinked his eyes a few times and with the palm of his hands rubbed the sides of his head.

"Thank you, sir."

"But I fear we may need to re-write history."

"Sir?"

"You are aware, master sergeant, that Article 23 of the Hague Convention provides that it is expressly forbidden to make improper use of a flag of truce, of an enemy's national flag, or of the military insignia and military uniform of the enemy? And that to do so is grounds for a court-martial under the Uniform Code of Military Justice?"

"Yes, sir," I said, lowering my head in shame.

"You can rest assured I won't be brining you up on charges."

"Thank you, sir."

"But that doesn't mean others won't."

"Sir?"

"The mission was accomplished. That should be all that matters. But, unfortunately, *how* the mission was accomplished *does* matter. McKim and Moellering and the convoy drivers all saw you in the enemy's uniform."

"Sorry, sir."

The colonel said we needed to change our story for General Loehr and everybody else at Joint Special Operations Command to protect me from court-martial.

I agreed that was a good idea.

The colonel signaled me to stand up. "Let's find some chow," he said.

He rummaged through the box of freeze-dried ready-to-eat meals. "Unrivaled MRE selection we've got here, master sergeant. Brisket . . . veggie omelet, which looks particularly foul . . . Mexican chicken stew. Oh, this one's got your name all over it." He handed me a packet. "Notice the 's' is missing from 'grits.' Typo, it looks like. Yes, a packet of Shrimp & Grit for the fiercest, grittiest, ass-kicking-est Southern girl ever to join the United States Armed Forces."

"I never had shrimp and grits. Nobody eats shrimp in West Virginia, where I'm from."

"Back in Virginia, I know a woman—her name is

Peaches—who makes a wicked shrimp and grits. Old family recipe, which her grandmother, who was born in South Carolina, taught her." The colonel inspected the MRE packet and scrunched up his nose. "Though I dare say her recipe didn't call for 'pulverized reconstituted krill, salt, whey protein concentrate, sodium phosphate, white hominy grits made from corn, niacin, thiamin mononitrate, folic acid . . .' Shall I continue?"

"I think I've heard enough, sir."

"Mmm, mmm, bad."

The colonel tore into the brisket; I attacked the shrimp and grits, which, in my view, were quite tasty. We didn't get much work done re-inventing our story during chowtime; neither of us realized we was starving until we dug in. But by the time we got to the lemon poppyseed cake, we had a version of events to present to General Loehr, generally along the lines of: *"After my grenade and sniper's bullet took out Hashmi's three balcony guards, I went in. The enemy was surprised to encounter a female soldier. They captured me when I come in and dressed me up as a jihadist, to taunt and humiliate me. But I broke away and got my fourth kill. Next I went to rescue the colonel, who didn't need no rescuing as it turned out, because Colonel Bland took out Hashimi's personal bodyguards, then snapped Hashmi's neck before I got there."*

Our story was not how events occurred, of course. Some soldiers would not approve of our historical re-writing. They'd have been mad that the colonel was going to get credit for three kills when he had none. But I didn't join the West Virginia National Guard as a teenager and, later, the United States Army, to win favor or medals; I joined to serve and to complete the mission—by any means necessary. And we completed the mission. With gusto.

"Sorry to deny you the additional kills, Tami," the colonel said as he tore into a second MRE. "But it's for your own protection."

"Four kills is plenty, sir. I don't need seven."

"Which brings you to . . . *how many?*"

"One thousand four hundred sixty-one official confirmed kills, sir."

"And the unofficial kills?"

"Another hundred or so, sir."

"I'll put you up for another medal."

"You don't need to, sir."

"Yes, I do."

The convoy bumped along and it got all quiet again. Despite that we had our story agreed on, the colonel was grumpy. "How long are we going to be in this goddamned convoy, master sergeant?"

"Four more hours, I reckon."

The colonel said we should get some shut-eye.

We spread out on the hard, splintered wood flooring, where I fell quickly to sleep.

When I woke, the colonel was pacing around, all wired and fidgety.

"You couldn't sleep, sir?"

"No."

"Permission requested to speak freely, sir."

"Permission granted, master sergeant."

"You've got the jitters worse than a piglet in the slaughter line, sir. It's like you hear the squealing piglet ahead of you go suddenly quiet when the bolt pistol strikes its forehead."

"As apt a description as any, I suppose."

"You're all riled up, sir."

"We've established that, master sergeant."

"You need calming down, sir. If you don't mind my saying."

"I don't."

A big thud sounded on the side of the truck. Somebody on the roadside hurling another brick at us, I reckoned.

"I was wondering, sir . . ."

"Wondering what?"

"Do you ever find yourself feeling frisky after combat?"

"Frisky?"

"Yes, sir. In combat, adrenaline levels are heightened. You are as close to an ugly, unnatural death as you will ever be. When the fighting is done, I find that I am greedy for good food, clean water, fresh air, and, frankly speaking, sir, a go. It's more than just stress-relief, sir. Coupling with another person, that is the opposite of a bullet to the head—life in all its purity and goodness. Permission requested to speak freely again, sir."

"Permission granted, master sergeant."

"Before Major Pstoka came in your tent with the news about Hashmi, we was gonna have another go. Remember?"

"Do I ever. If I recall correctly, you were going to 'coax' me."

"That was nine hours ago. I don't reckon you need coaxing no more, sir."

"I suppose there's only one way to find out, master sergeant."

Soon our uniforms were strewn on deck. We had two goes. I suggested a third go, but the colonel said he was out of juice again.

I fetched my pack.

The colonel, naked, sweaty and sprawled out, looked up at me. "You brought the munitions box?"

"You told me to bring all my gear, colonel," I said as I unhitched the lid.

"That's the thing you showed me back in the tent, isn't it?"

"Yes, sir. It's real brass. Got it in Basra."

"It looks old. Not just old. Ancient."

"It's from the 1700s, sir."

The colonel took it out of my hand and inspected it. "It looks like a . . . *diabolical tulip*."

"It goes up your—."

"—No it doesn't! It goes back in your munitions box, master sergeant."

"Right, sir."

The colonel took a big gulp of water. "I shudder when I contemplate what else you've got in that munitions box of yours?"

I showed him the lovemaking gadgets: a ball-crusher, a carved stimulator from Mogadishu, a glove made out of lamb belly with rosebush thorns sticking out of the fingers and palm.

He rolled his eyes. "I fear the potholes we keep plunging into would spoil the experience. Maybe we just go about it the old-fashioned way."

"Right, sir."

Two minutes later, the colonel's front side stood at attention, like his gear was about to be inspected by the head of the Joint Special Operations Command.

We had our go something fierce. From every which way. "Them potholes ain't so bad after all, are they, colonel?"

"I stand corrected," he said. Though, to be exact, he didn't say it so much as grunt it.

We plunged into a pothole as deep as a rock quarry—just

as the colonel reached his ecstasy moment. *"Tam-miiiiiiiiiiiii!"* he shouted as the truck tilted sideways.

The colonel laid on his back and rubbed his palms over his eye sockets. "Good God," he kept repeating. Finally, he hoisted himself up on off the floor and wobbled over to the cooler, where he dunked his head in ice water, then pulled it out and shook it, like after a dog gets out of a creek.

He returned to me and collapsed again.

"Another go, sir? I got coaxin' equipment here if you need it." I rummaged through the munitions box and handed him the ball-crusher.

The colonel scowled at the gadget presented him for inspection. "Every day I try to figure out how not to leave this wretched place on a stretcher, Tami. Much as I'd like to have yet another go, I fear that, if I did, I'd leave here on one—though, obviously, there are worse ways to die."

The colonel reached for his trousers, wadded them up in a ball, and wiped his underarms. He put the gadget back into the munitions box.

But something else in the munitions box caught his eye. His brow furrowed. "Boy, if you aren't full of pleasant surprises, master sergeant. Is all this stuff mixed in with the sex toys what I think it is?"

"What is it you think it is, sir?"

"Occult stuff?"

"For telling fortunes, sir."

He picked up the Magic 8-Ball, then tossed it in the air a few times, like a baseball. He put it back and sifted through the tarot cards and astrological charts. He chortled. "Where's the Ouija board?"

I didn't laugh, because the ability to read fortunes is not a joke. "Those don't work, sir."

"Why, look here," he said, "you've even got a crystal ball."

"It don't work. There's a crack in it, sir."

The colonel laughed. "I guess I'll never know my fate."

"You're making fun of me, colonel."

"Forgive me for poking fun at your hobby, master sergeant."

"It ain't no hobby, sir. It's a tradition. One that dates back centuries in my family, among my people. I have been schooled."

"Go on."

"I would be honored to tell your fortune. But you can't be a cynic, if you don't mind my saying so, sir. You must take this serious. If you don't, you're tempting fate."

He walked naked over to his pack, procured a cigar and lit up.

"If you put it that way, I'm not so sure I want to start seeing around corners."

"I don't blame you, sir."

He bit the cigar's tip and spat it out. "I do wonder about my post-military life."

"I took you for career military, sir."

"Like you?"

"There's no other life for me."

The colonel didn't say nothing, just fiddled with his cigar and gazed up at the roof of the truck.

"You want me to read your fortune or not, sir?"

"Why not?"

"Promise you won't laugh?"

"Promise." The colonel looked hard into my eyes. "So what do we use, tarot cards?"

"Have you ever been to a card- or palm-reader, sir?"

"No."

"Ninety-nine-point-nine percent of people get their futures read with their clothes on."

"And?"

"But you, sir, are in the nude."

"Indeed I am." The colonel glanced down, admiringly, at his gear.

"There is no more clear or honest reading than when someone before you is naked. They can conceal nothing. For this reason, I want to read every part of you. The lines on your face, few as there are. Palms, feet bottoms and, with your permission, sir, your private parts."

"By all means, master sergeant." The colonel flashed a grin. "Whenever you're ready."

"This is not a joke, sir."

"Sorry." The colonel cleared his throat. "I promise to be a good boy."

"Get on your back, sir. Legs splayed, hands to your side, palms up."

"Yea, ma'am!"

I read the face first. "Your large eyes mean you have a large heart, sir. People with small eyes are good in business."

"That explains my atrocious stock-picking record."

"Large eyes also mean you have strength and determination, sir."

"I'd like to think so, master sergeant."

After the face, I read his palms. "Earth hands are wide, with thick skin. Air hands are square with long fingers. Water hands have an oval-shaped palm. Fire hands got a square or rectangular palm and shorter fingers."

"Which am I?"

"Fire, sir."

"Which means . . . ?"

"High energy, short temper, big ambitions."

"Sounds like me," he said as he blew a puff of smoke.

I moved to his feet. The colonel was pleased to learn that his wealth lines were bold.

When I finished with the feet, the colonel clasped his hands behind his head, spreads his legs open wide, and said, "Tell me what you see in my gear."

"In a moment, sir."

From inside the munitions box I retrieved the little brown vials of oil I got while on a black ops mission in Yemen: oil of basil, cardamom, ginger, cinnamon, fennel, and frankincense. "Since your hair down there is ginger colored, we'll start with ginger oil."

"If you say so. I put my fate, literally, in your hands, master sergeant."

I rubbed in the oil all over the colonel's gear. "That's one mighty vein. Some life line you got, colonel."

"That mean I'm going to live to be a hundred?"

I traced my index finger across a second vein. "This is your 'Girdle of Venus.' People with thick Venus lines have wandering eyes. They're lusty."

"My heart belongs only to you, Tami," the colonel grinned.

"I need quiet, sir, if I'm to get a vision."

The colonel apologized and promised to keep quiet.

It took about five minutes, then my first vision arrived. "I see you young—age thirteen or fourteen. You are with boys. At school. Far from home. You don't want to be there. You begged your daddy not to make you go. You're upset something terrible. Wiping tears on your sleeve."

"That could be any ninth grader, Tami."

"You wasn't any ninth grader, sir. Quiet. Picked on." I looked up. "You and your mama? Close?"

"Yes."

"She died?"

"Yes. How did you know that?"

"Which is why your daddy sent you away to that school?"

A stern look came over the colonel's face. "How'd you know about my mother? Private Second Class McKim? Command Sergeant Major Moellering?"

"I had a vision."

"I'm not sure I like what you can see."

"Want me to stop?"

The colonel bit his fingernail. "No. Go on."

I pinched one of the beans in his bean bag. "Now I'm seeing you in your twenties. Outdoor event. Summer. I just saw a horse galloping by. You're surrounded by women. You've got a beer in your hand. But you seem bored." I looked up at the colonel: "You've never been in love, isn't that true, sir?"

The colonel paused for a moment, then said, "I suppose that's true. Just out of curiosity, how can you tell?"

"Your left ball, sir. It hangs lower than the right one. When a man's never known love, the left ball hangs lower."

The colonel was about to laugh but swallowed instead. "And what happens if the right ball hangs lower?"

"That's even worse, sir. It means a woman broke his heart. He thought he'd found his one true love: the girl he was fixin' to marry; the one whose unborn babies looked back at him every time he stared into her eyes; the one he'd nurse back to health if she ever got sick. But as him and her floated down the River of Love, unbeknownst to him, she always had one foot dangling over the side, looking for another canoe to jump into, reckoning its paddler might be stronger, or richer, or better-looking. And you know how this story ends, sir: when she finally jumped permanent to that other canoe, the canoe of the man with the broken heart tipped over and sunk—with him in it."

The colonel said he had known some men who let that happen to them, but they didn't know how to manage their affairs with women. It had never happened to him, the colonel insisted. He reached down and toggled his right ball. "And what happens if they hang even in the sac?"

"It's the highest form of true love. The rarest, too. The kind of love where a man's heart belongs to a woman completely—and hers belongs to him. When other people see them, they see only one being. When he runs out of money, she tells him how to make some. When she laments her looks have faded, he goes to Walmart and buys her a dress and makes her beautiful again, without being asked. When one mate dies, the other dies of natural causes about a week later, because he or she just can't go on living without the other one. True love is so rare because even-hanging balls is so rare."

"Mine hang even."

"Begging your pardon, sir, but no they don't. They never hang even, except on infant boys."

"And men in true love."

"That's right, sir."

The colonel jutted his jaw. "Mine have hung even. On many occasions."

"Begging your pardon again, sir. But no they don't. I been naked with you twice now, for long stretches, and that left ball of yours has been hanging low the whole time."

"It's just the heat over here. At home they hang even."

"They hang uneven in America too, sir. Except for after you just get out of a cold shower or a spring-fed pond."

"I'm sure mine hang evenly while I'm asleep."

"How do you know, sir? You don't sleep with your eyes open."

"Touché."

I squished his left ball, propelling it in various directions, the way you pinch the tail of a crawfish and it darts off every which way. I asked the colonel, "You ever seen a man's balls when he's sleeping, sir?"

"I'm delighted to tell you I have not, Tami."

"Well, sir, I have. That's when you see a man in his most natural state, when the real, true, honest him is most seeable. His innermost fears and desires—the ones he won't let himself even think about when he's awake—make a show. And one is *always* hanging way lower than the other. I've read me my share of them, and it's the rarest of rare sights."

"A 'black swan' moment in the annals of scrotal astrology, eh, Tami?"

"I don't understand, sir."

"Never mind," the colonel said. Then: "Well, by golly, will you take a look at that?" He glanced down at his gear. "I think there's another erection in my future."

"That ain't predicting. That's just what is. Now be quiet, sir, so I can concentrate."

"Yes, ma'am."

I put a big glob of the basil oil on my thumb and rubbed.

"Ohhhhhhhhh."

"Quiet, sir."

The next vision came quick. "I see a prince. A dark-haired prince. He comes out of the desert."

The colonel slapped the deck with the palm of his hand. "Oh, Christ, not another Arab prince! Ban them from my future, Tami."

"This is a young prince. The gentlest, kindest, handsomest prince there ever was."

"I've no use for a handsome prince at the moment."

"He brings despair."

"Tell me something I didn't know, darlin'. Everything these people have touched since the fourteenth century they've destroyed."

"Quiet, sir." I continued my reading. The colonel's breathing deepened. After a particularly loud moan his breathing leveled off. "Where'd you learn how to read men's fortunes?"

"The women in my clan been reading men's fortunes for as long back in time as anybody can remember, sir. Every first-born girl was taught by her mama, who was taught by her mama before her."

"Your *mother* taught you how to read a man's . . . *balls*?"

"She taught me cards, hands, feet and faces. She gave me a book on the extra parts and told me to learn the techniques on my own, in my room. It's an art passed down through twenty-five generations, all the way back to Petrești."

"Petrești?"

"It's a town in southern Romania, sir."

"You're Romanian? That explains those coal-black eyes of yours." The colonel splayed his knees even wider. "The first thing I noticed about you was your eyes. All the women where I'm from have blue or green eyes. Their hair is honey-blonde, or strawberry-blonde, or dishwater-blonde, or something-something-whatever blonde." The colonel shimmied up on his buttocks. "I always had a thing for brunettes, the darker the better. Not that I could find one in Charlottesville, mind you." He gently plucked a lock of my shiny black hair from my head. "I think I'm partial to Romanians now, Tami."

"I ain't Romanian, sir. Romani."

"Gypsy?"

"That's what they used to call us. But now they call us Romani."

"But your skin's milk-white."

"I'm Gypsy only on my mama's side. We was darker-skinned when in Romania, before our people was run out of the country. Across Europe at first. Our women have been in the United

States almost two hundred years now. We've coupled with all sorts of men since my grand-mama thirteen generations back, Luludja Văduva, came to America in 1823. Every firstborn woman in our clan is still called after her. You probably don't know it, but my real first name is Luludja, too. 'Tami' is just my affection name."

"You're right, I didn't know that," the colonel said as he reached down and scratched his gear.

"It was the same with the very first Luludja. Her affection name was Lulu. The naming habit kept on all the way down the bloodline through to my mama, Luludja—but everybody calls her Velvet."

"Velvet," he said, flicking cigar ash. "Nicknames are popular in my family, too. My Uncle was called 'The Captain;' my sister is called 'Sippy.' People at the club have known my daddy as 'Wand' for so many decades that most, if pressed, couldn't tell you his real name. Though how he acquired the nickname as an undergraduate at Hampden-Sydney has never been forgotten."

"I won't get another vision if we keep chattering, sir."

The colonel smoothed out the little tuft of hair on his chest. "My bad. Sorry I took you off-task, master sergeant. Carry on."

I dumped the whole vial of cardamom oil into my palm.

"You said your people were run out of Romania?" the colonel continued.

"Rival fortune-telling women in the next village put a spell on the Văduva clan, because we was getting too much business. Their hex made it impossible for our women to keep a man. So we kept moving to other villages, and later to other countries, searching for a man we could keep. But the hex stuck despite the Văduva women's efforts. It's just something my mama and her mama before her and her mama before accepted as permanent." I pulled my hand away from the colonel's gear and paused for a moment as I contemplated our women's history. "Though sometimes I wish it weren't."

"That's a sad story. Carry on, master sergeant."

I went to work on Colonel Bland's sword, which I was saving for last. Within seconds a vision: "A woman will come."

"Now you're talkin'."

"There is passion. Fire." I dabbed some frankincense on my thumb and swirled it around the business end of the colonel's spear.

"Even better!"

My thumb rubbed that little spot that drives men crazy. The colonel made an animal-like howl.

"Not yet, sir." I took the thumb away. The colonel inhaled deeply through his nose, held his breath and exhaled gently through his nostrils.

"What's she look like?"

"I can't tell. She looks blurry. She keeps changing: blonde as a wheat stalk one minute, black as mud the next. She's banging on a door. I'll return my attentions to your gear if you can promise to hold out."

"Promise." He widened his knees again. "So, let me get this straight: one day in the future, a goddess will show up at my doorstep and bang on my door? I like it!"

I pulled my hand away yet again. "You're making me mad as a box of frogs with all your talking."

The colonel apologized. I reached again for his gear, but the colonel grabbed my wrist. "You know, Tami, you've brought me so much good fortune today that I don't think I can stand—or deserve—anymore. What do you say you climb on board?"

Truth be told, that final go wasn't easy. But I got him there—thanks to a lesson my mama taught me. Every woman's got a secret muscle in her private area. It is a big mistake to overuse it, she told me, and should be flexed only in emergency situations so men don't get spoiled. I took mama's advice and employed said muscle.

"Ugggh!" the colonel groaned before his arms flopped to the side and he smiled, happy as a tick on a dog, before fading off to sleep.

All the goes had ginned up my appetite again. I got up in search of more RTE chow. When I returned to the colonel, a piece of pecan pie in hand, the colonel was snoring gently.

And that's when I saw it: the colonel's bag was firm and round, his balls floating even, high and proud, side by side.

The next morning, I went to Colonel Bland's tent. "Request permission to enter, sir."

From inside, the reply came quick and sharp: "Permission granted, Master Sergeant Vaduva."

I unzipped the flap and entered. I knew in an instant something was wrong. The tent was empty, stripped bare. No bunk, no table, no gear: the colonel's holsters, Cavalier sword, books, boots, and everything else was gone. At the opposite end of the tent, a soldier with his back to me was hunched over a big trunk, unpacking.

"Where's Colonel Bland?"

Major Psotka turned and looked up at me. "He's gone."

"Gone

"Colonel Bland rotated out today."

"When's he back, sir?"

"He's not."

The colonel didn't say nothing to me about leaving. "New posting, sir?"

"Back to the States."

"Pentagon, sir?"

"Home." The major unrolled a mat. It had the West Point seal stitched on it. "His tour of duty ended. Choppered over to Bagram, then took a C-130 back to Washington to brief the SECDEF. After that, our friend Colonel Bland will become just another civilian who does nothing but grill strip steaks and get fat and watch his pathetic Cavaliers lose. Lucky bastard."

"Did orders just come down?"

"He's known for weeks."

"So he ain't coming back?"

"Affirmative for the second time, master sergeant." The major walked towards me. My munitions box was cradled in his arms, like a baby's coffin. "Colonel Bland asked me to return this to you."

I thanked the major and turned towards the door. I felt a dollop of wetness in the eyes. I was sure to look away, outside the tent, as though I had just heard a distracting noise. To be sure, I'd been social with men during my many overseas tours. A soldier gets lonely—even worse, a soldier gets *bored.* I passed the time agreeably on many occasions with my fellow soldiers. I had the occasional go with fellas in the motor pool, a supply chain logistics officer, a translator, a public affairs officer, a telecom engineer, Private Second Class McKim, an optics technician, a small arms technician, a budget analyst, an electrician, the base's fuel manager, a radio systems engineer, a man from the dental corps, a cyber operations specialist, a Special Forces intelligence sergeant, a C-12 pilot, a radar operator, a carpentry specialist, Command Sergeant Major Moellering, a food safety officer, a biomedical equipment specialist, and once, when we was in Cairo, General Loehr. From JSOC. But not one of them was like Colonel Cletus Bland—the only man I had ever met with even-hanging balls. The one man to bring me True Love.

And now he was gone like a ghost.

I began to tilt, side to side. When I regained my balance,

from behind Major Psotka touched my shoulder. "If ever you need someone to talk to, I'm told I am a very good listener."

"Thank you, sir. I don't feel much like talking right now."

"You know," the major said as I turned the flap at the entrance, "it might be good for you to get out of here for a few days. Change of venue. Clear the head. This weekend I'm going to take a little R&R, at Konnos Bay, in Cyprus. You should come."

"That's real kind," I said halfheartedly to the major. I stepped out of the tent, into the dust and wind.

He followed me out. His hand brushed my hand discreetly. "Maybe you can bring your magic munitions box along?"

I looked down at the box and thought about my intimate times with Colonel Bland. "I don't think so, sir."

I tried a hundred which ways from Sunday to talk to the colonel after he shipped out, but all of his Army-issued communication devices were disconnected.

I went to Personnel and told them I needed to get the colonel's address and phone number back in America, but the Chief Warrant Officer, who during the course of our service never concealed her dislike of me, said we had to respect the colonel's privacy now that he was a civilian.

So I went online. There were innumerable Blands in Charlottesville, Virginia: Charlotte Blands and Emma Blands and Atticus Blands and Buford Blands and about ten thousand other Blands.

But no Cletus Bland.

For about a week I moped around the base like a sleepwalker, my eyes sunken from sleeplessness, my gait lethargic, and my voice reduced to a whisper. Major Psotka pulled me aside after P.T. "You've got to let him go, Master Sergeant Vaduva. You've got lot of other admirers around here." He invited me on a date again. This time to an upcoming military conference in Turkey.

"I'm not good company to any man right now," I told the major.

In the chow hall, on maneuvers, and even when I was dispatched over to Sari Pul Province, where I took out two enemy warlords while they were playing a game of panjpar, I couldn't get the colonel out of my mind. He was haunting me all through my days—and especially at night, when the dreams came. I saw the colonel riding a horse, swinging his Cavalier sword. I had visions of plantations I saw in the colonel's picture book—myself in a frilly dress walking through a big screen door into fancy gardens, the colonel standing beside me, in a white suit, drinking lemonade.

Dream after dream, night after night.

Four weeks after he left, in the middle of the night, I shot straight up in bed, gasping for air. My breasts were all swelled up, about to pop. I wiped the sweat off my face, went to the latrine, and pulled out one of a half dozen pregnancy tests I carried with me into my deployment to confirm what I already reckoned: I was pregnant with the Colonel's baby.

I was up all night, wondering what to do.

I knew what my mama would have me done. But I stopped listening to my mama the day I left home to join the West Virginia National Guard and walked away from the "family business." No disrespect intended, but there was no way I was going to end up like my mama and hers and hers before and every other Vaduva woman who traced her origins back to Petrești: I wasn't going to be no single mother. Nor would I get an abortion. Nor would I sell or trade the baby, as my Gypsy ancestors did without blinking. I was going to get married and start a family, like any woman with a bun in the oven deserves. And marry not just any man, but an officer and a gentleman: Colonel Cletus Bland III.

The next morning I marched into Major Psotka's tent and explained my predicament to my new C.O.

"Let me get this straight," he said as he looked down at my still-flat stomach in disgust. "You're requesting emergency leave in order to break a single-motherhood curse that you maintain dates back to nineteenth Century . . . *Romania*?"

I told him that was exactly what I was saying.

He said he was uninterested in hearing about the Vaduva women's misfortunes. I could request a non-combat assignment, he said, but DOD policy allowed only for maternity leave of up to six weeks—and I had to wait until the baby arrived for leave. I had another eighteen months on my contract and he wasn't granting me a second's leave until the baby was born.

Two days later, when I flagged General Loehr's chopper before takeoff, he told me I broke chain of command protocol and that I should work out the details with Major Psotka.

I was crushed. I loved the United States Army. These people had become my family. I spent times in foxholes with these men and women. But even if my baby was no bigger than a breadcrumb, I intended to love my new little Baby Bland even more than the United States Army. I was more determined than ever to marry Cletus Bland, raise a child together, and break the Vaduva curse. No rule or regulation was going to get in the way of me and Colonel Bland fulfilling our destiny. *Nothing.*

Like my mama and her mama and her mama before her had said to me since I was a little girl, "It's in the cards, sugar."

Five Weeks
LATER

(Charlottesville, Virginia)

I rolled five times before I finally came to a stop. I was dizzy. Shook up pretty bad. I finally found the munitions box, lodged in a sliver of creek bed.

By the time the taillights of Harlan's backing-up vehicle came into view, I was already deep in the woods.

From behind the trees I snuck along Route 947—what Harlan called "32 Curves Road"—back to the Blands' house. Every ten minutes or thereabouts I passed another fancy farm: "Crewe Hill" and "Leaping Colt Farm," and so on. But those guardhouses were all painted white, and the Blands' was painted green as I noticed upon our exit from the property.

When I finally located it, the guard at the gatehouse in front of Colonel Bland's house, called Derbyshire Farm, was wiggling on a stool, eating chicken out of a Bojangles chicken bag when he should have been watching the monitors. Surrounding the horse farm was a stone fence, three feet high. They must have been two hundred years old, the stones, all smooth and flat and fitted together as perfect as mating grasshoppers. I got over the stone fence easy and undetected.

The electric fence wires, some twenty yards beyond the stone fence, would on the other hand be trickier. But after sidestepping mines in Afghanistan, an electrical fence wasn't going to stop me.

Once through, pulled my night goggles out of my munitions box. After I applied a thick layer of camo paint to my face, I began the long journey on my belly up to the house.

I saw the little blonde girl first. Peaches was feeding her in the dining room. The colonel and that Ginny woman were in the kitchen. The colonel was scooping crackers into a bowl full of what looked like raw meat. Skinny Ginny stood next to him at a big kitchen table made out of quarry rock. Her hands were flailing. I reached in my munitions box and assembled the portable boom mic. Then I plugged the headphones in. Once the levels were set, I could hear them plain as day.

"No, Gin, I *have* explained it. Three times. You just don't like my answer." He gasped. "After that stunt she pulled in Kandahar, they were on the verge of sending her out on a DD 214. But if you're going to go for a mental discharge, you've got to go strictly by the book. Then there was the matter of whether she would be discharged honorably or dishonorably. I recommended dishonorable. But the public affairs officer was concerned about the bad P.R. we'd get: she was, after all, the most highly decorated soldier in the theatre. And one of very, very few women. They finally took my recommendation. But, naturally, that made it my task to deliver the news about her discharge."

"Which brought her to your . . . *tent*?"

"This isn't news you deliver in a mess hall, Gin."

Ginny opened the fridge, unscrewed the lid on a jar of pickled asparagus, took out two stalks, then screwed the lid back on tight.

"You're not having any of the tuna tartare?"

"You'll excuse me if I don't have much appetite tonight."

Or any night, from the looks of her.

"I think we left off at your tent, Cleet."

"We had one and only one conversation in my tent—and Major Psotka was with me the whole time, which is a mandatory protocol in situations like these—because the conversations have to be corroborated if the JAGs call upon you to testify, which, invariably, they do. Call him up. Ask him."

That Ginny scrunched her nose. "I intend to."

"Knock yourself out." The colonel yanked his phone out of his pocket and pressed buttons. "I just shared his contact info with you."

I'd been on my belly, perfectly still, when I noticed the underground hive a few feet away. It was starting to stir. I suspect the glow of my night goggles tricked the bees into thinking it was daylight. One landed on my wrist. I shooed it away.

That Ginny woman brought up me being pregnant again. "But if somebody *were* to have impregnated her, whom might you guess that would be?"

The colonel bit into another cracker. "How the hell should I know?"

"Surely there was one man on the base who *might* have been crazy enough to sleep with her?"

The colonel finished chewing. A look of deep thought came over his face. After he licked his finger, he said, "She slept with everybody. The men passed her around. Which is why, even if I were inclined to cheat—*which I am not*—I would have never touched her."

That wasn't true and he knew it. First, no men passed me around. *Ever.* I selected the men I hankered to have a go with—not the other way around. Second, the colonel told me, direct to my face, that from the first day he met me he wondered what was beneath my uniform.

"Maybe General Loehr," the colonel said as he sipped his beer. "Guys at his rank, they figure the women have it covered on birth control. Whereas the enlisted guys—guys who go into brothels when on leave—are scrupulous about protecting themselves."

I was with the general only once. And had my clothes on the whole time! A rub-and-tug in a helicopter flight out of Cairo.

"Contrary to the cliché, men do talk, and I hear that if it had a pulse, Loehr was after it." The colonel wrapped up the bowl of pink meat and put it back in the fridge. "If she *is* pregnant—which is highly doubtful considering her level of delusion—he's a potential candidate, I suppose."

"Let's call him and ask."

The colonel took another swig of beer. "Are you nuts, Gin? We're talking about a brigadier general in the United States Army. This conversation is *seriously* classified. And I damned well don't want to have to admit six months from now, under oath at Peter Loehr's court-martial, that an unauthorized civilian—as in *you*—was party to the allegation."

Ginny poured herself more white wine. She was drinking like a hairdresser on payday. "She's pregnant alright. A woman can tell. And now she's on the loose somewhere here in Albemarle County." She swallowed. "You're not concerned she's coming back to finish you off now that she knows she can't have you?"

"She's *not* coming back. And for the record, she never *had* me."

The colonel glanced at the window. He knew me well enough to know I was already in his yard.

Colonel Bland and the woman I was finally starting to realize was indeed his wife milled about. In the absence of conversation, they still made noise: plates banged, silverware drawers slammed, and empty beer and wine bottles crashed into the recycling tub.

"But you said it yourself," Ginny said, snapping the asparagus spear, which she still hadn't bitten into, "she's a psychopath, a natural-born killer. What's to stop her from coming back and doing God knows what?"

If my plan was to kill them, they'd have been dead by now.

"Gin, you're being ridiculous."

Peaches and the girl passed through. Everybody got a goodnight kiss. After they left Ginny kept harping. "You can't be sure of that. She killed—what was it?—fifteen hundred people, right?"

"I'm happy to have this conversation all over again in the morning, but right now I'm tired and, frankly, sick of being interrogated."

"Fine!" She went to the fridge and got more white wine. After she poured another glass, she just stood there, drinking and thinking. Finally she started talking, at first in a low voice, then at a fast clip, jumping from one topic to another, like a rock skipping across a pond: " . . . Piedmont Seafood Market is cutting corners on their jumbo lump crab. Peaches says it's loaded with shells. Not the first time, I've noticed . . . Flax was swarmed by those damned bees when I was riding this morning; you've really got to do something about them, Cleet . . . in the drop off queue at Digby, those adopted black kids of Shelby Nash and Davis Warren, whose manners are atrocious, were pounding on our car door, their way of greeting Augusta, I suppose . . . Bronwyn struts in late: 9:09 on Monday, 9:11

yesterday, 9:15 today—yes, I'm keeping track, so *sue* me—slapping her yoga mat on the hardwood floor, throwing everyone out of their poses; it's just so *rude* . . . bragging about a seven-thousand-dollar Hermès saddle she'd bought, thinking she was impressing us when of course we're all doing our best not to burst out laughing . . ."

"Pathetic," the colonel mumbled every time Ginny Bland paused between complaints to take a sip of wine.

" . . . I finally cornered the manager at Bounty, and asked if he could spare some of that yummy *pâté* they served at the Bastille Day Bash, and he has the gall to tell me it's too dear and I'm fuming as I remind him what we spend there, but he refuses to budge, so I say, 'Let me explain something to you, Harris,' and while I'm standing there, telling him off, No Caller ID pops up on my phone and, like an idiot, I pick up and this voice—this girl's voice—says 'Hi, Augusta.' I said,

'Excuse me?' And she says, 'Do you want to come to my house for a playdate?' And I said, 'Who *is* this?' and of course it's Shelby Nash's girl, Da'Shajay. I still can't pronounce her name. Did I tell you she has a fully developed chest? In fifth grade! Though Bronwyn swears she was held back a year. I don't know, Cleet, I consider myself an open-minded person, but I don't want to encourage a friendship between Augusta and the Warren-Nash girl. And I don't appreciate being put in the position of having to explain the whole 'two-dads' thing to Augusta." Ginny Bland bit her asparagus spear. "Speaking of Shelby Nash . . ." She went on and on about re-decorating the carriage house on their property like his carriage house, which was photographed for *Hound & Hammock* magazine. " . . . old heart pine flooring, beautifully pock-marked, this *amazing* brick and oyster-shell courtyard . . ."

She got all fired up and rushed out of the kitchen to fetch something.

After she left, the colonel spun around on his heel, like he was on parade ground, pulled down a bottle of whiskey from the cabinet and drank straight from the bottle—about five seconds' worth of gulping. When he was done, he shook his head something fierce and put the bottle away a full three seconds before that Ginny came back. She was waving the cover of *Hound & Hammock* magazine like a victory flag. "Shelby's going to rent it out . . . told me on good authority Bronwyn has her eye on it, a discreet little *pied-à-terre* for her and Dabney Hines, presumably, as if *everybody* in town doesn't already know . . ."

"Pathetic."

I was wishing she would run out of words, as the bees she complained of were back, a dozen of them swirling around my head, buzzing next to my ear.

"You sure you want Shelby working on our cottage, Gin?"

"Maybe it's time to let this Hatfield and McCoy nonsense go. At least for the sake of good taste. And Shelby most definitely has that, doesn't he, Cleet? It was a hundred years ago, for God's sake. Nobody can even remember what the grievance is *about* anymore. I'm sure Shelby's forgotten all about it. Besides, he did most of Willow's house. That sunroom they added is flawless."

They wrapped up their small talk and extinguished the lights. Ginny Bland and the colonel disappeared, then reappeared a few seconds later, in the library. I angled the boom mic towards the room where Colonel Bland told her tall tales about us. "Nighty night, Lady Astor," Ginny said.

"*Braaa,* she's not from here. *Braaa,* she's not from here."

Ginny draped a gray blanket that read LUFTHANSA over the top of the cage.

The colonel extinguished the library light. A half minute later, on went the bedroom lights on the second floor. I shimmied round to the other side of the house, retreating towards the perimeter to secure a better view. After I adjusted the field glasses, they came into focus. The colonel was in his skivvies, still tall and lean and plank-like. The vision of him half-naked stirred me. As for Skinny Ginny, she was equally plank-like, but in all the wrong ways. I angled the boom mic and picked up her voice. She was still complaining about that Bronwyn woman from yoga class. I had to adjust my goggles to zoom in on her blue pajamas, which appeared to be splattered with food stains from neck to ankle. The pink globs, it turns out, were little whales.

After the lights went out, it got quiet, and I started to break down my gear. Until I heard a low whispering voice in my headphones: "If you ever decide to destroy our family and humiliate me, will you promise *not* to hook up with some white trash psychopath who can't even string a coherent sentence together?"

I heard covers rumple. "My type has long blonde hair and green eyes."

That stung, his comment did. Until I realized he was just trying to appease her while he contemplated how he would get away from her and fulfill his destiny with me.

I heard little kissing pecks.

"No, Cleet. Please."

The pecking stopped.

"Ginny, I've been back a month."

"I'm just not ready. And Augusta . . ."

"Augusta can't hear a thing. She's all the way down the hall!"

"I just don't have it in me tonight."

"Or any night."

Sheets rustled again.

"What are you doing? Stop, Cleet!"

"What's the big deal?"

"I said STOP!"

It was silent for a spell. Then: "My God, those big, crazy eyes. Black as coal."

"Whose?"

"That lunatic who came to our home tonight!"

"Don't be so nasty, Gin," the colonel said. "She's a Goddamned hero. Just had a rough time of it." I knew he would stick up for me eventual. "A lot of us have," he continued.

Ginny Bland laughed.

"You think that's funny?"

"I actually wasn't even listening to you. I was thinking about her nose."

"Her nose?"

I heard someone punching a pillow.

"Not exactly what one might call an 'aristocratic nose.'"

"No. I suppose not," the colonel mumbled.

"You used to say my nose was aristocratic."

The colonel didn't answer.

"Cleet?"

Colonel Bland was gently snoring.

I packed my gear and evacuated.

"You can't sleep here!"

I scraped the granola out my eyes.

"Look at the sign," the postmaster said, pointing at the entry door. 'No Loitering.'"

"Forgive me, ma'am."

I rolled up my mat and tucked it in the corner of the El Camino's bed, next to my munitions box and the spare tire. After I paid $4 for a cup of coffee, I searched on my phone for a state park, where they always got lakes and rivers.

After a bath in the ice-cold waters of Lake Albemarle, I drove downtown.

SHELBY NASH & ASSOCIATES, ARCHITECTS AND INTERIOR DESIGN, my destination, was on one of those uneven cobblestone streets. I waited in my car until a man with a pink moon-shaped face rolled up around ten-thirty and unlocked the door.

"You Shelby Nash?"

"Who's asking?" said the man.

"I understand you got a cottage for rent?" His eyebrow went up. "How'd you know that?"

"Ginny Bland mentioned it."

He eyed me suspicious. "You and Mrs. Bland are . . . *friends*?"

I told him all about my time in Afghanistan with the colonel and why I'd come to Charlottesville. He looked at me all shock and awe, then snorted.

"I didn't think Cleet Bland had it in him."

Shelby Nash invited me into his office. It was an old house overstuffed with antique furniture, all of it with price tags dangling off the sides.

"Mrs. Bland wants you to do up her guest cottage all fancy like yours."

Shelby Nash sat at his desk, folding his hands like he was about to pray. "Lucky me."

"Who's Bronwyn?" I asked.

"Excuse me?"

"Bronwyn, who struts in to 9:00 o'clock yoga class between 9:09 and 9:15 on most days and plops her mat on the hardwood floors."

"Ah," he said, tilting his chair backward on its hind legs. "Since you spoke so frankly me to me about your situation, I'll speak candidly to you, Miss Vaduva. Bronwyn Fleming is the second biggest bitch in Albemarle County."

"Who's the first?"

Shelby Nash grinned. "Ginny Bland, of course."

"She don't like you much."

"Bronwyn or Ginny?"

I told him that Ginny Bland said his kids act badly at school drop off, and how her girl, Augusta, shouldn't friends with Da'Shajay because she has two daddies and her chest popped out early.

Shelby Nash burst out laughing. "Yes, the boob fairy came early to our house."

He swiveled in his chair, which made a long squeak, then

faced his computer. Stretching his fingers like a piano expert set to play a masterpiece, he banged on his keyboard with gusto. He finished up by pounding his index finger on the return key. He looked to me with his eyebrow raised. "So tell me, how did Ginny take the news about your lovechild with Cleet?"

I pulled up a chair, a needlepoint number stitched up with roses. "She was nice enough when I first came in. But later, when she didn't know I was listening, she called me white trash and said I didn't know how to string a sentence together."

"I'm sorry you had to hear that."

"Insults don't bother me," I told him. "I could tell you some phrases terrorists directed at me in Farsi before I shot them. About female goats' rotting private parts and so on."

"I'm sure. But that won't be necessary."

Shelby Nash rose, went to the window, and pulled apart a set of green velvet curtains. "Anti-black. Anti-gay. Anti-redneck, if you'll excuse the expression. That's my Ginny."

"She's a talker, Ginny Bland is."

Shelby Nash approached a table, where he arranged stacks of old books covered in leather. Moved ink wells around just so. Shuffled a tray overflowing with antique pens.

"How much is the cottage to rent?"

"That depends. How long are you planning to stay?"

"Fifteen days. Thirty max. Just until I marry Colonel Bland. After that we'll move in to his house, I reckon."

Shelby Nash was wiping dust off the cover of an antique book by some fella named Flannery O'Connor.

"You mean *my* house."

"Begging your pardon, sir?"

"I mean Derbyshire Farm was my family's home for nine generations," Shelby Nash said. It was the oldest, finest examples of Georgian architecture in America, he told me, modeled after a fancy house owned by the Duke of Something from the town in England where they invented Salisbury Steak TV dinners.

"If it's your house, how come Colonel Bland lives there?"

Shelby Nash laughed bitterly. The colonel's family stole Derbyshire Farm from his family in 1923, he said, after they got themselves indebted to the Blands. A dispute over mining rights in Nash County, in Southwest Virginia. At one point, someone in Shelby Nash's family put a gun in his mouth and blew his own head off, Shelby lamented. He picked up an antique pen and unscrewed, then re-screwed, the lid. "Just out of curiosity, once you marry Cleet Bland and move into Derbyshire Farm, what will become of Ginny Bland?"

"Her destiny isn't my concern, sir. Only mine and the colonel's is."

"I see." Shelby Nash waved the pen at me the way a schoolteacher waves a pointer. "And do you have grand redecorating plans for the house . . . once it's yours?"

"I like horses. I'm not a half-bad rider. But the house is bigger than I'm used to. I'd just as well move back to West Virginia, assuming the colonel is keen to do so after we marry. Build a cabin along the New River, with a wood-burning stove and a screened-in porch to keep the bugs out. Some place near Thurmond, close to my mama and grand-mamas, but not *too* close, if you know what I mean."

"I do." Shelby Nash crossed his arms over his chest. "I guess we need to discuss rent."

"After gas and the $4 coffee I had this morning, I got $97.81."

"Really?"

"I can do odd jobs," I told him. "I'm good at fixing cars and farm equipment, for example."

Shelby Nash said he had all that covered. "What else can you do?"

"Everything the Army taught me." I gave him a laundry list of my skills.

He pulled a big picture book off the shelf. *Virginia Plantation Homes*—that same book Colonel Bland had in his tent. "Maybe there's another arrangement we could make." His eyes twinkled. "I would be honored to have you as my guest if you could, perhaps, help me with something."

"Happy to help. I ain't looking for hand-outs."

"Of course not," he said. "It seems to me you and I are both looking for the same thing. To claim what's rightfully ours."

I nodded agreement.

"What's rightfully yours," continued Shelby, "is the love of a man, the father for your child."

I nodded again.

"What's rightfully mine," he said, laying his beefy palms over the glossy pictures of Colonel Bland's house, "rightfully, unquestionably, legitimately and justly mine . . . is Derbyshire Farm. Do you think you could help me regain what's mine if I were able to help you get what's rightfully yours?"

"I got no claim on the colonel's house, only the colonel."

"Splendid." Shelby Nash sat down in his chair and tilted backwards again. "Tell me about your plan."

"Plan, sir?"

"You didn't actually think you can just walk in, announce you're pregnant, and expect Cleet to divorce Ginny on the spot and marry you?"

"That's exactly my plan, sir. It's already underway."

"And how's it working for you so far, this plan?"

I swept away a few blades of dried grass from the Blands' lawn off my thigh. "Not so good, sir."

He shook his head. "Sharing your news is one thing. Cleet *acting* on it is quite another. You need a more comprehensive plan, a long-term plan."

"The colonel will do what's right. He's an officer and a gentleman."

"If you say so."

"He has no choice," I told him. "It's his destiny."

Shelby said he was impressed with my certitude, despite the fact that he was not. "Listen," he said, boring his eyes into mine. "The obstacles in your path are a lot bigger that you realize."

"I never met an obstacle I can't get around, sir. And with all due respect, folks around here don't scare me. It's not like they're gonna take me out with a MAS-49 assault rifle."

Shelby said where I was now, in what he referred to as "the highest echelons of Charlottesville society," was an entirely different theatre of warfare than what I was accustomed to. "It's one thing to conquer a mountain in Afghanistan," he said. "But quite another to conquer the molehill we call Albemarle County. Here they shoot you down with words—even looks—not bullets. Ginny and Cleet Bland—and the legion of idle, talentless, trust-funded relatives, who preceded them—have been kings of the molehill in Albemarle County for more than a century. And you should expect that they'll do *whatever* it takes to defend their position."

"I suppose I could always make him come with me. Intercept him, tie him up, and take him to West Virginia in the bed of my El Camino."

Shelby squished his thick buttocks against the side of his desk. "I think there might be more effective ways of helping Cleet see the light. If you'll allow me to guide you in the development of a few new skills to add to your fascinating portfolio."

I reckoned he was urging me to get more training. "When we drilled, Colonel Bland always quoted a Greek poet. 'We don't rise to the level of our expectations,' he always said, 'we fall to the level of our training.'"

Shelby Nash slapped his knee even harder this time. "Cleet Bland and I finally agree on something!"

Shelby Bland fluttered off his desk and told me he had some ideas for training. He scribbled out his address and instructed me to report at seventeen hundred hours.

"Welcome to Humbolt Farm," Shelby said when he opened the door. "It's not as grand as the Blands' spread, I assure you, but hopefully it passes muster."

"You got stables like the Blands. You rich, too?"

"Two horses doesn't exactly make you rich. They're for the girls."

"For you." I handed him a can of jalapeño cheddar cheese dip.

"Fortuitous!" Shelby Nash chuckled. "Malik," he shouted, "I have treasure for you!"

Shelby Nash escorted me to the kitchen to meet Aliyah and Malik and Elijah and Da'Shajay. They were cooking Mexican. Ginny Bland told the truth about Da'Shajay alright: girl looked to be about a 36C.

The screen door slammed and Dr. Davis Warren appeared. He looked like a United States Senator that one did: six-foot-two, strong jawline, black hair with gray specs at the temples. Shelby Nash told me while Dr. Warren was mixing margaritas that Davis knew the Blands, too. "He's actually a Bland himself—or once *was*—until his great-grandfather was excommunicated from the family, socially and, more importantly, financially, for marrying a Catholic."

"'Hate the sin, love the sinner,' that's always been my motto," the doctor quipped.

The kids were lovable at dinner—not at all rude, like Ginny Bland said. Aliyah, the youngest, did imitations of all her teachers at Digby Day. I could not say whether they were good or not, as I did not know any of the faculty at the kids' school. During the meal, I stuffed my face: nachos, tacos, enchiladas, and refried beans with melted cheese and sour cream. I was not impressed with my manners, but I had been without grub for two days.

After dinner was done, Shelby walked me over to the guest house.

"What's a brick oyster-shell courtyard?"

"You're standing in it," he said.

I looked down at what looked like run-over oysters in a bed of concrete. "I don't understand what all the fuss is about."

"It's all a matter of taste." He walked me inside the house. After showing me around a living room, done up mostly in white, we sat down. "I have a few questions for you," Shelby Nash said.

"I'll find a job by noon tomorrow. Until then," I said while rummaging through my munitions box, "here's $94.67. This morning I told you I had $97.81 for rent, but the jalapeño cheddar cheese dip was $3.14, which took me down to $94.67."

"I wasn't going to ask you about money. Different question."

"Fire."

"It's about your baby."

"Sir?"

"When will you start showing?"

"It's still real early. I got a hundred days, maybe one hundred and twenty I reckon, until I'm noticeable to strangers as with child."

"Don't most women show before that? Aliyah's mother was obviously pregnant sixty days in."

"The medium-built girls show early—especially if it's not their first. But the really fat ones hide it because they always look pregnant and the really fit ones stay skinny longer. Taut abdominal muscles."

"You look extremely fit."

"This morning, I ran ten miles, did 2,000 sit ups and a hundred pull ups."

Dr. Davis Warren, leaning in the doorway, overheard this. He looked at his husband. The two locked eyes. "We need to keep you on that workout regimen," the doctor said.

"Here's the deal, Tami," continued Shelby Nash. "In exchange for a place to stay—rent-free—you have to agree to let me teach you *everything* you'll need to know to conquer Cletus Bland."

"I already know how to infiltrate his compound."

"I'm sure. But you don't know how to infiltrate his *world*—which is ten times harder to penetrate than his compound." He swirled the margarita in his tulip-shaped glass. "But I do."

"You'll train me?"

"Yes, and it's going to be a form of combat training as intense as anything you experienced in the field." Shelby Nash gestured for Dr. Davis Warren to come over. The two sat together side by side. "If you're going to capture Cleet Bland, you've got to penetrate the fortress Ginny Bland has built around him. And you've got to get in *fast!* Because the minute you start to show, its game over—*for all of us.*"

"When do we commence the training, sir?"

"Tomorrow morning. Be ready at six."

We were driving up into the Blue Ridge Mountains for a sunup hike.

"I'm used to something hard under my back," I told Shelby Nash as I laced up my boots. "That bed of yours was like sleeping on a thatch of cotton candy."

"Yves Delorme linens. You've got to take out a second mortgage to afford them, but worth every penny."

As we ascended Afton Mountain in his car, Shelby wanted to know about my time in Afghanistan. I told him about my various missions—the ones I was authorized to discuss. Then we talked about all the different training exercises I had undertaken in the Army: advanced weapons, languages, PSYOPs, surveillance, and chemical weapons school. "I hated chemistry in high school. They know how to teach it better in the Army. Mix equal parts of difluoride and dichloride: you get sarin gas."

"I don't think we'll need to deploy chemical weapons to capture Cleet Bland."

Shelby Nash was thinking deeply while he parked the car. After his thinking period was complete, he said, "To infiltrate this new enemy territory, deception will be crucial."

I told him about infiltrating that seamstress group in Ghazni Province.

"After you get in and gain their trust, our version of PSYOPs begins. But let's not get too far ahead of ourselves."

"Train first, fight next."

"Exactly," he said. The leaves crunched beneath our feet as we entered the trail. "When you enlist, the first thing they do is de-program the old you and re-program a new one, am I right, Tami?"

I was following him onto a path marked with three notches. "It's called 'resocialization,' sir. The United States Army rewires a recruit's mind and emotions so he or she can survive in a hostile foreign environment."

"Well, that's exactly what we're going to do to you. To fit in with these people—especially the women—you can't have an ounce of fat on you, which, thankfully, you don't. But you need a yoga body, which you don't have. Yours is a warrior's body. Too much muscle. You need to become more *sinewy*."

"I don't know that term, sir."

"Have you ever noticed a professional tennis player's arms?"

"No, sir."

He looked around. "See that tree root? It's strong and tough—like you—but stretchy. I've got a stack of DVDs in the cottage. You need to start training in yoga poses tonight. Without yoga skills, I'm afraid it will be very difficult to infiltrate the enemy. And you can't possibly do tennis. Not with those ripped biceps of yours. They'll think you're some sort of dyke bodybuilder."

"I never done yoga."

"It's miserable. I *loathe* it; can't even touch my toes. But it's what all the women here do." Shelby Nash stabbed his walking stick into the mud. "Next is your uniform. In the military, you have fatigues, dress blues, and so on. And if even the tiniest element of the uniform is off—the shoes aren't shined properly, the hat is askew, whatever—it gets noticed, am I right?"

"If you're not squared away, the D.I. will make you drop and give him fifty."

"Well, it's the same with the people in the Blands' platoon. The women's yoga attire must be the right brand, fit, color, fabric, and so on."

"I follow."

"The jeans and tops that look so carelessly thrown together," Shelby Nash continued, "are in fact painstakingly selected—after hours or even weeks of shopping. We've got to get your wardrobe *exactly* right. Take cowboy boots, for example. There are a hundred ways to get a pair of cowboy boots wrong—and these women are trained to detect each and every one of them." Shelby Nash squatted on a tree stump to catch his breath. He took a big gulp of water. "Ginny and her tribe all get their boots from Cordwainers. They start at thirty-five hundred dollars."

"I never bought a pair in my life. Army-issue for me."

"Those won't do. "

"All I got is $94.67, sir. Even if I get a job doing auto-repair work or as a security guard, it'll take time for me to save up for all them fancy things you expect me to wear."

"No job!" he says. "Stop thinking about money! Definitely stop *talking* about it. The rich never talk about money—except to complain about how they don't have any. It's how you can always tell who's really got it. The rich – the old money rich, anyway – always talk poor despite all evidence to the contrary."

Shelby said he and Davis would cover all my expenses, then told a story about a woman in Ginny Bland's yoga class, a professor at the university, who went to Harvard University and became a Rhodes Scholar. The nonworking women in Ginny's yoga class called her a "striver" in secret and didn't invite her to the Bastille Day Bash. "The way these women assert their status over the women they perceive to be their inferiors is to earn a college degree – sometimes even multiple college degrees from very expensive private schools, then *not deign to work.*"

"Then why go in the first place?"

Shelby Nash laughed out loud and planted his walking stick firm into the ground. He hoisted himself off the tree stump and started walking again. "By the time I'm done educating you in their idiosyncratic ways, I promise you'll know the answer to that question."

I shook my head, confused.

Shelby kept talking. "Food. How they eat. And more importantly, what they don't eat. It's another huge tribal marker. When they're all picking on their kale salads at Bounty—it's always kale you order, never the Cobb. Ginny Bland and her friends don't *touch* bacon or blue cheese."

"Roger that."

He asked if I needed to write any of this down. I told him I had a memory like a camera.

Just as I had been advance-trained in military weapons, I had to get advance-trained in rich people's accessories, habits, and hobbies—what Shelby called "status badges"—which is for the women a form of weaponry: the right hair color, the right haircut, makeup, purses, jewels, furniture, which grocery store to buy from, which model iPhone to buy, and what kind of SUV to drive. ("Chevy Suburban, the fully loaded one, in white or navy blue—*never* black".)

We got to a clearing that was bright green and looked down

into the valley. "What do you know about horses? You said you know how to ride."

"I did six weeks' mountain warfare training with Special Forces. Pamir Mountains—in the Gorno-Badakhshan province of Tajikistan. Horse and mule riding. I learnt to canter a horse sideways up a forty-five degree incline."

"You'll do fine at the Foxtrot Races, I'm sure." Shelby remarked.

The sun had climbed high by this time and Shelby Nash was now perspiring heavy. He sat down again. Behind us, in the woods, I heard a rustle of leaves and braced my hand over the wet shirt clinging to Shelby Nash's chest to still him.

"What are you doing?" he whispered, looking around all fearful.

"Squirrel. Where I'm from, you never pass up an opportunity to get a squirrel. On any given day there's a half-dozen in my mama's freezer."

Shelby Nash sighed. "I brought sandwiches from Bounty. Turkey with cranberry relish and cheddar or country ham, Swiss and honey mustard." Shelby apologized for not remembering to feed me. He got all carried away, he said.

He took the sandwiches from his bag. "As part of your cover, we're going to need to give you a new name and a credible backstory."

"I done that a million times."

"There's one element of the training that we've got to do right away, and I'm not sure you're going to like it."

"Sir?"

"If you're going to infiltrate the Blands' inner circle, you'll need to make some . . . cosmetic changes."

"I don't wear makeup. Never have."

"Not just makeup, which you have to start wearing. But more. I'm afraid, *much* more."

"Like what?"

"It's not just your clothes and your, uh, haircut. There's an easy solution for that. And your eyes are a simple fix: a pair of tinted contact lenses and *voila*." He chewed slowly and broached the next subject with caution. "*Permanent* changes." He watched close for my reaction.

"Permanent?"

"Your teeth, for starters."

"I never went to a dentist before I got to the Army."

"I figured as much."

"What else?"

"Your under-bite." He pushed my chin backward. "Davis says you'll need jaw surgery."

I looked down at my chest.

"It's a simple procedure, really, and we can do it right after Davis fixes your nose."

"Nose?"

"That too, I'm afraid."

I reached up and touched my nose. "Could he make me an aristocratic nose? That's what the colonel likes."

Shelby Nash smiled. "You bet he can!"

I leaned back and took a big bite of my ham and cheese sandwich. "Change don't bother me none. I've been changing my appearance for one mission after the other," I said, whipping the honey-mustard sauce off my chin with my sleeve. Shelby handed me a napkin. "Effective immediately, your sleeve-wiping privileges are revoked."

He dabbed the corner of his mouth with his napkin and inspected the little red glob of cranberry on the napkin the way Ricky Ray Jeeter used to study the boogers on the tip if his index finger. "We've got another issue. A big one. Possibly the biggest. Fortunately, it requires no surgery to correct."

"What's that, sir?"

"Your dialect. An instant giveaway that you are—to use Ginny Bland's favorite expression—'not from here.' If she meets someone whose family has only lived in Virginia for say, 150 years, she'll pretend she's never heard of them and say they're 'not from here.' Virginia aristocrats—the truly old families—have an unmistakable accent. It's very subtle. Lilt-y. Elegant. They don't transfer planes in Charlotte, North Carolina, but in 'Shaw-luht.'"

Shelby told me I needed to see a woman for speech therapy counseling, a lady who usually worked with people who stuttered or lisped. She would teach me how to "speak Charlottesville," he said, before correcting himself. "'Shaw-lutz-vull,' I meant to say."

I told Shelby Nash I had a good ear for foreign languages and could mimic other people's sounds. I demonstrated my ululating skills, which I put to good use when we got Mehdi Hashmi. *"Aye-aye-aye-aye-aye-aye-aye!"*

Shelby Nash burst out laughing. "You're going to rock it." He suggested we head back to the car. "Look, Tami," he told me almost in a whisper. "This training is going to be all-consuming for us. Once we start, there's no turning back. Are you all in? One hundred percent in? If you're not, no hard feelings, but Davis and I need to know *now*—before a lot of time and money is invested."

"All in, sir. I do nothing at less than one hundred ten percent."

"That's been my impression."

On the way down the mountain, Shelby was fired up, making one phone call after another the whole time. There was a spring to his step. Sometimes he walked so fast I had to trot to keep up with him.

The next morning, at zero-eight hundred hours sharp, Dr. Davis Warren drove me to his office. Inside, he showed me a stack of pictures of women's noses. They all looked the same to me, so I told him to pick the most aristocrat-looking one. I changed into green PJs and Davis knocked me out with gas. Last thing I remembered before drifting into sleep was dreaming about Colonel Bland and him telling me to call him "Cleet."

When I woke up, I discovered I was in a different doctor's office in Dr. Davis Warren's building. His friend, an oral surgeon, had fixed my jaw while I was under, Dr. Warren told me as I reached up and felt the gauze wrapped around my head.

Back at the cottage, as twilight faded into evening, the fellas were the best nurses you ever saw. Shelby and Davis rubbed special lotions and creams all over my face, to control the swelling.

"Take this pain medication," said Davis Warren.

"I don't take medicine."

"You'll take this or regret it. We cut up the bottom half of your face today.

Shelby signaled me to hand him the pills. "On our hike today, Tami told me a story about her time in Afghanistan, when

ISIS or Taliban fighters—I can't remember which—hooked her up to a car battery with jumper cables. If she says she doesn't need pain meds, I'm inclined to believe her, Davis."

"I saw too many soldiers get hooked on dope," I slurred through the gauze, my face and mouth still numb.

The fellas told me to get some shut-eye and extinguished the lights.

The next morning, the fellas returned. Shelby gave me a protein smoothie for breakfast, made with peaches and yogurt. "You don't get out of bed today other than to go to the bathroom and back, doctor's orders," Davis said. "Sleep as much as you can."

"I'm wide awake and ready to start my training," I told them.

"Sleep."

I shrugged. "I'm just gonna sit here. Might as well train."

Shelby looked at Davis, then left the room and returned with a book, which he put on the nightstand. "Your assignment is to read this, cover to cover," he said.

The fellas left, to get the kids to school and go to work.

I studied the cover: *Antiquarian Assets: The Mythology of Inherited Wealth*. The back cover said the book was about rich people—people like the Blands and their set. It purported to be an "examination" of old-moneyed rich people's values, beliefs and behaviors. It looked like the most boring book in the history of books. I've never cared much about money. Nor did I care about Colonel Bland's money. Whether he was poor as a septic tank-emptier or rich as Dale Earnhardt, Jr. made no difference to me.

After I did some reading, I watched the yoga DVDs to learn the positions. I was keen to try them, but Dr. Warren said I wasn't allowed to get up except to pee.

So I read more *Antiquarian Assets* again. It was no more interesting the second time around.

I dozed off.

"More food for the body and mind," Shelby said when he come in at the end of the day and woke me. He brought me another smoothie—this time banana-strawberry—along with a big stack of ladies' clothing catalogs, *The Oxford Dictionary of Family Names in Britain and Ireland*, DVDs about food and travel, and a bunch of picture books on "dragoons"—British mounted infantrymen who rode horses into combat, parked them, then did all their fighting on foot.

"Listen to your body," Davis said later in the evening, after he put the kids down. "When you're tired, sleep."

I stayed up all night reading.

Next morning, Shelby came in, this time with a honeydew-almond smoothie. "The headmaster is in," he announced. "Do you have enough energy for tutoring?"

"Willing and ready, sir."

"The women in this town have to go to Bermuda for six months to convalesce after just getting their eyelids done. And you're 'willing and ready.' I love it. Let us begin. Time for your 'book report.' What is *Antiquarian Assets* about?"

"Rich people in America."

"What kind of rich people?"

"White Anglo-Saxon Protestants. Or 'WASPs.'"

"Go on."

"They're different than people who make their money from scratch—people with 'new money.'"

"Continue."

"New money is bad compared to old money."

"Correct. Why?"

"Old money people don't like nothing ever to change."

"And?"

"And they don't like strangers."

"Gold star! That's the most important message of the book, Tami. This we'll call the concept of *Always.* When Old Money is seventy it is still friends with the people it knew since it was six—and *only* them. In Charlottesville, Old Money children *always* attended Digby Day for elementary school, *always* took piano lessons from Mrs. Gammie, *always* went to the same town in Maine in summer, *always* attended Fourth of July fireworks at Worthington Country Club, *always* went to the Homestead at Christmas, and *always* went to the same stupid parties—Wild West parties, 1970s parties, Great Gatsby parties, Old Havana parties, and black and white galas."

"'*Always*' sounds like it'd get boring."

"Excruciatingly. But not to them. Continuity is a source of great comfort to these people."

I gave his pink-checked shirt, khaki pants, and bowtie a once-over. "You're one of them? An old money person?"

"Indeed I am." He put his hands behind his head, like he was stargazing. "What do you remember about their manners?"

"They got excellent manners."

"Yes. Which leads us to the next crucial concept for you to master: *grace.* Graciousness is the core value of old money. They are always excessively polite, especially to those they consider to be inferior—which is, of course, everyone who is not one of them."

He took his arms down and folded them across his lap,

like a professor. "So, if grace is what they value, what do you suppose they detest?"

"Rudeness."

"Second gold star. Vulgarity offends them. Deeply." Shelby then described the million ways to offend old money by being vulgar. Coarse language was vulgar. Modern homes and modern art were vulgar. People who drove flashy cars or wore flashy clothes were vulgar. Basically, any display of ostentatiousness—showing off—was vulgar, Shelby said. "The preferred term they use to describe vulgar people and things is 'shiny.'"

"Ginny Bland said a seven-thousand-dollar saddle from Herman Somebody was 'shiny.'"

"I bet she did. Ginny Bland's frenemy, Sloan Whittle, just bought a Hermès saddle. She's the laughingstock of the town."

"Then why do these women wear three thousand dollar cowboy boots?"

Shelby Nash clasped his hands together. "Excellent question! Again, it's a matter of appearances. Cowboy boots crafted by a local artisan, and exquisitely distressed, are lovingly beat up and made to look worn-in. Old."

"Like they was always owned."

"Precisely. Such boots are a subtle display of wealth, whereas a brand-name designer saddle is—"

"Shiny."

"Ginny may have been talking about the saddle, but what she *really* meant was Sloan Whittle, the saddle-owner. Shiny is bad because it attracts attention. Shiny stimulates envy. And the last thing Old Money can afford—figuratively or literally—is for people to get jealous of them. Because people who don't have anything don't like being reminded of that by people who have everything. The have-nots may lash out and make the have-everythings uncomfortable. And Old Money despises anything that makes them uncomfortable. Old Money people work very hard to project an image of modesty and humility. They are modest in speech; they don't yell. In attitude, they are self-effacing, never braggarts. They never waste money. Simple pot roast, not lobster and caviar. They may own six homes, but take great pride in plopping down a buy-one-get-one-free coupon at the grocery store."

"Why not enjoy your money?"

"Because you can never be seen by outsiders enjoying it. Let me tell you about Ginny Bland's great-grandfather's brother. He was governor of Virginia in the 1920s. He was worth then what today might be the equivalent of one hundred and fifty to two hundred million dollars. Legend has it a newspaper reporter came to interview him, and when the reporter entered his office, the governor was wearing a shirt and tie and a suit jacket—but no trousers, just boxers. Throughout the meeting the governor sat on a sofa, trousers in hand, sewing the split seams on a twenty-five-year-old suit, because to replace the suit would be wasteful when it could be repaired. And, besides—"

"—old is always better than new."

Shelby high-fived me.

After my latrine break, Shelby asked did I speak Italian.

"We refueled there once, at the base in Vicenza."

"There's a word in Italian—*sprezzatura*—which is defined as 'an art which does not seem to be an art, a carefully cultivated nonchalance, an elegant carelessness in attitude and personal behavior. Whatever is done or said appears to be without effort and almost without any thought about it.'"

"Colonel Bland was like that—except when he was in combat."

"All Old Money is always like that. So if being casual and elegant is what they value most, to be seen working too hard and wanting something too much—what the Italians call *'affettazione'* or affectation—is the height of what, Tami?"

"Vulgarity?"

"Third gold star." Shelby talked about how if I acted vulgar, in any way, I'd get caught. "They won't call it vulgar; they'll call it 'pathetic.' Wanting to be like them, when you were never one of them and never can *be* one of them, is vulgar." Shelby explained how self-made men and people like Ralph Lauren were all jealous of them—and how Old Money knew it and despised them for it. Asking people what they do for a living is vulgar because most of the people in the Blands' set don't really have jobs, he said. Not serious ones, anyway. "Nothing so offends those with inherited money as striving, or climbing, or clawing one's way up the corporate ladder," he said. "Even worse is *social* ambition, which may be the greatest form of vulgarity. This is why you must never appear the slightest bit interested in them." Shelby took a sip of his Coca-Cola. "There's a fifty-fifty chance we'll get away with it, but if you treat them with polite indifference, yet are duly intriguing and make them wonder if you might in fact be *even richer than them*, we might just be able to get them to come to *you*."

"I thought you said they don't care about money?"

I said they project the *appearance* of not caring about money. But make no mistake about it, they care very, very much."

"You have the skin of an angel," Dr. Davis Warren said after taking off my bandages. It was early in the morning – at least by Davis and Shelby's standards, though not mine: I'd been up since zero-four-hundred hours. They brought my smoothie. Shelby handed me a binder after he bade goodbye to his husband, who was dropping the kids at school early on his way to work.

"Get familiar with this."

I was worn out from all the reading about rich people, but I eagerly took it as there's no such thing as too much intel.

"It's a briefing book on Cleet. His interests and hobbies."

"I already know the colonel."

"No, you don't. You'll need to be an even bigger expert on all his favorite pastimes than he is."

I flipped the binder open to a random page. Shelby pointed to the picture of a bottle. "His favorite whisky is called 'Horsebit.' It's a precious little small-batch bourbon. They make it down in Charleston." He flipped a tab. "UVA football—players' bios, the coach, rivalries, mascots, legends and lore, stuff like that." Next tab: "Cleet's really into shooting. Quail hunting. Info on guns and shells and the best places to shoot."

I flipped through the tabs. "Nothing in here on that Ginny Bland."

"Should there be? I'm not so sure she qualifies as one of his 'favorite pastimes.'"

"Information on her hobbies and interests. Where she attended school and what not. Every time I did black ops—whether it was in Iraq, Kabul, Islamabad, Riyadh—we always had intel on the spouse. Good source of leverage."

Shelby Nash gave me an eye roll. "Ginny Bland is the most milquetoast vanilla woman in the county. She went to Digby Day—*like they all did.* She went to Sweet Briar—*like they all did.* She's blonde, insincere, excruciatingly well-mannered, and passive-aggressive—*like they all are.* Learn her favorite yoga pose and her brand of Chardonnay and you'll unlock whatever remaining mysteries there are about her."

I arched an eyebrow, just like Shelby. "She's having intimate relations with another man."

His mouth shot wide open, like someone just stuffed a whole potato in it.

"She's what?"

"Mr. Dabney Hines."

"That's impossible!"

"I put that Ginny Bland under surveillance." I got out of bed and retrieved my folder on Ginny Bland from my pack. I spread the pictures out like a deck of tarot cards.

"Where were these taken?"

"Magnolia Motor Lodge. Lynchburg."

"When?"

"The day I met you. You said go away until nightfall. I like to keep myself occupied." I showed him the time stamp on each photo. "Thirteen hundred hours: She gets there first and waits in her Suburban. Thirteen-twelve hours: a silver BMW enters the lot. Thirteen-fourteen hours: the man driving the silver BMW enters the room. Thirteen-fifteen hours: Ginny Bland enters the room."

"What's that she's carrying?"

"Sheets. That expensive kind you like, from the looks of them." I rubbed my hands over the Yves Delorme bedding. "Fourteen-forty-one hours: she comes out. Her face is all flush. Adjusting her blouse. The look of a woman who just had a go. Fourteen-forty-one hours: the gentleman exits, his hair wet from a shower."

Shelby Nash picked up the pictures, studying them like they were proof that UFOs exist. "I thought he was screwing his business partner's wife, not his best friend's wife."

"Is Bronwyn Fleming his business partner's wife?"

"Yes. How'd you guess?"

"Ginny said Bronwyn wants to rent your cottage to use as a love shack with Dabney Hines."

Shelby looked baffled. "It's like she's doing a triple-bank shot in a game of billiards. I didn't think Ginny was smart enough—or horny enough—to pull something like this off."

"Classic diversionary tactic, sir. Ginny Bland and Bronwyn Fleming are in cahoots, though Bronwyn would prefer not to be. Bronwyn chaired the Digby Day auction last year."

"Which I know all about. I wanted to donate a pair of old cast iron door-stoppers—two Confederate generals, a Robert E. Lee and a Stonewall Jackson, circa 1890s—just to get them out of my showroom. But Davis wisely talked me out of it."

"Bronwyn stole money. Ginny caught her. And keeps threatening to turn her in—unless Bronwyn does favors for Ginny."

"How could you possibly know this? You weren't here a

year ago. Did you tap their phones or something?" Shelby sipped his coffee and exhaled deeply. I smelled the aroma of whiskey on his breath.

"You told me they get all their yoga clothes at Goddess Kali. Yesterday, when I was reading that book about rich people, from my bed here I hacked into the store's security camera. I kept a live audio and video feed running all day, the volume turned down low, and glanced at the shop every few minutes, between my readings. Yesterday, about fifteen-thirty hours, the two women entered the store. They rummaged through stacks of yoga pants, looking like bored shoppers, but in truth they was in a nasty fight. Bronwyn said she was tired of having her reputation ruined to cover for Ginny, and Ginny said Bronwyn was about to learn the real meaning of reputation ruin when everybody found out she stole thirty-seven thousand dollars from Digby Day and blew it on a painting of herself with her three Maltese dogs on her lap."

Shelby picked up his spiked coffee again. "Ginny Bland and Dabney Hines. Wow. How long has *this* has been going on?"

"A decade or more."

"Shut the front door!"

I retrieved my iPhone. We scrolled through pictures of Ginny Bland's and Dabney Hines's love letters.

"How the hell did you get these?"

"They was in Dabney Hines's garage, hidden in a toolbox. That's where a man puts all of his secret things because he knows his wife won't look in there. They break up every few years and swear they won't never do it again. But then they wind up doing it again."

"When were you in his garage?"

"Last night. Middle of the night. Rode Malik's bike over to Dabney Hines's house after I located his address."

"You're not supposed to get out of bed!"

"I couldn't sleep."

Shelby was shaking his head. "Davis is never going to believe this." He pulled a cigarette out of a silver case with his initials on it. "Back in a minute."

"I don't care if you smoke in here," I tell him. "I grew up with smokers."

He said Davis would kill him if he knew he snuck one every once in a while. He had a nose like a bloodhound, the doctor did, Shelby said. He went outside, lit up, and texted his husband.

"I'm going to meet Davis for coffees. He says you are to take a hot bath with plenty of moisturizing mineral soak. And no spying today. Rest! Tomorrow's going to be a big day."

"Got it, sir!"

The next morning, Shelby opened the door.

I was naked, my back turned to him, having just emerged from my second doctor-ordered hot bath in twenty-four hours. I spun around to see him standing there, carrying my smoothie. He froze, nearly dropping the beverage on the rug.

"I beg your pardon, Tami." Shelby turned and looked out the window while I pulled up my sweatpants and yanked my VIRGINIA sweatshirt over my neck. "If it's any consolation," he said after I granted him permission to turn and face me, "that's the first time I've seen a naked woman since I was nineteen. And I'm delighted to report I remain as profoundly uninterested in them today as I was then." His face was still red. He handed me the smoothie. "We've got a little problem. Which I just discovered—not that that was my intent. I wish I would have known about it before we took you in for your nose and jaw work, because we could've killed three birds with one stone."

"What's that?"

"The tats."

"What about them?"

"The women in Ginny Bland's social circles don't have zippers tattooed over their pelvises. Or gigantic 'W's tattooed on their bums."

"When they gonna see me naked?"

"In the locker room, after yoga."

"I'll keep wrapped up in a towel."

Shelby tut-tutted me. "It's not a risk we can afford to take. The tats are the old you and we need to introduce the world to the new you. Davis can remove them. Erase the letters on the backside and the, uh, zipper."

"I'd like to keep that one."

"Which one?"

"The zipper. I'll just grow the hair back."

Shelby swallowed. His Adam's apple wiggled up and down. "You're sure?"

"It's a conversation-starter with men."

"I'm sure it is."

Shelby Nash was still fidgety.

"Sir?"

"I'm sorry to have to get so personal."

"Nothing's personal."

"When the hair grows back, it'll be . . . *jet black*, yes? Like your head-hair."

"Affirmative."

"Once we land on the perfect color—butter, or ash, or whatever—I'm afraid we'll have to color the hair down south, too."

"If that will advance the mission."

"It will."

Shelby Nash cracked open a can of Coke. "I can't believe we're having this conversation."

He sat down in the chair next to the bed. "Back to school," he said, and began the day's instruction.

He picked up the copy of *Antiquarian Assets*. "There's a very strict old money curriculum," began Shelby Nash. "The subjects a young person born into Old Money is tutored in, beginning in childhood—like the classes you take at school: math, science, and so on. From a young age, Old Money is trained to prepare for—and overcome—what are known as 'the three ordeals.' Do you remember those from the book? The first ordeal is . . . ?"

"Getting sent away to prep school and separated from your mama."

Shelby tapped his finger on my night table with purpose. "Cleet, Davis, Dabney Hines, and I—plus half the men at Worthington Country Club—were all shipped off to the Endicott-Woodland School for Boys. Grades six through twelve."

"I had a vision about that boys' school when I was with the colonel. He was bullied there, wasn't he?"

"Unspeakably. And deservedly. He was a spoiled little shit. Now, onto the second ordeal, which is . . . ?"

"Conquering nature. Old Money kids are sent off to the mountains or the West for the summer. Or made to walk the Appalachian Trail to raise money for a charity."

"Exactly. Contending with nature forces the pampered children of the very wealthy to toughen up. You have to pitch a tent, find wood for the fire, freeze when it goes out, survive thunderstorms, learn survival skills, and crap in the woods. When we cook up your backstory, we're going to have to ensure that we bolster your outdoor credentials."

"I know my way around the outdoors."

"There's a second reason they go outdoors. Extra credit. What is it?"

"They want to preserve that which is ancient and unspoiled. Which is why they are all trusteds—"

"—trustees—"

"Trustees of national parks, sit on the national board of the Boy Scouts, work to save the Chesapeake Bay, and so on." I sipped my smoothie. "Protect the *'always,'* I reckon."

"You continue to amaze and impress me, Tami. And the third ordeal?"

"Military service. Going to war."

"Right," he said. "Old Money has a strong sense of duty. For the men, military service checks several boxes. To be fair, our class feels a strong sense of obligation to the country and political system that made our families rich, but also to ideals that are bigger than simply trying to claw your way up the financial ladder. Second, combat credentials soft, rich, spoiled boys as tough fighting men. When they come home—and they don't always get back—"

"—they can get easy jobs and play golf for the next fifty years. But no one can ever really accuse them of being cowards."

"Bingo!"

16.

Dr. Davis Warren's friend the speech therapist told me I couldn't speak double negatives no more—*any* more. She drilled me in grammar and made me subscribe to podcasts: grammar and usage, vocabulary. As well as *Hound & Hammock* podcasts on Southern culture, art cooking, fine wines. "Listen very carefully to how they talk."

After she completed her tutorial, Shelby continued the language tutoring. He said that any question from anybody should whenever possible be answered with one, two, or at most three words.

"That's what I did when I was infiltrating terror cells," I assured him. "One wrong word—or mispronounced word—and you're dead. I said as little as possible."

"Same principle applies here. Besides, they will misinterpret your silence as aloofness, which is what we're going for. They're used to ingratiating social climbers trying to hitch their wagons to their stars. Strivers always sucking up to them. So you want to communicate polite indifference on most occasions, mild contempt when you sense they're getting particularly nosy. That will make you intriguing in their eyes!"

He taught me stock phrases I was to employ during my interactions with Colonel Bland's set. I was to say "I don't want to bore you," in hopes they'd beg for more information, which I was under no circumstances supposed to supply. I was to wave them away to show how I didn't like to talk about myself, as gracious persons always make others feel good and don't talk about themselves. "If someone asks you a question," Shelby advised, "turn the tables and say, 'Why do you ask?'—as if you're tired of everyone treating you like a celebrity."

If someone said something such as, "I like chocolate" or "It's two o'clock," I was to cast doubt on their opinions and facts, replying with something like, "If you say so" or "I'm not so sure about that." In total, Shelby gave me about a dozen new words and phrases to memorize, which he said would work in almost any situation. "Intimidation phrases," "affirming statements," "deflective phrases," and so on.

After Shelby left for his client meeting, I practiced the day's yoga position—"hanumanasana"—splits done front to back instead of sideways.

When Shelby and Davis came in after dinner with a big cocktail shaker, Davis, who saw me posed, said, "You just learned that today? It takes people ten years to learn how to do that."

"Tore a hamstring, but they heal. It's happened before."

The boys poured their cocktails. After Shelby took a long pull from the glass, he said, *"Ahhhhh."* Then he looked at me and said, "Tonight's the night we formulate your backstory, Tami."

"This is my infiltration story?"

"Correct," said Davis as he sucked the blue cheese out of

the pit of his martini olive. "A new biography that will make you credible in the Blands' social circle."

"Everything has to be impossible to verify, naturally," Shelby added. "The first part is easy: they're all Anglophiles—most trace their ancestry to England. So we'll start by making you more British than they are themselves. A real-deal Englishwoman."

"But not *too* English," Davis warned. "Because we'll never get the accent perfect. We need to give you an accent that's got an English lilt but is deliberately off—one informed by all the places you've lived in your life."

"On the Continent, in Asia, South America, every exotic port of call we can think of," Shelby added as he took another gulp.

Davis bit through the olive. "From places we can be certain they've never visited, or are inexpert in, or we can be reasonably assured they don't know people there who can verify your pedigree claims."

"Her daddy needs to be a diplomat," Davis said to Shelby.

The first thing we did is come up with a name for me. Shelby plopped a gigantic book on the coffee table *The Oxford Dictionary of Family Names in Britain and Ireland.*

"Obviously, we won't be doing Irish," Davis sniffed as he opened the book.

The two men started with last names—what Davis called "surnames." Davis read aloud to Shelby:

"Winkworth?"

Shelby Nash wrinkled his nose. "Too cute."

"Smith?"

"Too common."

"Tunley?"

"Too pompous."

"Wright?"

"Not pompous enough."

And so on, through about 200 names. Then we started on first names: Agnes, Agatha, Beatrix, Edna, Edwina, Enid, Felicity, Primrose, Rosalind.

An hour later, we finally settled on a name with my initials, so I could remember it. I was to be called: Tamsin Euphemia Venables.

After the naming ritual was done, the boys were half-drunk. It was now time to invent all the places my pretend mama, papa, and I supposedly lived when I was a child. We flipped through the *National Geographic Atlas of the World* for ideas. I lived in embassies in Tajikistan, Zimbabwe, and Indonesia, I was instructed to say. Went on beach vacations at the Caspian Sea and ski trips in the Carpathian Mountains in Slovakia. Attended horseback-riding schools in Dubai and Singapore.

By late evening, we settled on a story that, after making me tell it fifty times in a row and firing questions at me, I knew as solidly as if I were about to undercover penetrate a terrorist cell in Lahore.

When everyone was satisfied that I was almost ready to make my debut in Charlottesville high society, Shelby stood up, losing his balance. Davis, who drank half as much as Shelby, rescued him. "Tomorrow we go to work on your accent," Shelby slurred.

"Which better be more comprehensible than Shelby's," Davis groaned as he guided his husband to the door.

The next morning, before work, Shelby came in with a stack of DVDs. "Time for a film festival," he announced. "These are foreign films. Old movies from England and Sweden and India and France. You're watching movies all day." I was ordered to listen closely and learn how to inflect my voice like the actors in those movies, so I could say words and phrases in what he called an "Anglo-Swiss-Hungarian accent with a dash of Bombay." He said getting the accent down would be the hardest part.

"I'm not so sure about that," I replied.

Shelby laughed. "Pay attention to how they use different phrases to express things. If something is 'excellent' in America, it's 'brilliant' in England. In America, we say 'goodbye.' In Europe, they wave a hand and say '*ciao.*'"

"Like dog chow?"

"Exactly."

"If you say so."

"After movie-viewing, we go shopping."

"I don't like shopping. The best part of military service is having Uncle Sam pick out all my clothes."

"You don't have to like shopping; Marion, my sister, will

pick everything out. She knows exactly what you'll need to look as if you fit in here."

While I was watching *A Room With a View*, Marion Nash-Bonner came in. She was blonde and yoga-attired. She set her wine down and nudged me to move over and got comfy on my pillow beside me before opening her laptop. "We're going to do some damage," she said.

We spent a couple of hours on eBay buying cowboy boots from Argentina, blue jeans from Tennessee, embroidered dresses from Hong Kong, a duffle bag from Rome, sunglasses from Japan, makeup from Paris, horse-riding gear from Scotland, and rings and bracelets from Turkey. All of it had to be what Shelby called "gently worn." I called it used. By the time we were finished, she had spent nearly a year's salary in the U.S. Army. "Follow me to the bathroom," she said. She opened a white box containing contact lenses. "Shelby said they had to be green, but there were ten shades of green to choose from: 'verde' and 'ocre' and so on." She took her lenses in and out of her eyes, teaching me how to do it. "I think I've picked just the winning shade!" she said after me trying on several colors. "'Envy!'"

The following day, she told me, we'd dye my hair and connect the hair extensions.

Shelby arrived with my dinner tray.

"This is horrible!" I said, wanting to spit out the food but mindful I was not permitted to do so.

"It's kale salad. You'll need to acquire a taste for it. *Quickly*, as it will soon become your go-to dish in about ninety-nine percent of dining situations."

Davis appeared. "The good news is that you're chewing solid food." He looked at Shelby. They two men give each other a look. Shelby texted one of the kids. Malik arrived minutes later with a DVD that instructed good table manners. "Watch this five times tonight," Shelby said.

Davis got all serious suddenly, putting his hand on mine. "You're going to be on your own soon. Are you sure you're ready?"

"I was born ready, sir. This isn't going to be hard at all. I've had far tougher missions with one one-hundredth the amount of training."

"Say it in your new accent," Shelby commanded.

I repeated myself in my new Anglo-Swiss-Hungarian with a dash of Bombay accent.

"That's astonishing," Davis said, looking at his husband. "Even with your jaw clamped tight your accent is nearly flawless."

"It's flawless precisely *because* her jaw is clamped tight," Shelby replied. "Make sure you keep it tight, even after you're healed and it loosens up," Shelby added.

"Like I said, I got a good ear," I said in my regular voice.

Davis got serious again. "You understand the time pressure you're under?"

"To capture the colonel? Yes. I've got approximately ninety days before I start showing."

He squeezed my hand. "A week from Monday, first thing, we're sending you into the viper's pit."

"Where's that, sir?"

"Yoga class."

"I've been arranging everything," Shelby interjected. "Getting you fast-tracked on membership approval; it helps that I'm a trustee at Worthington. Not that they wouldn't be begging for a new member anyway. There was a time when it was nothing but Old Money Virginia Aristocrats. But there's a lot less Old Money around here than there used to be, let me tell you."

"Plenty of new though," laughed Davis.

"But even though they've let Catholics, Jews, Latinos, and homosexuals like us in, they're still short on members. The club's running a gigantic operating deficit—$2.1 million."

"It could actually go under," Davis said, not in a lamenting but gleeful way.

Shelby fussed with the fancy handkerchief popping out of his jacket. He folded it, refolded it, stuffed it back in the pocket, and fiddled with it just so. Then he took a big, deep breath and looked over at his husband first, then me. "We've got one last problem."

"Sir?"

"Your car. I don't want you pulling onto Worthington's lot next Monday morning in your . . . El Camino."

"Too 'shiny,' sir?"

"Not shiny enough," the men said in unison.

I scratched the left nostril of my new nose.

"We could buy you a new car tomorrow morning," Davis said. "The trouble is, new is—"

"—bad and old is good."

Shelby told Davis he'd been car-shopping online. "I've found it rather a challenge so far to find the *right* 'gently-worn' luxury sedan that's in good shape but not *too-good*-a-shape."

"I got—I mean *have*—an idea," I said. "Just leave everything to me."

Shelby and Dr. Davis didn't look too convinced. But since

they hadn't found the right car yet, they didn't have much choice but to take a wait-and-see attitude about my ability to pick out – or *discern*, as they'd say – a vehicle that would make my infiltration story believable.

~

When D-Day finally arrived, nearly two weeks later, Shelby was screaming in the phone at me. "Yoga starts in forty minutes. Where the hell are you?"

"On 32 Curves Road. I'll be home in thirteen minutes."

"Hurry!"

When I rolled up, Shelby was in the courtyard waiting for me. His jaw just about fell off his face and landed on the crushed oyster shell he was so proud of. "Where on earth did you find *that?"* he said as I exited the vehicle.

"In a barn. A place call Potomac, Maryland. Saw the driver in Washington, D.C. and followed him home."

"And he traded *that* for the El Camino?"

"I traded it," I said with lament, as I was deeply fond of my El Camino. "Without his authorization, after he was in bed. Pulled the plates and ripped the VIN tag off the El Camino. Wiped it down for prints and left the keys in the ignition."

Shelby looked up at the sky like he was beseeching the Lord. "Wait until Davis sees this."

"I passed him on the road two minutes ago and waved, but he didn't recognize me."

"Great," he said. "So now you're driving a stolen car. What *is* it? French?"

"English. You said the people in the Blands' circle are obsessed with things English and old. So I got an old English car. 1971 Rover P5B. A 3.5 litre saloon. V8. Automatic. Power steering. Not a car I'd normally pick. Horsepower don't stack up to the El Camino."

"Horsepower *doesn't* stack up to the El Camino's. I want you listening to those grammar podcasts every minute you can."

"I listened the whole drive. Both ways. And don't you worry none. Once I'm in infiltration mode, my grammar will be perfect."

Shelby grumbled, then poked his head inside the car. "The steering wheel is on the right side! I love it."

"Not too shiny, is it?"

"No. It's . . . *perfect*. It's not a Jag or, God forbid, a Rolls or Bentley. The black paint is exquisitely faded. The burled walnut is cracked and stained in all the right places. The seats are amazing—their color, perfectly distressed and faded—like . . . *grandmother's pearls*. Perfectly distressed."

"You didn't think I was paying attention," I told him. "Old Money's first rule: 'always repair, never restore.'"

Shelby Nash clapped his hands. "Go get changed," he said. He ran inside the house and corralled the kids. "Out to the car. Now! Or it'll be medical experiments for all of you!" Shelby said to the kids, who laughed at their daddy.

"Whoa!" said Malik the second he caught sight of me.

"Look at your hair, girl!" Da'Shajay screamed. She ran her fingers through my new, long honey-blonde hair.

Malik kept looking me up and down, like I was the hot new girl who just transferred to Digby Day. I looked different in my skintight yoga outfit, Cutler and Gross sunglasses with my all-scuffed-up Roman duffel bag slung over my shoulder. "Dad," he said to Shelby. "If I were you, I'd seriously consider switching teams."

Shelby waved him away. 'Remember what I told you," Shelby said to me. "Say as little as possible. Mystery, mystery, mystery."

I zipped my lips shut and with an extended pinkie finger pushed away a strand of ash-blonde hair dangling in front of my new envy-green eye. "It's just another mission, sir. Not my first. Not my last."

18.

There was a big convoy heading into Worthington Country Club. I fell in near the rear. All the cars had school stickers on the back window: Digby-Emmanuel Day School, Endicott-Woodland School for Boys, Sweet Briar College, Hampden-Sydney College, University of Virginia. I watched the women get out of their gigantic SUVs, holding big, clunky sets of keys like they worked maintenance in an office building. Baseball caps were their head gear of choice in soft, fruity colors. All the caps had words or slogans I had never heard of above the bills: Kiawah, Pinehurst, Bay Creek. From behind each cap, above the slide buckle, all the women had short, blonde ponytails sticking out—though there was some variation in shade.

My heart skipped a beat when I saw that Ginny Bland, who paid me no mind whatsoever as I followed her and the other ladies, mat tucked under my armpit.

Ginny Bland was complaining to her friend that she had a bee problem at Derbyshire Farm, which I knew all about.

"What about Harlan? Can't he kill them?" asked the lady in the lemon-colored Kiawah hat.

"Not at his age. At this point, he's best suited for collecting the mail," Ginny Bland explained.

"Cleet?"

"You've got to be joking," Ginny Bland said to Lemon-Colored Kiawah Hat. "He can't operate a chainsaw unless Harlan starts it for him."

"We used Gordon's Pest Control to get rid of the termites that ate up our sun porch."

"I've called them—and ten other exterminators," Ginny Bland complained. "Only two came to look at the nests. But neither of them ever came back with a bid, much less to actually do the job."

"It's so hard to find anyone willing to actually do any work in this town," Lemon-Colored Kiawah Hat lamented. "Most of these day-laborers' families have had three centuries to ascend. I suppose if they were going to make something of themselves, they would have by now."

We filed into the yoga studio. The ladies rolled out their mats. I copied their every move.

"Ladies," the instructor said, "let's extend a warm Worthington welcome to the newest member of our club, Tamsin Venables." The ladies greeted me with the "polite indifference" Shelby told me to expect. I treated them like they was invisible and said not a thing, like Shelby Nash told me to do.

Nine minutes into class, as we shifted into warrior one sequence, Ginny Bland's "friend" Bronwyn came in and slapped her mat on the wood floor. "Good morning, Bronwyn," the instructor said, a faint chill in her voice. From the nose of Ginny Bland and all the women in her row, a disapproving exhale was issued.

Without much effort, thanks to my training, I was able to bend myself into all the positions: lotus, hanuman, bird of paradise, and the rest.

After class, as the women rolled up their mats, all the women chattered away—though not with me.

I said nothing as I collected my gear and headed for the door.

"Are you new to Charlottesville?" Bronwyn asked as we approached the door.

"Hardly," I said, careful to avoid eye contact.

She gazed down in a way she thought was accidental but was obvious and inspected my ring finger, to see if I was married. "Tamsin . . . is it?"

"Mmm," I said, using one of my new "acknowledging phrases."

"I'm Bronwyn."

I extended a limp hand and said nothing.

"Where are you living?"

"A cottage."

'Really?"

"While I look for something suitable."

"Oh," she said. "Are you looking for a house?"

"Horse farm."

"Go either to the east or west side of the county. The north and south are full of rednecks and downtown is crammed with those detestable university people. Perhaps I can introduce you to an agent, my husband's brother, Dabney—"

"—I hope you'll excuse me. But I'm late for an appointment. *Ciao!*"

I scurried down the corridor, mindful not to look back. As I approached the glass double-doors, I saw in its reflection that the yoga women behind me were all standing in a cluster, looking in my direction.

Mission accomplished.

For the next several days, the pattern was repeated as I was gradually, politely interrogated by each woman in the class—except Ginny Bland, who expressed no interest in me whatsoever. When asked what brought me to Charlottesville, or if I played tennis, I replied with a one-word answer to the yoga lady in the tangerine-colored Pinehurst hat . . . or the lady in the lemon-colored Kiawah hat . . . or the lime-colored Bay Creek hat, followed by what Shelby called my "Exit Phrase."

"Goddess Kali," I said when they asked me where I got my yoga pants. Then: "I hope you'll excuse me. But I'm late for an appointment. *Ciao!*"

They asked me my impression of Worthington Country Club.

"What do *you* think?" I replied, turning the tables.

They gushed about Worthington.

I shrugged. "If you say so."

Lime-Colored Bay Creek Hat asked, "Where were you before Charlottesville?"

I use the "BENJI" trick Shelby taught me: "Brunei, Ecuador, Nigeria, Japan, and Indonesia," pronouncing Indonesia the way Shelby taught me: *"In—doe—nee—zee—yah."*

A few days in, after yoga, I was walking to my car. A man with golf clubs slung over his shoulder was inspecting it. I was ready to ask, in a nasty voice, if I could be of assistance, when he turned around and faced me. It was Colonel Bland. My heart rate went haywire. The colonel looked fine. He surely did. I re-collected myself and faced him. The few words I was permitted to say got stuck in my throat. "Good day," was all I could muster.

The colonel's green eyes twinkled as he looked me up and

down, slow and lustful. My knees started wobbling. "Your car is magnificent," he said. Then he raised an eyebrow. "Late sixties?"

"She's a '71, sir."

I shouldn't have said "sir." But he didn't seem to notice, as his eyes were busy scanning back and forth, between my car and my body. He ducked his head and inspected the front seat. "That leather upholstery. That shade of gray. It's magnificent," he said, using the word "magnificent" a second time, though I had never heard him use it once when we were deployed. "Like raw oysters."

"If you say so."

"I say so." He walked in front of the car and appraised its grill. Then he looked up at me. Then looked me up and down. "I'll bet there's a lot of power under that hood."

"V8."

He smiled. "I'd expect nothing less." Then he got all serious. "Forgive my atrocious manners. I'm Cletus Bland."

He extended his warm hand, which I accepted and squeezed for a few seconds longer than customary. It was like there was an electrical current. "Tamsin Venables," I said, pronouncing my new name in my Anglo-Swiss-Hungarian with a dash of Bombay accent.

"Are you a member here?"

I reckoned if I stayed too long he might recognize me. Further, I was to cultivate my mystery. "Excuse me," I said. "But I'm late for an appointment. *Ciao!*"

"I'm sure I'll be seeing you around," the colonel said, tipping his UVA baseball cap.

I climbed in the Rover and backed out. I checked the rearview mirror, slyly, without being noticed, as I drove away.

He just stood there, the colonel did, grinning like a frog on a log.

Contact established. Phase One completed.

19.

Every morning after yoga, the ladies probed and prodded a little further. Their inquiries were always casual, delivered with a warm smile or gentle laugh—not exactly the "enhanced interrogation techniques" I was trained in, which, in the case of those two terrorists I water-boarded in Fallujah, were not accompanied with a warm smile or gentle laugh. I revealed a little more information each time. A slow drip, drip, drip of intel for the ladies.

After their interrogations of me, the ladies always went to Marketplace Margaret for coffees, though I was never invited.

But that didn't stop me from accidentally "bumping into them" on occasion. I strolled into the hundred-year-old former tobacco warehouse with rickety floors and tin ceilings after I knew they were seated—though never two days in a row. I pretended to browse the women's boutiques, the chocolate shop, the fancy cheese shop, the wine shop, the kitchen store, the fireplace store, and the bird store.

They always sat at the same table in the coffee bar, in a place that looked like they didn't want to be seen but were sure to be seen. I made sure they saw me buying fancy objects with Shelby Nash's credit card—which Shelby's sister, Marion, returned at the end of the day.

Eavesdropping from the next table over not being an option, I bugged the rusty old Folgers coffee can stuffed with packets of artificial sweeteners on "their" table. I roamed through the shops, pretending my hair was caught in my earring as I wiggled my earpiece into position and monitored their conversations:

"Very accomplished horsewoman, from the sound of it," said Bronwyn, who interrogated me *daily.* "Her grandfather or great-grandfather—I can't remember which—was a rider in something called "Earl Herriman's Light Dragoons'—some sort of elite British cavalry. She told me about these uniforms they all wore—cherry trousers, baby blue tunics, and feathered caps."

"She said something about a family home in Wiltshire—which I guarantee you is some sort of castle," said Tangerine-Colored Pinehurst Hat. "The Venables family apparently dates back to, like, fifteenth century England."

The scene replayed itself the next morning:

"She didn't say it outright—it's impossible to get a straight answer out of her—but I'm guessing her dad was in the British diplomatic corps. A bunch of "Ambassador Venables" pop up when you Google the name. My God, can you imagine what it'd be like to live in the British embassy in . . . *Tajikistan* of all places?" asked Lemon-Colored Kiawah Hat.

"That explains the car," said Lime-Colored Bay Creek Hat as she sipped her coffee. "It's called a Rover. Whit says it was a favorite of high-ranking Government Ministers, and served as Prime Ministerial transport for Harold Wilson, Edward Heath, James Callaghan, and Margaret Thatcher."

Whit would know, they all agreed: his grandfather was Ambassador to the Court of St. James.

"Can you imagine what a fortune it'd cost to bring it with you everywhere? Ship it across five continents?" Bronwyn asked.

The morning after that:

"I love the way the British spell favorite with a 'u' in it," said Tangerine-Colored Pinehurst Hat.

Day after day, Ginny Bland sat there, still and silent the whole hour as they yammered on about me. Finally, Lime-Colored Bay Creek Hat asked Ginny what she thought.

Ginny Bland looked down at her cappuccino and swirled it around with a skinny wood-stir stick. "All I know is she's not from here. So I'm not so sure she's worth knowing at all."

"Or maybe she's decided that *you're* not worth knowing at all," Bronwyn giggled.

Ginny sipped her coffee. After she swallowed, she smiled an even wider smile and looked up at her frenemy. "Careful, Bronwyn. Be very, very careful."

Shelby stood in the doorway of my cottage. "Have you been listening to your vocabulary and diction podcasts?"

"Every day. During P.T., in the car on my way to and from yoga, and for a few hours before bed," I assured him.

"French lessons, too?"

"Oui."

He pointed to the tray in his hand. "Know what this is?"

"Looks like bear crap."

"No, it's not bear *scat* or bear *excrement.* Imagine you join the Blands' for dinner at Le Perroquet. A waiter arrives, puts one of these before you, and says, 'The chef thought you might enjoy this Armagnac-soaked prune stuffed with a mousse of duck foie gras.' What did the waiter just bring you?"

"An appetizer."

"No. An appetizer is something fried you order off the menu at Chili's. This single, bite-sized *hors d'oeuvre* was a free gift from your host. What's it called?"

"An *amuse-bouche*!"

"Exactly. Which, literally translated into English, means . . . ?"

"A 'mouth-amuser.'"

"Outstanding!"

We talked about my progress infiltrating the yoga ladies' circle as we nibbled *amuse-bouche, fromage, escargots a la bourguignonne, tapenade noir a la figue, tartare de filet de boeuf,* and *pissaladieres*. I dabbed a napkin at the corner of my mouth just like he taught me and explained that progress was slow. The yoga ladies were mighty curious about me, alright, but they still weren't talking to me. Or inviting me to join them for coffees.

"I warned you," he said. "These circles aren't easily penetrated."

"You know what General Patton said?"

"No."

"'A good battle plan that you act on today is better than a perfect one tomorrow.' Our boss in the desert, General Loehr, had a Patton quote for every day of the week."

"What are you suggesting?"

I asked Shelby if maybe it was time for me to confront them directly.

"Absolutely not."

"We've got to *force* them to come to me, not just *hope* they come to me."

Shelby stuffed a wad of bread into the escargot tray and moped up garlic-herb butter. "How do you propose we do that?" he asked, stuffing the wad of bread into his mouth in an unmannerly fashion.

"When the enemy's hiding, you've got to flush him out. You can bomb him—that always flushes him out—or you can lure him into a trap."

Shelby stood and started pacing around. "What's the best way to lure the yoga ladies out since, sadly, we're not allowed to bomb them?"

I popped a chunk of honey-dipped *fromage* into my mouth. "They'll come out to make a rescue."

He finished chewing and swallowed. "What are you suggesting? We kidnap one of their children?"

"That's an option. But there are other things besides women and children the enemy will surface to rescue. They'll surface to defend food supplies, fuel supplies, weapons inventory, homes, and mosques. You said Worthington is the yoga ladies' 'golden temple,' isn't that what you called it?"

"Gilded temple."

"You keep telling me it's the center of their social universe, their Mecca. Their holiest place on earth. One they'll come out of any spider hole they're hiding in to rescue it if it's threatened, right?"

"I suppose." His eyes darted around, wondering what I was about to propose.

"You said Worthington is going under from unpaid bills."

"I did." A smile crept across his face.

"Let's rescue Worthington—and invite the yoga ladies to join us."

Shelby made a fist. "Are you proposing you – we – bail out the club?"

I nodded.

"That's $2.1 million dollars in debt? I think you've overestimated Davis's and my resources."

I scraped the wad of honey out of the corner of my mouth with a corner of the napkin. "It's not going to cost you and Davis a penny. We'll get 'Tamsin Venables' to pay. But not actually pay, of course. Just *promise* to pay. We did that all the time in Afghanistan. You infiltrate an enemy and promise to give their warlords weapons or whatever. As soon as you acquire the intel you need, you exit, order the drone strike, and they never get their weapons."

"But if you don't pay, you'll be disgraced. Run out of the club."

"The club can wait ninety days, or as long as I choose, for Tamsin to pay, which will be never. Besides, once I've got my wedding ring, the colonel and me will be leaving for West Virginia, to build a cabin along the banks of the New River. If we stay, I'm sure Colonel Bland has the cash."

"Did you ever see that documentary about the French guy who, in the 1970s, walked a high wire between the Twin Towers of the World Trade Center?"

"No."

"This will be harder."

"But I saw the one about the terrorists who blew up the towers. This won't be as hard as that. They don't scare me, the squishy men at Worthington and their toothpick wives."

20.

Two days later, at sixteen hundred hours in the afternoon, the hundred most important members of Worthington Country Club—the "Golden Circle," as Shelby called them—were crammed into the library. In addition to Shelby was Dr. Davis Warren, Colonel & Ginny Bland, Bronwyn Fleming, Lemon-Colored Kiawah Hat, Tangerine-Colored Pinehurst Hat, Lime-Colored Bay Creek Hat, and their husbands, who always seemed to be blinking, like they had dust in their eyes, plus a lot of other people I did not know who looked exactly like all the people I did know: wives in dresses with big leaves or vines or flowers on them, husbands dressed in khaki pants and checked shirts and blue blazers.

Shelby put me on a chair next to the patio doors, away from the other guests. He made me dress in my fancy "new" clothes, which were of course "gently used:" a plain tan skirt, white silk blouse, and a pale green cardigan sweater. The pearls, from Shelby's shop, belonged to President Wilson's wife some hundred years before, he claimed.

Ginny Bland didn't look my way, though Lime-Colored Bay Creek Hat stopped and told me my necklace was "exquisite."

"I'm not so sure about that," I said.

Shelby approached the podium and thanked everyone for

coming on such short notice. He said the people gathered there that afternoon were the "spine" of the club and he wanted them to hear good news before everyone else did.

Everyone settled in to their seats. Shelby talked about Club debts and his job as head of the club's Finance Committee. "If we don't wipe this debt clean and begin anew, it will threaten the existence of this wonderful place. A club generations of families and friends have *always* belonged to." Boy, was he laying it on thick. He talked about all the parties and fireworks and New Year's Eve dinners and "Wine and Whiskey Wednesdays," and so on. After a long speech about the need to preserve that which was old and good, he said, "Which is why I'm delighted to announce that our newest member of the club, Tamsin Venables, intendeds to donate $1.1 million to relieve half of our debt."

There was a gasp in the room, like right before a militant is about to spray the area with gunfire. Then everybody broke into applause.

Then, finally, he detonated the bomb: "But there's a catch," Shelby cautioned the audience. "Tamsin Venables will help eliminate our debt—but *only* on the condition that each of you match her gesture." The club members froze up. "Don't panic; nobody has to write a $1.1 million check. Instead, In exchange for her $1.1 million, each of you—the hundred leading members of the club—is on the hook for a mere ten thousand dollars per family—which will cover the other half of the debt." Shelby pulled a check for ten thousand dollars out of his pocket and waved it in the air. "Now's the moment of truth, my friends. Kindly raise your hand if you're willing to rescue the club from ruin?"

From the corner of my eye, I saw the husbands standing

still and clueless as deer as their wives rammed elbows into their ribs. Frowning men gradually stuck their hands up. The husband of Tangerine-Colored Pinehurst Hat walked to the podium and handed a check to Shelby, followed by Lime-Colored Bay Creek Hat's, husband, and a parade of other husbands, including Bronwyn Fleming's, who looked like he was marching to the guillotine.

After all the checks were walked up, Shelby called me up to the podium. I cast my eyes down, pretending to tame flyaway hairs at my ear when in truth I was adjusting my earpiece.

Shelby kissed me on both cheeks, European-style, and whispered, "Just listen and repeat."

I stood at the podium, pretending to review the notes before me while Shelby scurried out to the portico. "If you can hear me, tug gently at the strand of pearls," Shelby said.

I tugged, just like he said, and looked at the audience. Outside, Shelby Nash was lighting a cigarette, which he always did when he was nervous, all while talking into the microphone in the cuff of his jacket. "Smile condescendingly at the crowd."

I did as commanded.

"When you're ready to speak, gently fold your hands in front of you."

I folded my hands.

Shelby started talking in my ear, and his words spilled out of my mouth about a half second later: "I will begin by answering the question I know is foremost in everyone's mind," I said in my Anglo-Swiss-Hungarian accent with a dash of Bombay. "Why would a new member of Worthington, someone not even *from* here, donate $1.1 million to the club?"

I paused and stared suspiciously at the audience, who nodded in agreement. "The answer is simple: because the Venables family has been a member of this community for more than four hundred years."

The eyebrows of husbands and wives furrowed.

"To be sure, you won't find my family's name in your history books, or on university buildings, or in your telephone directory. But we have always been here. *Always.*" I peeked over at Shelby and he gave me a sly thumbs up. "While the story of the Venables family in England dates back before the Norman Conquest, the story of the Venables family in Virginia begins in 1607, when Cornelius Venables, a confidential advisor to King James I of England, was dispatched here to spy on the men establishing the Colony of Virginia and report back to the king."

That statement pricked their ears. I might as well have been reading out the winning numbers to the Powerball. For the next five minutes, Shelby had me explaining the next four hundred years' worth of Venables comings and goings in and out of Charlottesville—all of them unverifiable, of course: Venables men visiting Mr. Jefferson's home, Monticello; Venables men buying up millions of acres across Virginia, always under relatives' names to keep their financial affairs and tax obligations secret from the kings and queens they served throughout the 1700s and 1800s; Venables men playing golf in the 1900s at Worthington with prominent Virginia gentlemen who later became senators and governors and presidents, and so on. "For me, this is a sort of homecoming, then," I said to the group.

"I'm pretty sure I remember my grandfather telling me a story about playing golf with one of the Venables men," Lime-Colored Bay Creek Hat blurted out.

"Ask 'Was his name Henry Holt?'"

"Was his name Henry Holt?" I repeated.

Lime-Colored Bay Creek Hat gasped. "Yes!"

Other club members said they had heard of my fictitious granddaddy, too.

Shelby made a big cigarette-smoke exhaling sound. "Now pause and smile," Shelby instructed.

A man with a shiny forehead raised his hand. "I'm Dabney Hines, Miss Venables, we haven't formally met but, on behalf of all of us, I can't say how delighted we are to meet you."

I shifted my eyes ever so slightly to see Ginny Bland's reaction. As predicted, it was not positive.

"There's some mystery landowner in Crozet sitting on sixty-one thousand undeveloped acres," Dabney Hines continued. "I've been trying for two decades to find the owner and talk him into selling, but the guy's as slippery as an eel in Vaseline. Taxes paid every year by some untraceable corporation in the Virgin Islands. Might 'Nautical Resources, LTD' be a Venables holding?" He said it like he was kidding, but I could tell he really wanted to know.

In my ear the voice of Shelby. "Say, 'The Venables family's holdings are vast and multi-continental.' Then wink at him."

I did. The crowd broke out in laughter.

"So I imagine this isn't *your* first time at Worthington?" asked Ginny Bland, her voice creamy. "Certainly not given your four hundred years of history in our town." It was some sort of trick question.

"My first visit to Worthington was with my governess, when I was five."

"And what year was that?" Ginny Bland asked, smiling.

"I beg your pardon, madam, but I'm perfectly within my rights to smoke outside the club."

The words come tumbling out of my mouth before I had a chance to stop myself.

Everyone in the audience looked at me funny.

"I beg your pardon?" Ginny Bland said.

I squinted out the corner of my eye through the window at Shelby. He was in an argument with a woman in a bright green dress with big white tulips all over it. "Read the sign," her voice boomed in my ear. "It says: 'No smoking within fifty feet.'" I stood there stiff and silent. Shelby and the lady were now in a full-scale fight. It was time to think fast, like that time I was cornered inside that chemical weapons plant in As-Safira. I lifted my chin up high, like Shelby taught me, then looked down my nose at Ginny Bland. "When I was here as a girl, we were inside this very room." I pointed to where Lime-Colored Bay Creek Hat was seated. "Daddy was drinking a double whiskey neat, blowing a big puff of smoke from his cigar. A woman passing by complained about the smoke. My daddy, who loved cigars, said to her, 'I beg your pardon, madam, but I'm perfectly within my rights to smoke inside the club.'"

"Can't say times have much changed," quipped Dabney Hines as the group erupted.

Ginny Bland was not amused.

"My father said it was outrage," I continued. "He grabbed me by the wrist and stormed out. Said he was never coming back. But me, I have a soft spot for this place." A long pause followed. "As I hope I have shown you today."

The room burst into applause.

"Now, if you'll excuse me," I said, "I'm late for an appointment. *Ciao!*"

21.

An hour later, Shelby slid into the booth beside me. "You were supposed to hang around and schmooze the donors!"

"I never overstay my welcome in hostile territory."

"Were you nervous?"

"I was hungry."

He looked down at my combo and scowled. "You should be eating the fresh fruit and lean meats we've been buying for you—not fried chicken sandwiches at Bojangles."

"It's Cajun catfish filet. Fish is health food."

"You'll show faster if you eat that junk."

"I'm still P.T.-ing every day. Ten miles before breakfast. Then yoga. Sit ups and pull-ups before bed." I patted my stomach. "Flat as sheetrock." Then bit into my sandwich. "Besides, I got a good metabolism."

"I've *got* a good metabolism." Shelby reached over and snatched one of my French fries. "Thirty-six members made pledges after you left," he said as he chewed. "We raised three hundred and sixty thousand dollars on the strength of a ten-minute speech, which shamed a bunch of cheap bastards into prying open their wallets. You and I ought to go into politics."

I wiped a speck of Bo's Special Sauce off my chin with the tip of my finger. "I've no interest in politics," I told him as I licked the tip and tore open another packet of sauce. "Only the colonel."

"You're a sight to behold: you in Mrs. Wilson's pearls and my mother's cashmere cardigan, at Bojangles' Famous Chicken 'n Biscuits on Lee Highway, lapping Bo's sauce out of the palm of your hand like a dog at his bowl."

"I was craving Bo's Special Sauce something fierce."

Shelby stole another French fry. "Your strategy worked, Tami. We flushed them out. You jump-started the game. Now the whole town's talking about you."

"I overheard Ginny Bland talking about me to Bronwyn."

"When?"

"Five minutes ago. Just before you got here."

"You saw them *here*?"

"No. Ginny Bland was in her car and Bronwyn was at the grocery store. I installed bugging apps on their cellphones yesterday morning, after yoga, when they were showering. They got in a big argument over me, Ginny Bland and Bronwyn did. Bronwyn said skinny Ginny should invite me to the Fox Hunt Fundraiser, but that Ginny Bland said she would do no such thing. Ginny Bland said she's known everybody coming to her Fox Hunt Fundraiser her whole lifetime, but she doesn't know Tamsin Venables and has no interest in getting to know her. Then Bronwyn said Ginny Bland had to invite me, because a) I stepped up at Worthington and made that big donation and b) I might write Ginny a big check for her fundraiser since it was clear Tamsin Venables is now the richest woman in town. Bronwyn said that with my money, they could pay for medical research that will find a cure for kids with peanut allergies. Ginny huffed and said she had an appointment at Scandinavian Skin Spa and hung up. After Ginny Bland hung up, Bronwyn called that woman who wears the Bay Creek hat all the time—her name is either Willow or Caroline—and said that Ginny was jealous of Tamsin Venables and Ginny was getting too much botox, which you could tell if you looked close. Then Bronwyn said Ginny Bland was going to need more than a forehead with no wrinkles in it if she expected to remain the doily of Charlottesville society."

"I bet she said 'doyenne.'"

"Huh?"

"It's a woman at the top of her particular heap. The most important female banker, or politician, or in Ginny Bland's case, socialite."

I bit into the second sandwich. When done chewing, I said to Shelby: "I don't think Ginny Bland likes Tamsin Venables. And that's not good. When you're trying to infiltrate the enemy, you've got to build trust and goodwill. If the enemy gets suspicious, you wind up dead. How am I supposed to infiltrate this Fox Hunt Fundraiser if that Ginny Bland isn't going to send me an invitation? Can you or Davis get me in?"

Shelby laughed. "I'm even further down the invite list than you. There hasn't been a person with Nash DNA who has stepped foot on Derbyshire Farm in decades."

I took a long, slurpy sip of my sweet tea. "I'm getting in that party," I told him.

The Scandinavian Skin Spa was just five minutes north of Bojangles, next to Dr. Davis Warren's medical office building.

After I changed and retrieved my gear from the trunk, I drove up Lee Highway and located Ginny Bland's vehicle.

No one saw me when I slid underneath it.

When Ginny Bland exited the spa forty-five minutes later, she climbed up into her vehicle and headed back down Lee Highway.

I trailed from behind, listening in as she chattered away on the phone with the woman whose voice I recognized as Lemon-Colored Kiawah Hat's. Both women were worried that Bronwyn might have an eating disorder. Ginny Bland asked her fellow yogi if she had not noticed how Bronwyn always went to the ladies' room right after she had her chocolate croissant at Marketplace Margaret, and how her breath was always rancid bad when she came back to the table, like she'd been throwing up? Lemon-Colored Kiawah Hat said she had noticed that. They both said they were worried for Bronwyn.

Ginny Bland was just past Marketplace Margaret when her car engine started howling and rattling. "What the . . . ?" Ginny Bland said before she told Lemon-Colored Kiawah Hat she'd call her back.

I pulled off the highway, onto the 7-Eleven parking lot, where I hacked into Ginny Bland's phone and disabled it permanently. Then, because I needed to kill two minutes, I sifted through my Bojangles' bag until I found the Bo-Berry Biscuit. I finished it off in three bites and re-started the Rover.

I found Ginny Bland two miles down the highway, roadside, standing behind the car. She'd just thrown her cellphone on the ground when I roll up behind her. I walked up to her and pretended not to know who she was. "You okay, ma'am?"

Ginny Bland stiffened up. "I'm sure I'll be fine."

I cocked my head, the way Ricky Ray Jeeter's dog, Jerimiah,

did when he heard someone tear the seal on a bag of potato chips. “Don’t I know you?”

Ginny Bland pretended not to—as if she had already forgotten the woman who donated $1.1 million to her club two hours earlier. “I’m not sure. Maybe.”

“Do you do yoga?”

“I do,” she said, pretending to be surprised that I guessed correctly. “You?”

“Yes.”

“Where do you practice?”

“Worthington Country Club.”

“Of course,” she said, tugging at the fabric around her waist. “You’re the new member. The one who made that generous donation today. Forgive me that I don’t recall your name.”

“Tamsin Venables.”

“Of course!”

I nodded my head in the direction of her vehicle. “Car trouble?”

“Before it died, the motor sounded like someone dropped a fork into a blender and hit the puree button.”

I indicated just the right amount of sympathy to show Ginny Bland that I didn’t care too much but felt an obligation to appear like I did. “Need a lift? To a garage? Home?”

Ginny Bland graciously declined, saying she would not dream of inconveniencing me. “But perhaps I could borrow your phone to call my husband and have him come collect me?”

“Sadly, I don’t carry a phone,” I told her. Shelby said I should say “sadly” whenever possible, as it made me sound insincere and British.

She watched passing drivers on the highway, hoping she’d

see someone she knew. I needed to strike quick. "Let me look under the hood."

Ginny Bland looked at me all crazy. "You know about car engines?"

"I learned about cars in Zimbabwe, as a girl. Papa said if we ever broke down, I could be kidnapped and God knows what else. He said it was better for a girl to know how to fix a car than speak French."

"Qui pourrait être en désaccord?"

"Pas moi," I shrugged.

I popped the hood and rolled up the sleeves of my cashmere cardigan.

Ginny Bland strode up to the front of the vehicle and watched me as I fiddled around. "What's wrong with it?"

I wiped the dipstick and put it back in place. "When's the last time you put oil in this car?"

"I don't service this car."

I pointed to the crankshaft. "See that?"

"What exactly am I supposed to be looking at?"

I pretended that she knew what I was talking about. "You threw a rod."

"Is that bad?"

"The engine's ruined. You'll never drive this car again. Turn the hazards on. I'm driving you home."

22.

Ginny Bland was looking out the passenger window, staring at one car dealership lot after another. I needed to make a connection, build trust, but didn't want to seem too eager. "Have you been doing yoga for a long time?" I asked.

"Hmm."

"After I pulled my hamstring riding, it took me forever to be able to do Hanuman again."

"Oh."

We drove on in silence for another few minutes, except for occasional light coughing and throat-clearing from my passenger. Just as we passed Bojangles, Ginny Bland said she was "parched" and could we pull into Freshly Pressed, the juice store? Five minutes later she was back, with six bottles of Kale Koncoction. Stuff looked like engine coolant.

"What's in that?" I asked, reminding myself to look admiringly rather than disgustedly.

She rattled off the ingredients in her bottles of green sludge: kale puree, cucumber juice, spinach juice, celery puree, ginger juice, lemon juice, mango puree, broccoli, wheat grass, parsley, ginger root, algae, garlic, parsnips, collard greens, Boston lettuce, iceberg lettuce, arugula, and beet stems.

"You drink a lot of it?"

"Daily."

Time for flattery. "That explains your skin. It's amazing."

She smiled. First time I ever saw her do that. "It's loaded with antioxidants."

"Does it make your hair shiny, too?"

"It does." She brushed a strand of hair behind her ear.

She said no more but was in a better mood as we drove past one big farm after another along 32 Curves Road. Ginny Bland was looking at the cows, probably counting them, the way kids do on long car rides, to kill time. "Once Worthington pays its bills, maybe they'll build a new yoga studio," I said, desperate to make conversation.

"Most of us prefer the old studio," she said to the cows.

"If you say so."

Ginny Bland was not an easy woman to get familiar with.

After the man at the gatehouse let us in, we drove up to the Blands' home. About halfway up the drive, I saw the colonel. He was in the field, riding horseback. He wore those skintight khaki pants horsemen wear, the ones that fit like skin in the seat and thighs. When he saw us, he gave the horse a kick and raced us up to the house.

I slowed down and let the colonel win.

I killed the Rover's engine and rolled across the pea gravel, in Neutral. Like an Indian chief circling a wagon, Colonel Bland circled the Rover, the horse cantering this way and that.

Ginny Bland got out of the car hastily and started barking orders at the colonel. "Call Harlan and tell him my car broke down on Lee Highway, near Marketplace Margret."

The colonel ignored Ginny and leaned sideways on the horse to get a better look at me. "You're the woman who donated all that money today."

I didn't smile but was sure to forge strong eye contact as I made a face that verified, yes, I made a million-dollar pledge, but please don't make a fuss about it.

"And you were kind enough to give my wife a ride home after she experienced engine trouble. Seems you're like an angel on our shoulder."

"She threw a rod," I report to the colonel.

"Oh my," the colonel said.

"We've really taken enough of her time, Cleet," Ginny burst in. "Again, thank you so much for the ride."

Colonel Bland's prancing horse click-clacked up to my car window and stuck its snout inside, sniffing at me. "You'll have to forgive Marlborough's manners," the colonel said as he dismounted.

"I don't expect soldiers' horses to have good manners. He's a Cleveland Bay?"

Colonel Bland puts his hands on his hips. "How on earth did you know that?"

"Really, Cleet, we ought to let her go. We've monopolized so much of her time." Ginny Bland came up beside the colonel, arms folded across her chest.

The colonel ignored her and awaited my reply.

"The dragoons' favorite, if I recall. He's far better suited for getting you in and out of combat situations than prancing around your front yard," I said, keeping my eyes locked on the colonel.

"Remarkable."

"You certainly seem to know a lot about the military," the colonel said. The colonel looked over at his wife. "Did you hear that, Ginny? At least somebody around here likes the military."

"Venables men have been riding for King, Queen, and

Country for centuries. We rode with the 1st Troop of Horse Guards at the Battle of Dettingen. The 14th Dragoons that put down the Jacobite rebellion. My great-great uncle was killed in Burma. 1942. The last British mounted cavalry charge, against the Japanese. They cut out the horses' voice boxes on that campaign, so they couldn't alert the enemy with their brays."

Ginny Bland said the colonel needed to get showered up to join her for dinner.

The colonel ignored her. "Do you ride?"

"Of course," I replied.

"There'll be a few horses like this one at the Fox Hunt Fundraiser," he said. "A buddy of mine up in Middleburg breeds them. Temple Dunsmore. His family's been here so long they probably sailed over to the colonies with yours. You should come and try one out."

"I'm not sure our new friend would find the company very stimulating, Cleet," Ginny Bland said. "She's only just arrived in town after – however long it's been – and wouldn't know a soul."

The colonel looked at me. "Well, at least you know the Blands after your good Samaritan works today, first at the club and then recusing Ginny. There'll be riding competitions all afternoon. Classical dressage. Steeplechase. Though it's really just an excuse to get loaded on champagne and have a big party."

Recalling what Shelby told me about never appearing too interested, I tried to sound bored when I said, "I'm not much of a drinker."

Ginny Bland's nostrils flared. "It's actually a dull affair. Another boring fundraiser, with the same old boring donors."

Colonel Bland looked between me and his wife. His look suggested that it would make him glad if I attended for no other reason than it would make his wife mad. "It's good to support worthy causes, don't you think, Miss Venables?"

"One wouldn't dream of pressuring her to attend—not after the generous donation she made today at Worthington," Ginny Bland said, trying to shut down the conversation.

Ginny Bland and her set never said my name aloud in my presence, for fear, I suspect, that I might mistake manners as familiarity. "There's only one cause that could make me open my purse—especially after the donation I made today," I said to the colonel.

The colonel sat up on his horse. What's that?"

"I don't want to bore you."

"I'm curious."

Ginny Bland was not.

I got all serious. "My brother. Esmond," I said in a low voice. "He died when he was five. When we were in Nigeria."

"I'm sorry," the colonel whispered. "You know, my middle name is Esmond. Pretty rare name – even in Virginia. What happened in Nigeria, if you don't mind my asking?"

Ginny Bland shooed away a bee. "Cleet, I thought you were going to do something about these bees."

"I'm working on it, Gin." The colonel looked back at me. "Go on. Your brother."

I braced my hand on the car door, as if to steady myself. "Esmond ate something he shouldn't have, while we were at dinner with a local tribal leader and his family."

Ginny Bland winced. "You dined with African warlords?"

"My father was a diplomat who served in Africa, among other places."

"Your brother?" Colonel Bland pressed.

"These villages. Their diets are hardly fancy. No caviar or

steaks. Simple food. We ate peanut soup. A staple of the diet over there. Esmond couldn't breathe. Lost consciousness. And never came back . . ."

"Anaphylactic shock," Ginny Bland said, like a doctor.

"To be sure," I said, trotting out one of Shelby's "affirming statements."

"Our daughter's allergic, too," the colonel says. "We're raising money to find a cure." He looked sternly at his wife. "It's settled. You're coming to the Fox Hunt."

Ginny Bland looked like she just swallowed one of them bees. Her lips parted. She was about to say something. Then she smiled. "I'll drop off an invitation tomorrow at yoga."

"You're too kind," I said as I fired up the Rover. "Good evening, Mrs. Bland."

She nodded.

"Goodbye, Miss Venables," the colonel said. He squeezed his thighs against the horse and tugged at the reins. Marlborough cantered backwards. "See you 'on the hunt,' as it were."

23.

We were eating breakfast on the boys' outside table on the morning of the fox hunting fundraiser.

"Show me the fixture card," Shelby demanded.

"The what?"

"The invitation to the hunt."

I took the thick card out of my vest, careful not to get any mayonnaise smudges on it. "Ms. Tamsin Venables'" Shelby said in a deep voice. "Your name looks as regal as it sounds when it's rendered in calligraphy. Okay, test time: What's the 'mask'?"

"The head of the fox."

"'Breast high'?"

"When the scent is good the hounds run with their heads high."

"'Cold hunting'?"

"The opposite: the scent's gone cold."

"'Brush'?"

"The fox's tail."

"'Vixen'?"

"A girl fox."

"You're not going to do anything reckless, like steeple-chase?" asked Dr. Davis Warren in a worried voice.

"I'll trot around a little. But, mostly, I'll be in the house."

I swallowed the last bite of my sandwich and washed it down with sweet tea.

"Doing what inside the house?" Shelby asked.

"I've got a long to-do list," I said as I shoveled a fork-load of hash into my mouth. "PSYOPs tactics: disrupt the environment. Sow confusion. Destabilize the targets."

"This is probably your one and only shot at Ginny and Cleet in an unguarded environment," said Shelby Nash.

Dr. Warren glanced at my belly. "We don't have a lot of time left."

"Less than thirty days, I reckon. Correction: *fewer* than thirty. Less pertains to amount, fewer to quantity."

"You were up and out of here early this morning," Davis said as he handed me a paper napkin.

"Quick trip up to the Blue Ridge."

"For P.T.?"

"No. To get a hostess's gift for that Ginny Bland."

Shelby leaned in all conspiratorial. "Is that 'something' in that leather satchel in the cottage?"

"Yes, sir."

Davis looked at Shelby, who was sipping a glass of grapefruit juice which, unbeknownst to Davis, was spiked with gin, then looked at me. "What's in the bag?"

"You fellas," I said as I took a big gulp of gin-free grapefruit juice, "are on what in the military we call a 'need-to-know basis.'"

Fifteen minutes later, Davis turned onto 32 Curves Road, which was closed for the day to automotive traffic. The horse trailer behind Davis's Volvo station wagon rattled as we came to a halt.

"Who's she riding?" asked Shelby as he opened the hitch.

"Mister Buzz," said Davis.

"He's so old he can't even get up the driveway."

"That's the point, Shelby. She's not getting thrown off a horse today."

After I mounted the horse, Shelby slapped its rump and I cantered down the road.

Riders approached the Blands' estate from both directions. A caravan of hundred-year-old horse-drawn carriages shuttled old people and children.

Everyone was dressed in their hunting attire: black helmets, black boots, tan breeches, the men in scarlet coats, the women in black coats.

A man at the gatehouse inspected my invitation then waved me in. Inside the Blands' estate, I cantered up the long driveway. I knew every nook and cranny of the property, having crawled across every inch of it on my belly, more than a dozen times. Davis and Shelby did not know it, but I paid numerable visits to the Derbyshire Farm during my convalescence. The Blands' spread was overwhelmed by people: on horses, standing under tents, sipping apple cider, eating under the many food tents scattered across the estate. Jumping contests were underway. Kids rode on the back of hay-wagons. The hounds, all of them crammed in a makeshift kennel on the west side of the property, howled and yelped.

About halfway up the drive, I detoured left. One of the half-dozen or so beehives on the property was at the foot of the mighty oak near the airplane hangar. With a long stick I casually agitated the nests. Nobody noticed. I did the same to the nests behind the house, near the pond, and behind the out-building where Harlan kept the tractor much to the displeasure of Mister Buzz, who wheezed the whole time.

I heard the hoofs of another horse behind me and was soon riding side-to-side with Lemon-Colored Kiawah Hat—who was not, for once, actually wearing her lemon-colored Kiawah hat but was instead wearing a black riding helmet, like everybody else. "Oh my God, Tamsin, those boots are fabulous. Are they from Cordwainers?"

"Argentina."

"And that bag," she continued. "I'm trying to place it: is it from that place in Charleston that advertises in *Hound & Hammock*?"

"It's from the Battle of the Somme."

"Huh?"

"It was my great-great-grandfather's."

"You have the coolest accessories."

We made more small talk on our way up to the house. Just as we arrived, she said what I did to rescue the club's finances was an incredibly generous act.

"If you say so."

We dismounted. Grooms tied up the horses. Through the screen door came Ginny Bland, who walked down the front steps of her house and greeted us. A waiter was wandering around, offering snacks from a silver tray. "Fortify yourselves, ladies," Ginny said, "the horn doesn't sound for another ninety minutes. The ham and biscuit sandwiches are rather a disappointment—dried out. But the cranberry pecan brie bites are heavenly."

Ginny told us where to go to get our apple ciders, explaining that the outdoor lavatories were for men-only and ladies should use the first floor, and so on. To be more precise, Ginny issued her instructions not to us but to Lemon-Colored Kiawah Hat, as she refused to make eye contact with me. Lemon-Colored Kiawah Hat excused herself to use the lav and I was glad to see her go; unlike that Ginny Bland, she never shut up.

Ginny Bland and I stood there, unsure what to say to each other. As one of the grooms escorted Lemon-Colored Kiawah Hat's horse past us, Ginny Bland pointed at it and said, "That's some saddle on Sloan's horse."

"I'm not so sure about that."

"Oh?"

"Hermès, is it?" I asked, mimicking Ginny's blasé speech style and cadence.

"I can't be certain, as I don't shop there. But . . . yes . . . I believe it is Hermès. You like it?"

"A bit . . . *shiny* for my tastes." I said as I shifted my satchel from one shoulder to the other. I kept peeking out of the corner of my eye for a glimpse of the colonel, but I had yet to see him on the grounds. "Where's Cleet?"

"The colonel," she said, in a frosty, formal tone, "is busy with his obligations as host. Sadly, he's not going to have much time—"

"—Lucy Corter just got stung!" shrieked the grinning boy who bolted toward us. "Five times! Lucy Corter just got stung! Lucy Corter just got stung!"

"Where?" Ginny Bland asked.

"On the face, arms, thighs—"

"—Where *is* she, Caleb?!"

Ginny Bland didn't run to the barn but walked faster than any woman I have ever seen. I walked briskly behind her, as close as I could get without getting too close. Ginny commanded her phone to "Call Cleet!"

"I'm going to kill you," she hissed into the phone. "The governor's daughter just got stung. Multiple times, I'm told. You need to get to the barn and we've got to smooth things over with the Corters ASAP!"

Behind the barn, the whimpering child sat motionless atop a John Deere tractor, next to the Blands' daughter, Augusta.

Lucy Corter's mother burst onto the scene. "Oh, sugar!" The stung child wrapped her arms around the neck of her mama as Ginny Bland begged forgiveness.

"Shall I go and get some sting treatments?"

"Thanks, Tamsin," Ginny Bland said, saying my name for the first time ever. "There's an EpiPen above the refrigerator. Grab it, please—just to be safe."

I broke into a sprint, then slowed myself down a bit, mindful that it was not in my interest to overly agitate the contents of the leather satchel flapping against my shoulder. I reckon I had eight minutes to complete my task. Any longer, and someone would come looking for me.

Nobody was on the second floor, so getting the Colonel's bedroom bugged and photographing the list of Ginny Bland's computer passwords was done in less than two minutes. Back on the ground floor, I entered the library. Lady Astor, Ginny Bland's bird, flapped and fluttered when I opened the door. "*Braaa,* she's not from here. *Braaa,* she's not from here." After I got the bug installed, I yanked on all the file cabinet drawers until I found the locked one, broke it open, and procured the paperwork I needed. The bird kept flapping its wings inside Ginny Bland's fancy birdcage. "Shut up, Lady Astor!" I whispered.

A man with a black moustache was standing in the doorway, nibbling on a cranberry-brie cracker.

"Find what you're looking for?"

I reached behind me and adjusted the flap of my coat, making sure it concealed the manila folders stuffed beneath the waistline of my riding breeches. "No. Ginny Bland sent me to find an EpiPen. The governor's daughter got stung."

"Look in the kitchen or the bathroom, that's where people usually keep them."

I started to bolt for the door, but he casually blocked it. "The kid's not going to die. Ginny overreacts to everything."

"If you say so."

He pointed at Lady Astor. "Gorgeous parrot, isn't he?"

"What makes you so certain it's a him and not a her?" I asked, deploying one of my doubt-casting questions.

"I'm not, come to think of it." He aimed his bloodshot eyes at me like a sniper beading a target. "All I know is that that bird is an asshole. Killed its mate a couple of years ago. Ripped the creature to pieces, leaving nothing but feathers.

"Ooh. So shiny!" Lady Astor squawked. *"Ooh. So shiny!"*

"I told you so." He approached the cage and flicked the bird's beak. "Asshole parrot." The bird's feathers fluttered as it hopped backwards.

"Hyacinth macaw—not a parrot."

He fiddled with a brass button on his riding coat. "You're an ornithologist?"

I had no idea what he was asking, so I gave him one of Shelby's phrases: "If you say so."

"Dabney Hines," he said, extending his hand.

Like I didn't know; I had photographed this man entering and exiting motels in Lynchburg and broke into his garage. "I'm Tamsin Ven—"

"—Oh, I know who *you* are, sweetie. Everyone in this county knows who you are," he laughed.

I shrugged.

"Maybe we could get together for a drink sometime. You know, talk about the birds . . . and maybe even the bees?"

"The governor's daughter was just stung. I need to get there with treatments."

"That's tragic. How about that drink?"

"No alcohol before the hunt."

"We'll have a cider."

I pointed out the window to the drinks-tent on the lawn. "Go get me one. I'll meet you outside in a second, after I look again in the kitchen for sting treatments."

I re-opened the door to the birdcage and lodged several thimble-sized wireless microphones, transmitters, and speakers into the rafters of the birdhouse. Lady Astor bristled. "*Braaa,* she's not from here," the bird squawked.

"Nor is this fella," I whispered to the bird as I carefully unzipped the satchel and pried open the bag's mouth with my riding crop.

"You two play nice," I said as I inched backwards towards the door.

24.

The kitchen was empty, except for a member of the catering crew. "Mrs. Bland is furious," I said. "Half the tents are out of food. She wants replacement trays right away."

"Yes, ma'am," the caterer said. With shaky hands she grabbed two food trays off the island and bolted towards the exit. I had thirty seconds, max. I opened the fridge, unscrewed the lids on four bottles of Ginny's Kale Koncoction and with my syringe dosed each with fifteen ccs of a compound I leaned to make at chemical weapons school—a combination of antigens, enzymes, hormones, lipids, and fatty acids.

With EpiPen and other sting treatments in hand, five seconds later I was strutting down the front steps. Clutched against my chest were plastic jugs filled with ammonia and vinegar, a bottle of Fiji Water, a box of baking soda, meat tenderizer, cotton balls, and a stainless steel mixing bowl. I ran past Dabney Hines, a cider in each paw, and barreled towards the barn.

Colonel Bland was standing near the tractor, next to his wife.

"She's hyperventilating," Ginny said when I arrived. She swiped the EpiPen out of my hand and was about to stab it in the governor's daughter's thigh when the colonel grabbed it out of his wife's hand and said, "No, she's not, Gin."

He took the treatments from me and mixed up his own concoction and dabbed it on the girl's thigh as the governor's wife worriedly observed.

After the girl calmed down, the governor stood next to the colonel as he surveyed the property. His gaze was steely, fixed to the southwest, like he was carved into Mount Rushmore, staring out over South Dakota. "Do you see them out there, Cleet?"

"Who?" the colonel asked.

"Watch their flight pattern. A straight military formation. All headed in the same direction. Those aren't bees. They're wasps. Yellowjackets."

"I'm sorry Lucy was stung," Colonel Bland said. He was genuinely sympathetic. "But I'm confident they won't be coming back."

"Harlan got stung Wednesday," said Augusta Bland, now standing next to her daddy.

The colonel shot her a look.

"Who's Harlan?" the governor's wife asked.

"The caretaker," Ginny explained to the governor's wife. "He's been with us forever."

"He's in hospital," Augusta Bland said.

Ginny Bland looked like she was about to smack her daughter, which I knew for a fact she had never done, despite the fact that the girl, a disrespectful and unpleasant child, would have benefitted mightily from the action.

"What the devil happened to him?" the governor demanded.

"He's not in the hospital . . . *anymore*," Ginny Bland explained. "He's home and fit as a fiddle."

I kneeled down and poured some meat tenderizer into my palm, splashed a few drops of Fiji Water atop it, and made a paste. I smiled at the girl, Lucy, and applied it to her stings. She let out an *aahh.*

The governor's wife's eyes were as big and hard as black walnuts. "You knew this property was infested with yellowjackets? And you hosted a fox hunt anyway? With *children* present?"

"We're on top of it, Bitsy," Ginny Bland said to the governor's wife. "We brought in a fogger Thursday and again yesterday." It was the first time I had ever seen Ginny Bland groveling instead of being snooty.

"A 'fogger?' And I'm supposed to feel better knowing that—in addition to the stings she sustained—Lucy and the rest of your guests have been exposed to DDT or God knows what kind of toxic chemicals?"

"Everything's under control, Bitsy," Colonel Bland assured the governor's wife. "Ginny uses an organic pest service."

"Yet you knew you had—"

"—Sorry, Bitsy, I've got to take this." The colonel put his phone to his ear. *"What?"* the colonel shouted. "Get everybody out!"

Ginny bit a fingernail as she looked at her husband. "Cleet?"

The colonel grabbed Ginny Bland's wrist and started dragging her along the graveled path. "We've got to get up to the house. *Now!"*

"I need to stay behind and make amends—"

"—No! Now! Come with me!" He whispered confidentially to his wife, though I was still within earshot. "That was Dabney. There's a rattlesnake in the house."

"What!?"

"Lower your voice. Don't panic. Nobody's been bitten. It's contained. In the library."

"Lady Astor's in there!" Ginny screamed.

"She's protected behind the bars."

I fell in with the Blands as we ran across the pasture.

"You need to secure the perimeter, sir," I huffed. "Men at the front and back doors, and the sliding doors in the sunroom and off the library."

The colonel called Dabney and relayed the orders.

"And station someone on the second floor with a broom—just in case that rascal gets out of the library and tries to go upstairs."

"Right." The colonel shouted again into the phone. "Get somebody on the upstairs landing with a broom or a stick so he doesn't get any ideas about going to our bedrooms, Dabney."

After he hung up, the colonel turned and stared at me before breaking into a run.

"What is it?" Ginny Bland called after him.

"I don't know. Nothing. Just this weird sense of . . . *déjà vu*."

Were we still in a military theatre, Master Sergeant Tami Vaduva would have cast her eyes downward in subordination to her C.O. But since I was on a covert operation that called for deception, I flipped my hair instead, Tamsin Venables-style, and said, "We had snakes all the time in Africa."

Both the colonel and his wife nodded in deference to my expertise.

Just as the house came into view we saw a bunch of people running. Whether you were drone-striking a spice market in Yemen, collapsing the ceiling on a chemical weapons plant in Syria, or releasing a venomous snake into a stately plantation home in Charlottesville, Virginia, people always panicked in the same, predictable way: hysterical moms clutched babies and adults dropped food and drink as they bolted from the scene.

"My party is destroyed!" Ginny Bland shouted.

"Can we focus on the snake for now, Gin?"

"How will you kill it?" Ginny Bland demanded to know as we skipped up the front porch stairs.

"Shoot it," the colonel said.

"But all the guns are in the library, Cleet. And the snake's in the library."

The colonel froze, pivoted and said, "I'll get a spade or hatchet."

"There isn't time, Cleet! He's probably made his way up to Augusta's bedroom already!"

I stepped forward. "I know how to lure him out."

"Miss Venables, thank you for that offer, but I'd prefer not to put you in harm's way. I've got this situation well in hand."

"Shut up, Cleet. What's your idea, Tamsin?"

I brushed past the colonel and his wife, burst into the house, and headed for the library.

25.

During the summer of my ninth year, Mama and me moved downstate, into the dank, fear-provoking basement of West Virginia: McDowell County. We relocated soon after Mama befriended the pastor at the Pentecostal Tabernacle of the Holy Ghost's Testimony church, on whom she smelled the aroma of economic opportunity. In that ungodly place I was apprenticed in the art of snake-handling.

I learned two things behind the pastor's house, where thirty screened boxes were filled with copperheads and rattlers. First, not to fear snakes, for they are easily distracted cowards. Second, how to pick one up without getting bit.

Inside the Blands' library, I got the rattler's attention by playing rock-scissors-paper with him real fast—just to keep him guessing. He darted side to side in confusion. Then, from behind, I grabbed him by the tail and turned him upside down. I kept my arm stretched lengthwise to keep him from coiling up on me, though that didn't stop him from lunging at my belly. But I sucked in my three-months-pregnant tummy and, like a girl at a square dance, jumped backwards when he tried to strike. With my other hand, I pinched my fingers behind his head. He was tamed.

When I came out the front door holding him in a U-shape, people gasped. Then applauded.

Dabney Hines overturned a Coleman cooler filled with soda. I dropped the snake into the box and sealed it up tight.

"Kill it!" Ginny Bland shrieked.

"We just need to send him home, back up the mountain," I told her.

"You're a better conservationist than me," Bronwyn said. "I'd have chopped his head off."

"Had someone else do it, more likely," snorted Dabney Hines.

"He's not going to bother anybody in that cooler," I promised. "Leave it to me to get rid of him. I know the best way."

Ninety minutes later, after everyone fled the Blands' estate and Ginny had her big meltdown on the front porch, I was sitting outside my cottage. I'd just finished skinning the snake when I heard a noise erupt in my earpiece: a slamming door.

I heard the glass top of the colonel's whiskey decanter clink against the crystal and the glug-glug of whiskey being poured into tumblers.

"She lived in Indonesia, too?" a man's voice said. It was a muffled voice, but I recognized it as Dabney Hines's.

"That's what she told me," said Colonel's Bland. "Her daddy was some kind of diplomat or military attaché. She lived in Africa as a small girl, Jakarta as a teenager. Snakes were everywhere in both countries, apparently."

"So she comes to town and makes a million-dollar pledge and—"

"$1.1 million."

"Excuse me, $1.1 million donation. And can handle snakes."

"She also knows how to diagnose a blown rod in a GMC Yukon," the colonel laughed. "Not a girl from this county, Dabney."

I chopped the rattlesnake into cubes, dunked one in egg batter, and swirled it around to ensure the salt and tabasco got on it.

"Not a girl from this *galaxy,* Cleet," Dabney Hines replied.

"Ginny and her crew have been working to get the whole story," the colonel continued. "Every day at yoga, they take turns teasing out one detail after another –never trying to seem too interested, of course. You know Ginny. Bronwyn picked up some tidbit from her about spending summers on the Caspian Sea. Sloan heard she owned horses in Dubai. And what's her name—that blonde woman who always wears the Pinehurst hat, I can't remember her name for the life of me—she said something about the Venables family owning a castle in Wiltshire."

I shook the iron skillet. The oil was not yet shimmery.

Dabney Hines said, "Did you see the *ass* on her? The way she was packed into that dress! And those tits!"

"Hard not to," the colonel said.

I reached down and massaged my sore, swelling-by-the-day breasts.

"The seams on her dress looked about to burst. Lurid and elegant at the same time," the colonel added.

I looked up the word "lurid" as the men continued talking.

"I've never seen anything like her," Dabney Hines said.

"I have. Once," the colonel said.

"Where?"

I heard one of the men swallow whiskey. "In Afghanistan."

"Lurid and elegant . . . in Afghanistan?"

"Well, maybe not elegant, exactly, but definitely impressive in her own right."

"And?"

"And what?"

"Did you tap it?"

"As a married man, I won't dignify that question with a response." There was silence for about five seconds. Then the men laughed and Dabney Hines said: *"Dawg!"*

I dropped a fistful of snake meat into the skillet and it popped like gunfire.

"Dabney, she was the most magnificent piece of ass of my life. She even kind of looks like Tamsin—the body I mean, more than the face. A little harder in the ass and shoulders, she was. Tough. A real soldier."

"And beneath the uniform?"

The colonel made a gasping noise. "A sight to behold. She had these wild tattoos." Colonel Bland told Dabney Hines about my zipper-tattoo: how it opened from the bottom up instead of the top down.

"Nooo!"

"That was nothing, my friend. Let me tell you about her ass-tattoos."

"Whoa!"

"She did things to me I didn't know were possible. Most of them illegal until recently—at least here in Virginia."

I smiled as I recalled our intimate times together.

"She was a sweetheart," the colonel added. "Hard worker, too. But simple, Dabney. West Virginia. Not somebody well suited to our world."

I heard the library door burst open.

The colonel quickly shifted conversational gears: " . . . and so I pull a 5 iron out of my bag and Harrison said, 'You should be using a 6 at this distance sir,' like he just put on the green blazer at the Masters." There was a split-second pause then: "Oh, hi, Gin." Then, after a longer pause: "Is everything okay? You look a little peaked."

26.

The next morning at yoga, all the ladies were there—except for Ginny Bland. Which must have explained why, for the first time, I was invited to coffee.

After everyone was done congratulating me for getting rid of the snake, Lemon-Colored Kiawah Hat took a big sip of her soy vanilla latte and asked the group: "Has anyone talked to Ginny?"

"She's gone completely dark," Tangerine-Colored Pinehurst Hat said. "I tried her a dozen times. Texts, calls. I drove over to her house last night just to see how she was holding up, the hunt being canceled and all. They always wave me in at the gate straightaway, but last night the guard made me wait until he called up. I heard her on the intercom. She was slurring badly. He said she was already asleep and turned me away."

"Bless her heart," said Bronwyn.

"She's not responding to me either," said Lime-Colored Bay Creek Hat before she took a big gulp of her chai tea latte.

"Sounds like she's in full lockdown mode," Lemon-Colored Kiawah Hat added.

"I think she maintained extraordinary composure during what I imagine was a very difficult day," Bronwyn said. "If the live rattlesnake crashing the party wasn't enough, little Lucy

Corter was attacked by killer bees. And then Governor and Bitsy Corter stormed out very publicly—escorted by four state troopers. Crushing, totally humiliating—especially since Bitsy has been snubbing Ginny since they were at Sweet Briar. Add to that the hordes of crying kids when the hayrides had to be stopped. And the caterers' refusal to reenter the house, even after the snake was captured. It's all so sad." Bronwyn had a trace of a smile on her face as she skimmed the foam off her nonfat cappuccino with the back of her spoon. "I, for one, was really looking forward to hearing Ginny's speech, which she put so much work into, about the urgent need to find a cure for peanut allergies. What is traditionally a ten-hour event—one Ginny plans for a year—came to a grinding halt less than two hours after it started." Bronwyn looked deep into her coffee mug. "All that said, I think it was nonetheless a lovely party."

"Oh my God!" said Lime-Colored Bay Creek Hat as she scrolled through her text messages.

"What?" asked Tangerine-Colored Pinehurst Hat as she stirred a packet of Splenda into her nonfat caramel macchiato.

"From Juju, our helper. She's good friends with Peaches, who works for Ginny and Cleet. Very bad situation at the Blands. Cleet has taken Ginny up to D.C., to see some doctor he knows from his time in the military."

"Bless her heart," Bronwyn said again.

Then, like one of those Kit-Cat clocks in Mama's trailer, Lemon-Colored Kiawah Hat's eyes shifted sideways, real slow. They were soon met by Lime-Colored Bay Creek Hat's eyes, which also shifted sideways real slow. Both women smiled. Just a trace of a smile. A smile so small you'd need facial-recognition software from Langley to detect it unless—like me—you are trained to detect it.

"She really needs our support right now," Tangerine-Colored Pinehurst Hat said.

I sipped my apple juice. "Maybe somebody can post a get-well message on her Facebook page?"

"That may be a bit more supportive than Ginny would prefer," Bronwyn said.

"Of course, *you* could post that," Lemon-Colored Kiawah Hat said to me.

"I'm not on Facebook." I told the ladies I would instead make her a get-well card. Something homemade, not store-bought. Could any of them recommend a good arts and crafts store? One with excellent parchment paper, markers, X-ACTO knives, and the like?

"Foster Art and Design. It's in that alley that runs between Goddess Kali and Bounty. When Wyatt and all his friends were still at Hampden–Sydney, they bought their fake I.D. supplies there."

I thanked her and said, "Thanks, lovely ladies, for the invitation to coffee but now you must excuse me. I'm late for an appointment. *Ciao!*"

Everyone at the table said they had appointments to keep, too. Outside Marketplace Margaret, Bronwyn pulled me aside as I climbed into the Rover. "You need to get on Facebook. Half the fundraising happens there."

"If you say so."

Why would I get a Facebook account, I thought to myself on the drive to Foster Art and Design, when I had Ginny Bland's Facebook page at my disposal? I now had her password—to Facebook, and a dozen other websites that Ginny regularly visited: the Digby-Emmanuel Day School parent portal, shopping sites like Cordwainers.com and GoddessKali.

com, her by-invitation-only Charlottesville Wine Mommies club, her fitness and diet tips groups, her Sweet Briar College alumni site – all of them. Every single one.

Back at Shelby's cottage, I spread the art supplies over the harvest table. Shelby arrived just before dinner. "That's some haul you got from the Blands' library," he said as he sorted through the paperwork. "Birth records, medical records, military discharge papers, school transcripts, stocks, bonds, real estate deeds, and bank statements. Oh my, what's this?" he asked as he thumbed through bank statements. "They're a lot richer than I realized." News of the Blands' wealth seemed to make him sad.

"Here's our treasure," he said a few minutes later. He handed me Ginny Bland's birth certificate. "I take it you've done this sort of thing before?"

"This pass muster?" I handed him my phony Tamsin Venables passport, birth certificate, and baptismal certificate.

He flipped open the passport. "Where did you learn how to do this? Wait, let me guess . . . the Army."

I saluted smartly. "I forged a passport for a Syrian counter-insurgent once. Got her out. We both crossed the border, pretending to be fancy food-buyers who wanted to import Syrian hummus into Romania. Made passports for girls in Riyadh and Karachi, too." I started cutting out the Illinois state seal with my X-ACTO knife while Shelby did internet research.

Thirty minutes later, I was done.

"The document is flawless," Shelby said approvingly.

I walked over to the stereo cabinet. "I almost forgot. The

Blands are up in D.C." I loaded the CD and the sound exploded from the speakers. Shelby cupped his hands over his ears. "What on God's green earth are you listening to?"

"It's called 'House Dog: Barking and Growling Sounds for Added Home Security.'"

I showed Shelby the CD case. On the cover was a picture of the biggest, meanest German shepherd you ever saw, fangs bared. I walked over to the stereo cabinet and turned my mobile phone about thirty degrees, bringing the microphone closer to the speaker. Then I turned up the volume to its highest setting: *"G-r-r-r-r-r-r-r-r-r-r-r-r-r-r-r-r-r . . . ruff, ruff, ruff, ruff, ruff, ruff, ruff, ruff, ruff, ruff, ruff, ruff . . . g-r-r-r-r-r-r-r-r-r-r-r-r-r-r-r-r-r . . . arf, arf, arf, arf, arf, arf, arf, arf, arf, arf, arf, arf . . . g-r-r-r-r-r-r-r-r-r-r-r-r-r-r-r-r-r-r."*

"You're playing a barking dog CD over the phone? To whom?"

"Keep it down!" I said in a loud whisper. "To Lady Astor."

"Who's she?"

"Ginny Bland's Hyacinth Macaw. I'm piping the noise into her cage."

"Why?"

"To break her. Loud music is used in psychological operations. Five minutes of screeching heavy metal music on. Then two minutes off. Then six minutes on. Then three minutes off. Until the subject breaks."

"And the subject you're torturing is . . . *Ginny Bland's bird*?"

"If Lady Astor is upset, it'll make Ginny Bland upset." I hit the pause button on the CD player and motioned Shelby to zip his lips, then handed him the phone. "Listen," I whispered. "What do you hear?"

Shelby scratched the whiskers on his chin as he listened.

"A hysterical bird flapping feathers, squealing, making crashing noises."

I took the phone away from him. "That's the objective of the mission."

After the barking and growling noises started up again, Shelby asked, "How long do you keep at this?"

"Until the bird makes noise no more."

Shelby gave me a disapproving look. "Killing animals is a line-crosser for me. Davis, too."

"In war, there's collateral damage—there's no way around it," I explained. "Besides, I'm told Lady Astor is a murderess who ripped her mate apart, leaving only a pile of feathers above an empty carcass."

"So that justifies killing her?"

"What comes around goes around."

Shelby made a face like he just swallowed spoiled milk. "That's one way of looking at it."

~

The next morning, after yoga, I was invited to coffees for the second day in a row.

"Ginny updates? Anybody?" Tangerine-Colored Pinehurst Hat demanded.

"They're still up in D.C.," said Lime-Colored Bay Creek Hat. "Due home tonight."

After everyone said how sad they were for Ginny Bland, everybody got on their phones.

"Has anybody seen Ginny's Facebook page today?" Tangerine-Colored Pinehurst Hat asked casually.

All the ladies checked Facebook.

"It looks like a family tree of some kind," Lime-Colored Bay Creek Hat said as she sipped her chai tea latte.

"Whose?" Lemon-Colored Kiawah Hat asked.

As best she could manage the pronunciation, Lime-Colored Bay Creek Hat said: "Irenka Běla Prochazkova. Born to Ewunia Grażyna Mieszkowski and married James Gooch Stith of Charlottesville, Virginia."

"I don't get it," Tangerine-Colored Pinehurst Hat said.

A moment later, Lemon-Colored Kiawah Hat spat her skinny vanilla latte out of her mouth. "OH. MY. GOD! Look at the document next to it; the one from *DNA and ME!* It says Virginia Gooch Stith is fifty-eight percent Polish ancestry, twenty-five percent Ashkenazi Jew, and fifteen percent Italian!"

"Ginny told me her family landed at Jamestown in 1607! There's a replica of the boat they sailed over on, the *Discovery*, in Cleet's library!" shouted Lime-Colored Bay Creek Hat, her mouth wide open.

"It says her mother wasn't even born in Virginia," declared Bronwyn, whose ancestors emigrated from Newcastle to Surry County, Virginia, in 1663.

"She came from someplace called Berwyn, Illinois. What's Berwyn?" asked Tangerine-Colored Pinehurst Hat, whose ancestors emigrated from Leicester to Prince George County, Virginia, in 1709.

None of the ladies knew what "Berwyn" was.

"Her surname was 'Mieszkowski'," said Lime-Colored Bay Creek Hat, whose ancestors emigrated from Glasgow to Gloucester County, Virginia, in 1804. "Not only that, her daddy's mother was of Jewish origin – Goochman was the name – and converted to the Episcopal faith upon her marriage to Ezekiel Stith."

"Does anybody know if Cleet knows? Or is this something she's been hiding from him?" wondered Lemon-Colored Kiawah Hat, whose ancestors emigrated from Leeds to Williamsburg, Virginia, in 1795.

"Well, she certainly hid it from us!" sneered Bronwyn.

For the next fifteen minutes, the ladies discussed whether they should like the post or not, and whether to post emojis that showed a smile, a surprised face, or a sad face.

I hastily stood. "I hope you'll excuse me, ladies. But I'm late for an appointment. *Ciao!*" I said to them after the mission was accomplished.

I returned to Shelby's cottage.

After he was briefed, I dialed up Ginny Bland's bird, Lady Astor, for some more chit-chat.

"Is more bird-torture really necessary?"

"In battle, victory must be definitive," I told him.

27.

I was in my bed at Shelby's cottage, pouring my morning coffee from the French press and reading Ginny Bland's emails, when in my earphone I heard the Colonel and Ginny. They were in Charlottesville, up in their bedroom, fighting up a storm.

"So you're just going to pack up and leave for God knows how long to Bermuda?"

"That's exactly what I intend to do, Cleet."

"And what about Augusta?"

"What about her?"

"You don't think she needs her mother?"

"To drop her off and pick her up at Digby Day? Then bring her to piano lessons and dance lessons? And haul around her lacrosse equipment? And bring her to her allergist? That's something a father is equally capable of doing, Cleet."

"That's not what I mean and you know it."

"Well, she got on fine all those years her father was away doing God-knows-what with God-knows-who."

"I'm not going to dignify that. But I will tell you one thing: women who don't screw their husbands for a decade shouldn't be surprised if, eventually, husbands start to stray."

Ginny Bland said, "Whatever you say, Cleet. But either

way, I assure you Augusta will be fine with me away for once. This will be a good opportunity for you to get to know your daughter. To bond. Maybe a little less golf and bourbon and a little more help with homework." There was a pause. "Like I've been doing for the past ten years."

I heard suitcase latches pop open. "I fly out this evening. Will you be taking me to the airport, or should I ask Harlan?"

Their arguments migrated from one combat theater to another: the bedroom, the library, the kitchen. They still were at it, like pecking chickens, an hour later when I logged out of Ginny Bland's email and headed to yoga.

I was on the mat at zero-nine-hundred hours sharp. Bronwyn strutted in twelve minutes late, slapping down her mat during our sun salutations. A few months in Afghanistan is what that woman needed: the Army would square her away double-quick when it came to reporting to reveille on time.

The instructor ordered us to into chair pose. As we squatted, Lime-Colored Bay Creek Hat said to Bronwyn, "Juju talked to Peaches again. Ginny's back."

Bronwyn said she was so relieved.

Lime-Colored Bay Creek Hat leaned over again and said, "You didn't hear it from me, but, apparently, she's totally unhinged."

"How so?" Bronwyn asked. It was like the Hindu God of Gloating stroked both their heads.

"She refuses to show her face."

After we completed our chaturanga push-ups, we all moved into downward dog position. Bronwyn sighed. "She's got to get over this. It's not like we all haven't thrown a party at least *once* in our lives that wasn't a resounding success."

"We should go and cheer her up after yoga, Lime-Colored Bay Creek Hat said.

"Join us, Tamsin?" asked Bronwyn.

"If you think it would be useful," I said in an indifferent way, so they'd conclude I found all of this Ginny business boring.

After coffees, we bought gifts for Ginny Bland at Marketplace Margaret: turquoise pillar candles, a silver picture frame, and a lacquer bar tray with flamingoes on it. Bronwyn picked out a green serving tray shaped like a cabbage. "Bunny Mellon collected these. She had, like, hundred variations of these on her farm in Middleburg."

The yoga ladies *oohed;* it was the ugliest plate ever seen.

With our gifts we piled into the Rover and drove to Derbyshire Farm.

"We're not taking no for an answer," Bronwyn said when we arrived at the gatehouse.

Peaches accepted the gifts on "Miss Ginny's" behalf and told us we were all so sweet for coming by while trying to get us to leave.

"We're not leaving," Bronwyn insisted. "No true friend would leave at a time like this."

The quibbling and squabbling continued until, finally, a voice from upstairs said, "Show them to the library, Peaches, and bring coffee."

A few minutes later Ginny Bland entered the library. The yoga ladies gasped. Mrs. Bland's face was concealed behind a tan ski mask with red and black stripes crisscrossing it.

"I know that mask! You wore it to the Cops and Robbers Ball," said Lemon-Colored Kiawah Hat.

Tangerine-Colored Pinehurst Hat nodded approvingly. "Burberry."

Behind the little round hole covering the mouth, Mrs. Bland's lips were pursed. Her bloodshot eyes, peering through the even smaller eyeholes, blinked heavily as she sat down next to Bronwyn.

The yoga ladies pretended that everything was normal and said nothing more about Ginny's choice of headgear.

We made small talk and told Ginny we missed her at yoga, and had she been out of town? Like we all didn't know.

Ginny talked about her trip to D.C. and said everything about it was dreadful: the colonel booked them in at a boutique hotel a few blocks from the White House. When they checked into their room, Ginny waved a black-light over the bed's comforter, like she always does when she goes to a hotel, and found body-fluid stains on it, which required her to send the colonel to Bed, Bath, & Beyond to get a new comforter. For dinner, she ordered a $29 plate of asparagus because she wanted to treat herself to a big splash of hollandaise sauce after all she'd been through at the Fox Hunt Fundraiser. But the sauce was runny. "You're telling me a Michelin three-star-rated French restaurant in the capital city of the most powerful nation on earth can't make a decent *hollandaise* sauce?" She was also mad about the traffic and how *pathetic it was* how the women of Washington, D.C. try way too hard to look powerful. She didn't mention visits with head-shrinkers—the purpose of her trip.

The ladies knew better than to bring that up.

"The only thing that made the trip bearable was getting a little time to myself in the mornings. Cleet would go out for a run on the National Mall and I'd sit on my balcony reading

Hound & Hammock. I'd drink a Kale Koncoction, then do yoga, then a scalding-hot bath."

When there was nothing left to discuss about her trip to Washington, Lemon-Colored Kiawah Hat finally asked what all the yoga ladies were thinking: "Is everything all right, Ginny?" she asked as Peaches set a rattling, antique sterling silver coffee tray on the table.

"I don't want to talk about it."

Peaches poured coffee for the ladies.

After everyone doctored the beverages to their liking, Tangerine-Colored Pinehurst Hat said, "Sloan didn't mean any harm, Ginny. We're just so worried about you. When you greet us in a ski mask, and we're not in Aspen or Gstaad, well, you can't blame us for not knowing what to think."

"Whatever it is that's got you so blue you feel you can't show your face, we can help you get through it. We're you're friends and have been forever," Bronwyn said.

Everybody touched Ginny Bland ever so lightly: on the hands, the forearms, the shoulders. I could not determine if she welcomed their affections, as her facial expressions were concealed behind the ski mask.

Lime-Colored Bay Creek Hat asked if Ginny had cold cream under her mask, which might explain the headgear.

"No."

It was awkward quiet again. The front door's screen door slammed and I heard thick heels clomping across the flooring. Colonel Bland waltzed into the library in his cowboy boots and his painted-on jeans—just like that fella in the Dolly Parton song. I felt my body heating up as I took him in.

The colonel smiled when he saw me. "Be careful, Tamsin,"

he chuckled. "You don't want these wicked women to conscript you into their coven."

"I've met women who practice witchcraft, Colonel Bland. It's a dark art."

"Call me Cleet."

Ginny caught the colonel staring at my getting-bigger-by-the-hour breasts. He cleared his throat and turned towards his wife. In a low, sympathetic whisper he said, "It's done, Gin."

Ginny Bland lowered her head. I heard sniffles. The colonel retrieved a folded bandana from his back pocket and handed it to his wife.

Bronwyn scooted in close, next to her best friend. "What is it?"

Colonel Bland pointed at the birdcage. The gray blanket that read LUFTHANSA was draped over the top.

"Where's Lady Astor?" asked Lime-Colored Bay Creek Hat.

"Out behind the barn," the colonel said. "At rest in the pet cemetery—alongside five decades' worth of Bland family mastiffs: Ambrose, Barlow, Arthur, Hinsley, and Wilbur."

"Don't parrots live to be, like, fifty?" asked Lemon-Colored Kiawah Hat.

"She was thirteen," Ginny Bland mumbled.

"Disease?" asked Lime-Colored Bay Creek Hat.

"No. We came home from D.C. and . . ." Ginny's voice faded. She rubbed the pads of her index fingers into the eye-holes of her mask, wiping away the tears.

"Oh, sweetie," Bronwyn said. "You don't need to hide. We've all lost pets."

Ginny Bland brought the cup of coffee to her lips.

"Let us help you, Ginny," said Bronwyn, who reached over to brush her fingers against Ginny Bland's masked cheek, but accidentally—or so it appeared—knocked Ginny's wrist, spilling scalding coffee over the jaw of the mask.

The porcelain coffee sup crashed to the floor as Ginny shrieked "Ow!" With her hands she fanned the bottom of her coffee-soaked mask.

"For Christ's sake, Gin, take off the goddamned mask before you get third-degree burns on top of what you've already got!" the colonel said.

Ginny Bland glanced over at the colonel and slowly removed the ski mask. The colonel averted his eyes as she did so.

Big blue veins—thick and jagged, as if they'd been drawn with Sharpie markers—crisscrossed her forehead. Normally as hard and smooth as ice, her face was covered with lesions and sores. Little droplets of yellow-green pus oozed out of the fresh sores; the closed-up sores had dried pus crusted on them.

Tangerine-Colored Pinehurst Hat, Lime-Colored Bay Creek Hat, and Lemon-Colored Kiawah Hat each gasped, then looked down into their coffee cups. Bronwyn studied Ginny Bland's forehead. The colonel, still frowning, asked to be excused, saying he and Harlan had to contend with yet another yellowjackets nest.

Lime-Colored Bay Creek Hat tried to be reassuring: "When I'm under extreme stress, I break out all over my chin. My hormones go completely insane."

"This is hardly an acne breakout," Ginny Bland said.

"Oh, Ginny, don't tell me you went back to that awful aesthetician in Richmond," Lemon-Colored Kiawah Hat said.

Ginny shook her head slowly. "I was exposed to a chemical, a rare neurotoxin. Something called "tekokorisinotoxin." My dermatologist told me it's not a substance that occurs naturally in nature. It's synthetic. Lab-made."

"Is it a poison?" Lime-Colored Bay Creek Hat asked.

"No. Not on its own. In and of itself it's harmless. Unless, that is, it comes into contact with certain *other* neurotoxins."

"I don't understand," Lemon-Colored Kiawah Hat said, eager for every last bit of information.

"Remember those chemistry experiments we used to do on Fridays when we were all at Digby Day?" Ginny asked the yoga ladies. "When Mr. Osbourne would have us fill one beaker with baking soda and another with vinegar? On their own, each substance was perfectly safe. But when you mixed them—"

"—it caused a chemical reaction," Bronwyn said triumphantly as she sipped her sweet tea.

"Like a volcano erupting," Tangerine-Colored Pinehurst Hat recalled.

The tip of Ginny's index finger dabbed at one of her sores. "That's what happened to me."

Lemon-Colored Kiawah Hat was still confused. "You eat organic; you don't touch sugar or flour; you do yoga seven days a week and have, like, ten percent body fat. You can't *possibly* have toxins in your body, Ginny!"

One side of Ginny Bland's mouth curled. "Apparently, there's what's called an incumbent neurotoxin in my system. One that co-mingled with the rare neurotoxin I was exposed to. A neurotoxin that goes by the name Botulinum toxin type A. Better known as—

"—Botox!" Bronwyn shrieked.

The yoga ladies placed their hands over their foreheads reflexively to search for lesions, the way men cup their hands over their groin to protect their privates when about to receive a swift kick.

"Is it permanent?" Lime-Colored Bay Creek Hat asked.

"No," Ginny Bland said. "But I'm leaving town. Tonight at six. And I'm not coming back until it clears up."

Bronwyn bit her lip and said she supposed that was best, especially after all that business with Ginny's Facebook page.

"Facebook?"

The ladies glanced at each other. I kept my expression as plain as white bread.

"Oh, it's nothing," Bronwyn said. "Loads of people are just concerned about you, that's all."

The yoga ladies took turns looking at each other out of the corners of their eyes.

Bronwyn said it was time to let Ginny be and everyone had commitments for the day. Everyone hugged Ginny, careful not to come into contact with her cheeks.

We were pulling out of the Blands' driveway onto 32 Curves Road and Tangerine-Colored Pinehurst Hat was already on the phone with Brandi, the appointments girl at Scandinavian Skin Spa. All the ladies were hunched forward, hanging on to every word. "Brandi said there isn't an opening for four months, but that she'll put us on the list if anybody cancels," said Tangerine-Colored Pinehurst Hat, her own face a mask of terror that gave Ginny's a run for her money.

Bronwyn snatched the phone out of Tangerine-Colored Pinehurst Hat's hand. "Listen to me, Brandi, and you listen good: it's Bronwyn Fleming. In fifteen minutes, me, Sloan Whittle, Caroline Skipwith, and Willow Holt will be at your office. Whatever Dr. Goulb is doing is about to come to a crashing halt, because he's going to remove every drop of Botox injected into our foreheads—even if that means he has to *suck* it out."

28.

At seventeen-thirty hours, I was sitting on the sofa in Shelby's cottage, braiding his daughter Da'Shaja's hair, when my earpiece crackled. Colonel Bland told Ginny Bland to get her gear and head out to the car, as she didn't want to miss her flight.

"It's a charter, Cleet. It leaves when I'm ready."

Ginny told Peaches to find Harlan and send him to her bedroom to collect her luggage.

Goodbyes were exchanged and the Blands left for the airport. After I heard Peaches close and lock the front door at Derbyshire Farm, I hacked into Ginny's computer again and commenced the next phase of my "Shock and Awe" campaign.

An hour later, once I was confident Ginny Bland was wheels up, I pushed the POST button, booted-down my laptop, and headed over to Worthington Country Club, where, according to intel captured earlier in the day, Colonel Bland was soon expected for a squash game with Dabney Hines and whiskey-drinking afterwards.

I waited in the club's bar, the Framers, for the colonel and Dabney Hines, who arrived, as expected, after their squash match.

When he noticed me, the colonel waltzed over to my

little table, where I was pretending to read a brochure about a quail-hunting lodge in Georgia.

"On the hunt, are you, Tamsin?" the colonel asked. His so-called friend Dabney Hines licked his lips.

I handed him the Wynfield Plantation brochure. "Have you shot there, Colonel Bland?"

"Of course. They have these great bird buggies down there. Open-air Jeeps with dual La-Z-Boy recliners mounted on a big grill-tray that juts out from the front bumper. Best shooting in the Red Hills."

"I'm not so sure about that."

"Really?" Dabney Hines asked. "Did Ted Turner invite you to his place, or something?"

I shrugged. "I prefer Tipiliuke Lodge."

"Huh?" Dabney Hines grunted.

"In Argentina. It's a fifty-thousand--acre estancia in the Andes foothills. *That's* the best quail-shooting you'll find in *this* hemisphere."

The colonel sized me up. "Join us at the bar for a drink, Tamsin?"

"It's unseemly for a lady to sit at the bar," I said. "Why don't you gentlemen have a seat here at my table?"

The men sat down. An old white-gloved black man limped over to the table. "Horsebit bourbon for me," I said, demanding it be prepared to the colonel's exact specifications: "Double, neat, water-back, no ice with a little lemon peel, please." Colonel Bland's and Dabney Hines's eyes widened. "Same for us, Caesar," the colonel said.

"Normally, I'm a single malt girl. But I think I'm becoming a convert to your—what is it called?—'hooch,' is it?"

The drinks were served. I took the smallest sip, and reckoned

I was about to puke; a pregnant woman's body somehow knows alcohol is pure poison. Fortunately, the colonel didn't notice. Instead, he discussed Horsebit bourbon's distillation process, which he had studied in his spare time. When a man is an expert at something—whether he makes whiskey or taxidermies bear paws—he loves to talk about it. And if you're a woman, you listen. Mama taught me that.

The colonel swirled his bourbon as he explained how the brown liquid was ricked, aged, and staved. Just when he started explaining how it was bottled, I noticed Tangerine-Colored Pinehurst Hat and Lemon-Colored Kiawah Hat were standing at the entrance to the bar, both of them fidgety, white as ghosts. It looked like the yoga ladies were having some sort of argument, as one kept pushing the other forward and the other stepped backward and pushed the other woman out in front. Finally, they approached the table, with Tangerine-Colored Pinehurst Hat in front.

After the ladies said their hellos, Tangerine-Colored Pinehurst Hat said to the colonel, "So I see from her Facebook post that Ginny's left town."

He sipped his bourbon. "Some well-deserved R&R."

"She went to Bermuda?" I asked, as though I didn't already know.

The colonel affirmed, grunting a half-hearted "uh-huh." He pointed to my drink and started talking about how the bourbon's color was related to how it was aged.

Tangerine-Colored Pinehurst Hat said to Dabney Hines: "You might want to take a look at her Facebook page."

"I'm delighted to say I'm not on Facebook. Nor have I any intention of ever being on it," Dabney Hines snorted.

The colonel, who couldn't stand Tangerine-Colored

Pinehurst Hat, zoomed in on me and continued his lecture on whiskey-distilling.

I flirted with the colonel as, from the corner of my eye, I watched Lemon-Colored Kiawah Hat lean down, clinch her teeth and mumble, "Some people may get the impression Ginny's not in Bermuda, Dab, but down in Lynchburg at the moment—with *you.*" She handed him her iPhone. *"Look!"*

The colonel pointed to my drink. "Everybody thinks it's all about the barrels. But weather is a huge factor, too. Temperature-controlled warehouses are rare. And the temperature variance between bourbons aged at the ground level versus a few floors up can be as much as fifteen degrees."

I watched Dabney Hines and Lemon-Colored Kiawah Hat out of the corner of my eye. His mouth was wide open as he looked at the pictures of him and Ginny Bland cavorting at the Magnolia Motor Lodge. "Holy shit," Dabney Hines muttered, glancing up at the colonel, who paid him no mind. He stood up and sauntered away like a wounded cat as the colonel explained moisture levels, and what happened when water evaporated from the barrels.

When Tangerine-Colored Pinehurst Hat and Lemon-Colored Kiawah Hat interrupted, saying they had important news that the colonel should hear, the colonel told the yoga ladies he was not in the market for news—neither good nor bad—as he was "on vacation." This was the first night of peace he'd had in three months, he said as he waved them away. They looked at each other, not sure what they should do next. Finally, they shrugged and left the bar.

For the next four hours, the colonel and I talked each other's ears off: about whiskey, about the colonel's Henry .30-30 lever-action rifle, about fly-fishing, about cigars, and about

University of Virginia football legends whose numbers had been retired. The colonel said "Bullet" Bill Dudley from the class of '41 was the biggest legend of them all. I disagreed, reckoning that 1968's Frank Qualye was better, but was denied the credit he was due.

Time plays tricks on people when in combat or in love. Every second of combat is in slow motion. A single minute feels like eternity as bullets whip past your ear. When you're in love, it's the opposite: every hour spent with someone you love feels like a minute.

We were just starting to talk about military matters when the old black man announced the bar was closed.

I stood up real slow to let the colonel get a good look at me. I held out my hand lady-like and shook with the colonel, wishing him a good night.

"The night doesn't have to end," he said as I walked away, pretending not to hear.

Twenty-four hours later, I was back at Worthington Country Club. I glided into the Framers bar and pretended to act surprised when I saw the colonel was already here. He'd been here for a few hours by the looks of him. I went to the bar and sat down beside him.

"Isn't it *unseemly* for you to be up here on a bar stool?"

"I pick and choose which rules to follow."

The colonel called out to Caesar and ordered another double Horsebit for himself and one for me.

"You should eat something, colonel," I said. "Let me buy you a burger."

"No one around here calls me 'colonel.' It's nice to hear it once in a while."

"I honor our servicemen and women."

After Caesar delivered the drinks, the colonel said nothing as he sipped. Until, finally, "Did you see Ginny's Facebook page today?"

"I'm delighted to say I'm not on Facebook. Nor have I any intention of ever being on it." I faked a big sip of whiskey.

"I'm the biggest sucker in the history of suckers."

"That can't be true." I flagged down Caesar and ordered each of us a double cheeseburger, rare, with fries and mayo on the side.

"How did you know that's how I like my burger?" the colonel said.

"I didn't," I lied. "It's how *I* like them."

He took a swig of whiskey and for the next half hour told me about the affair his wife had been conducting—for two decades—with his best friend, Dabney Hines. He told me about the time they disappeared during the wedding reception in Lexington . . . how Dabney somehow always managed to be on Pawleys Island the same time they were, year after year. He shook his head. "I'm not saying I've been the best husband, but I tried." The colonel directed his remarks to the mouth of the whiskey tumbler. "I'm the laughingstock of town," he said, hoisting the drink to his lips.

"I'm surprised you'd come here, where everybody knows." I wasn't surprised in the least he was drinking at his club. While most men would hide in their library, humiliated, and drink whiskey when they found out their wife cheated on them with their best friend, I knew the colonel would come out for drinks because, for once, he got to be the victim instead of the villain.

Besides, with his wife away, and secure in the knowledge he'd find me at the bar, I reckoned he thought there was a chance of me giving him a 'sympathy go.'" I touched his wrist. "What will you do?" I asked.

"That's to be determined."

When Caesar delivered the burgers he changed the subject to quail-hunting.

After dipping a French fry in mayo I steered it back to the matter of the colonel's future—*our* future. "You say you weren't the best husband you could've been. What did you mean? Were you faithful?"

The colonel took a deep breath as he picked at a fry. He studied it rather than ate it. "Yes. Well, actually, no. I mean, I lasted almost two decades, if you include high school. There was absolutely no sex then, of course. In college, Ginny and I fooled around, but I always got the impression she was holding her nose and suffering through it. The first years of our marriage were hardly a tale of sheets set on fire. Then, after Augusta was born, Ginny 'retired' from her marital duties. I only cheated once, when I was in the Army. Twice, technically, but it was all in the course of one twenty-four hour period, and with the same woman. Got laid for the first time in a decade since I knew I wasn't going to get laid for another decade when I got home." The colonel finished his bourbon and slammed the whiskey tumbler on the bar. Then he looked at me. His ears and face were red. "That was vulgar. I'm sorry."

In accordance with my training, I over-chewed and waited until every last morsel of burger was down my gullet before I spoke, which I was keen to do. "Would you be happier apart?"

"That's not really an option for me."

"You were in the military. There are always options."

"There aren't in Charlottesville, Virginia," the colonel said. "There just isn't anybody on the market right now. And being married is better than being alone."

Spoken like a drunken fool. "Colonel Bland," I said. "That woman you were with. Did you love her?"

He looked down. "We came from very different worlds," he whispered.

I looked down at Tamsin Venables's manicured hands, hardly recognizing them: trimmed nails painted up in clear, glossy polish, the rose cut emerald ring – an antique courtesy of Shelby Nash's aunt. Then I looked closer: I saw a wisp of a scar from when I ran through a plate glass window in elementary school. A raised spot on the back of my hand, courtesy of shrapnel. I'm still here, I thought to myself. I will always be here. *Always.* "If she was rich and well-educated like you, might you have loved her?" I asked.

A new whiskey was placed before the colonel. "Anything's possible." He swirled and sniffed the bourbon, then gazed at me. "You know, she actually reminds me of you a little bit. Obviously, your manners, education, and erudition are quite different. And you look different, your nose and jawline are more . . . regal. But what you share is comportment. She was fiery. A lot of spirit. Uninterested in anyone else's approval. And totally at home in a man's world." He looked me up and down. "You don't strike me as ever having been 'one of the girls.'"

"Women bore me. Especially the women of Charlottesville."

We looked at the dessert menu. Colonel Bland ordered the chocolate pecan pie, to split.

"Maybe there's somebody out there that it's your destiny to be with. Your one true love," I offered.

"I didn't take you for a romantic," the colonel grunted.

"You don't believe in the kind of love where a man's heart belongs to a woman's completely—and hers belongs to his? When one mate dies, the other dies of devastation?"

"A woman once told me the definition of true love was when a woman gave money to a man after he'd squandered all of his. That is not, I assure you, the way things work here in Charlottesville. And the man bought the woman a dress at Walmart after her looks faded."

"As good a definition as any, I suppose. Did this woman happen to be that one you slept with?"

The colonel gave me a look. "I can't put my finger on it. But every time I'm around you, I feel like I know you—from some other time or place."

"If you say so, colonel."

"I say so."

The dessert arrived. Each of us stabbed a fork into the pecan pie.

"You're the most interesting woman I've met in a very long time, Tamsin Venables," he said. "Who am I kidding? You're the most interesting woman I've *ever* met. I hope you plan to stick around here for a while. Charlottesville could use someone like you."

"Oh, I'm not going anywhere. I assure you." After hogging most of the pie, I pushed the plate aside. "Now come along," I said, "I'm driving you home and you're not arguing. You don't want to see pictures of your DWI mugshot photo on Facebook twenty-four hours from now."

The colonel saluted smartly. "Yes, ma'am!"

On the drive up to the house, the colonel said, "Peaches took Augusta to Disneyworld."

A fun place for a child, we agreed.

"You have an old caretaker on hand, don't you? Harmon, is it?"

"Harlan. He's here, alright. But long before he got old and started going to bed at eight, Harlan taught himself not to see and hear so well." The colonel winked.

Of course, I knew what he was thinking. Which was the same as what I was thinking since I first saluted this man as my commanding officer.

The Rover rolled quietly over the gravel up to the front door of the house. "Home safe and sound." I shifted the engine into neutral—a signal to the colonel I had no intention of coming inside.

"No nightcap?"

"You've had plenty and I have to drive home."

"Then a cup of tea?"

"You don't drink tea."

"I don't?"

"You drink three espressos every morning."

"How on earth do you know that?"

Second mistake of the night: bad manners with the pecan pie and now the espresso. I could hardly tell the colonel I knew what he drank at breakfast because I bugged his house. "Strong men drink strong coffee."

"Bullshit. That was no lucky guess."

Busted red-handed. Time to think fast. "Your wife was complaining about your coffee-drinking habits at Marketplace Margaret. Said too much espresso gets you all revved up, makes you argument-prone."

"She complains about a lot," the colonel snorted. Then he grinned. "Would you care to come in for an espresso?"

"No."

"Why not?"

"I don't go into married men's homes when their wives are away."

The colonel looked forlorn. "I don't think I'm going to be married for long."

"You're still married now."

"What if I told you I was planning to get a divorce?"

"I'd tell you to invite me in once the divorce was final."

The colonel leaned over and kissed me on the neck.

"Stop." I needed to drag this out.

He tucked a long strand of hair back behind my ear.

"Don't. You really should go in, colonel." He pecked at my earlobe. My heart was thumping. My loins were moistening. "We shouldn't be doing this," I said as I jumped him and thrust my tongue down his throat. He started massaging my breasts, swirling them around in circles, like he did in that tent, and later in the convoy, in Afghanistan.

"Let's go in the house."

"No," I said as I unbuttoned his shirt. "I won't go inside

a married man's house." I slid the palm of my hand under his belt, below the elastic waistband of his skivvies, into the nest that surrounded his privates. "But I never said anything about not going into a married man's barn."

~

The colonel lit the oil lantern and the whole barn turned gold. By the haystack he reached for the top button on my blouse and started to undress me.

"No."

"Huh?"

"I'll bet you gave out a lot of orders when you were a colonel."

His mouth twisted. "Your point?"

"I'm giving the orders tonight."

He raised an eyebrow. "Are you?"

"Affirmative, sir."

"And why should I let you boss me around?"

"Because I've got something you want."

"You're right about that, darlin'."

"Shut up, colonel."

"Yes, ma'am."

"Attention!"

The colonel saluted.

I stepped forward and placed my palms against his cheek. I stroked gently as I gazed into his eyes. "Give me your wedding ring."

He pried it off his finger. "One gold wedding band, ma'am."

"Now the watch."

He unclasped it and placed it in the palm of my hand. "One Rolex Daytona."

"Shirt."

He peeled it off, revealing the same muscular upper body I remembered. "One gingham long sleeve shirt, ma'am."

"Trousers."

He unbuckled the belt, removed his trousers, and folded them neatly. "One pair of khaki trousers, ma'am."

After the socks and shoes came off, he was down to his skivvies, which he began to lower.

"Stop! I did not grant permission to remove the skivvies."

"Huh?"

"That's my prerogative. As your commanding officer."

"Yes, ma'am."

I reached for the waistband.

He panted as I tugged the boxers down to his ankles slow—just like he did to me in the tent.

"Step out of them."

"Yes, ma'am."

I stood before him and looked down on his privates, like I was conducting an inspection on parade grounds. I fixed a disapproving look on my face, when in fact I approved mightily of what was presented before me.

"Permission requested to undress you, Tamsin."

"Permission denied. Right face."

He was still plank-thin, his compass arrow pointing north. I walked about ten feet in front of him, my back turned to him the whole time, and stepped out of one high heel at a time. I removed my blouse and stood still, forcing the colonel to stare at my bare back. Then I removed my bra and pulled the skirt high up my thighs.

One of the horses brayed.

"You like pantyhose and garters, colonel?"

"You bet I do, ma'am."

I unfastened the garters on each leg, then rolled down the stockings and peeled them off at the toe.

"Am I passing inspection, colonel?"

"Yes, ma'am!"

I took my time with the skirt. I hoisted it up over my hips, revealing the lower half of my backside. "Seen one like this before, colonel?"

"I certainly have not and I want very much to see the whole thing!"

"Who's giving the orders?"

"You are, ma'am."

"Don't forget it!"

"No, ma'am!"

I unzipped my skirt and shook my hips until it fell to the floor, revealing my backside complete. I could hear the colonel groaning behind me.

"My backside meets with your approval, colonel?"

"It's astonishing, ma'am."

"I've got something else to show you. Would you like to see it?"

"Yes, ma'am!"

With my backside still facing him, I bent over, into one of my yoga poses. My legs ramrod straight, I looped my thumb and forefinger around each toe, revealing to the colonel my most intimate secrets.

"Good God!"

"Do you know what this yoga position is called?"

His breathing was jagged. "No, ma'am."

"'Padangusthasana,' Or big toe pose. Do you do yoga, colonel?"

"No, ma'am. I'd put a gun in my mouth before I'd do yoga, ma'am."

"Colonel, I recall asking if you did yoga. I do not recall asking your opinions about yoga."

"No ma'am. Sorry, ma'am."

"Are you glad that *I* do yoga?"

"Eminently, ma'am."

I unfolded myself and stood erect. "Ready to see the front side, colonel?"

"Oh, God yes, please!"

"You're sure?"

"Certain!"

I covered my privates with folded hands, like girl statues in museums covered with fig leaves. Then I turned to the colonel. The strand of pearls, all that was left on me, reached all the way down to my navel.

"I've got to have you, Tamsin."

"Not until I say so, colonel."

"Please say so. Please. Say it now!"

I slowly pulled my hands away from my pelvis, revealing a patch of ash-blonde hair dyed to match my up-top hair. "Attention!" I said sharply.

"I'm done playing Army, Tamsin."

"There is one final command."

"Hurry."

I cleared my throat. "I said, 'There is one final command. To which you reply . . . ?"

"Yes, ma'am!"

"That's right. Close your eyes."

The colonel obeyed the command.

I approached him and took the bandana out of the colonel's

pants pocket and tied it over his eyes. I just let him stand there, at attention—every bodily part of him—for two minutes. "Okay," I said when I was ready, "you can open them now."

He ripped the bandana off his face and tossed it to the ground. When he saw me, his face slackened. "No! No! What are you doing?" The colonel looked like a boy who just learned his beagle has been run down by a car. You're dressed!"

I gave him his watch and wedding ring. "I'm leaving."

"Why?"

"I told you, colonel: I don't sleep with married men. I just needed you to see what you are missing, what could be yours one day. Yours, that is, if you're willing to surrender to true love."

"So, you'd sleep with me if I was single?"

I smiled coyly. "I'd sleep with you if we were married."

The colonel swallowed hard. "You'd marry me if I was . . . available?"

"Do you intend to become 'available' sometime in the near future?"

"Yes."

"We're a good fit you and me, as you said, Cletus Bland. Similar backgrounds. Similar interests. You also happen to be the finest looking man I've ever met. So my answer is yes—not that I consider this conversation a formal marriage proposal."

"There's not some international billionaire you're pulling along on a string out there?"

"Money doesn't interest me. Just you."

"You, too," the colonel mumbled as he cupped his privates and groaned like a wounded animal, which, given the ache he must have been experiencing in his private area, was warranted.

"And if we do marry," I continued, "I promise that by the

end of our honeymoon you're going to be walking on crutches. What do you think about that, Colonel Bland?"

The colonel slumped to the ground. "I think I'm in love."

I blew the colonel a kiss as I walked out of the barn.

30.

I was in bed an hour later at Shelby Nash's cottage when my phone rang. It was Colonel Bland. "I must see you tomorrow."

"Will you still be married tomorrow?"

"The best divorce lawyer in Virginia is a fraternity brother of mine. My divorce will be final in fourteen days, and Ginny's not going to make a peep about it."

"Is that so?"

"She plans to stay at her skin clinic for at least another three months. After that, her doctors tell her it'll take a year before she looks like herself again. She's not even letting Dabney see her, I hear."

I took a breath, curling myself up in a ball.

"What about Augusta?"

I heard the colonel drum his fingers on the burled wood table in his library. "Peaches has done most of her mothering." There was long silence on the phone. "Tamsin, I can't be a husband to Ginny. I'm not sure I ever could be. But I'm sure as hell going to be a father to Augusta. I will put her in the best boarding school in the world if I have to. Anything to do right by her."

"Then I'll see you in fourteen days," I say.

"I need to see you tomorrow. It's urgent."

"Why?"

"We're getting married in fifteen days. We need to plan."

I blinked uncomfortable, a reminder that I had forgotten to take out my

envy-green contact lenses before bed. I pinched them out of my eyes and set them in their case on the nightstand. I let him stew in the silence. Then: "Tomorrow night. Six. Framer's Bar."

~

At after-yoga coffees the next morning, Lemon-Colored Kiawah Hat asked if there was any news of Ginny.

Bronwyn looked around to make sure no one was listening, then lowered her voice and said, "I talked to her last night. At two-thirty in the morning."

"Have they fixed her forehead yet?" Tangerine-Colored Pinehurst Hat asked.

"No. And her forehead is the *least* of her problems."

"Her genealogy problems?" asked Lemon-Colored Kiawah Hat.

Bronwyn leaned back, crossing her arms over her chest. "Pedigree problems are even further down the list, believe it or not. She and Cleet are getting divorced."

"They can't!" said Lime-Colored Bay Creek Hat.

"No!" winced Tangerine-Colored Pinehurst Hat.

"She's *thrilled* about it, actually. Said things have been loveless for years, and they haven't even had sex since forever, and when they did it was terrible. She just couldn't take it anymore, she said. And he really let her down at the Fox Hunt Fundraiser.

If he had fixed the bee problem, she said, the event would have gone off without a hitch."

The yoga ladies nodded agreement.

"She's been carrying him for a long time. He has zero social skills," Lemon-Colored Kiawah Hat said.

"Like having a conversation with a slab of concrete," said Tangerine-Colored Pinehurst Hat.

The ladies lamented how hard it was going to be for Ginny Bland at her age when she returned to Albemarle County as a divorced woman. How that Dabney Hines was a player and there was no way he'd ever marry her. Besides, he didn't need her money.

"She's in no hurry to get back here," Bronwyn continued. "Talked about getting additional treatments in Switzerland." She looked over at me. "What do you make of all of this, Tamsin?"

"Why do you ask?"

"I don't know. I suppose because you're new here. Fresh set of eyes."

"If you say so."

"Just interested in your impressions."

"I believe in destiny. What is meant to be is meant to be."

The women nodded as they sipped coffee.

"Poor Augusta," Tangerine-Colored Pinehurst Hat said. "It's the kids who always suffer most in these situations."

"She and Cleet have already spoken about transferring her to some all-girls' boarding school in Montreux," said Bronwyn.

"And leave Digby Day?" Tangerine-Colored Pinehurst Hat said.

"Unfathomable," added Lime-Colored Bay Creek Hat.

"Well," Bronwyn said, all philosophical-like. "I suppose it's better than staying here. Go away for a year or two. By then, the whiff of family scandal will be all but forgotten."

"When they smell blood, the kids at Digby Day can be nastier than the parents," Lemon-Colored Kiawah Hat said.

They all agreed that in sending Augusta away the colonel and Ginny were keeping their daughter's best interests at heart.

Caesar delivered two Horsebit whiskies.

"I've never been married before. I have no idea how to plan a wedding," I confessed.

"Me neither," the colonel said. "At my first one, I just showed up, wore what I was told, and stood where they told me to stand. I do know that Ginny's dad spent a hundred grand."

"It's the bride's job to pay for the wedding, isn't it?"

"That's the custom, yes. But the rules are relaxed on second weddings."

I thought about my paltry savings. "A hundred grand on a wedding seems kind of . . . *shiny*, don't you think?"

The colonel clinked his glass of whiskey with mine. "I think."

I palmed my knees as I leaned in towards the colonel. "Our family weddings were always small and simple affairs. A vicar, a chapel, and a light lunch afterwards."

"I'm not much of a church-goer myself," the colonel told me. "How would you feel about being married by a judge? Or better yet, the governor?"

"Isn't he mad at you after his girl got stung?"

The colonel waved such nonsense away. "He won't hold a grudge if my request is accompanied by a fat contribution to his re-election fund."

I plucked a peanut from the silver bowl. "If you say so."

"Indoors or outdoors?"

"Outdoors. *Always.*"

"Done. We'll do it outside, at Derbyshire Farm." Then, as an afterthought, he looked up from his whiskey. "I almost forgot. Anyone you want to bring over from the UK or somewhere else? Siblings, aunts, best friends from childhood?"

I leaned over and planted a gentle kiss on him. "Just you and me."

I was devouring my yogurt in Shelby's cottage when my ear piece picked up the colonel's voice. He was in his library at Derbyshire Farm.

"As your attorney, I must advise that you're being a complete fucking idiot, Cleet. She breezes into town and a month later you're going to marry her? You need a prenup."

"It's a moot point, Cameron. Trust me, this woman can buy and sell me ten times over."

"You and Ginny had one," the attorney said.

"Yeah and look what happened. That was our problem from the outset, Cameron. Her bank accounts, my bank accounts. Her stock portfolio, my stock portfolio. Everything was always separate. Separate money, friends, interests, lives."

The attorney finished chewing whatever it was he was eating for breakfast, swallowed, and said, "I hear what you're saying, Cleet, but you know nothing about this woman."

"I know everything I need to know. Ginny and her friends did their due diligence, Cameron. Trust me. They ran every trap across four continents. Internet searches, calls to college roommates whose husbands now work in the City of London. Sloan Whittle's plugged in to the international art scene. Sotheby's and Christies in London, Paris, Hong Kong—where the Venables have been regulars on that circuit for generations, apparently. Bronwyn Fleming traced the Venables family back to the Norman Conquest. Generals, diplomats, advisors to kings and queens, and philanthropists: the Venables family has been at the top of the British food chain for ten centuries. Her family's the real deal. Her pedigree is impeccable. And my *feelings* for her are real—more real than anything I've felt my entire life."

"Well, judging by my very limited peek into the Venables name, it seems to me there are rather a lot of them . . . and all over," the attorney said. "Families that old, especially European ones, are often, by this point, high on prestige and low on cash. Have you seen any *proof* of money? I mean apart from the money she promised to give to Worthington?"

Silence on the colonel's end.

"We're talking about a $70 million estate," the attorney said. "One your family built over three centuries. An estate over which you are custodian."

The colonel's voice was tinged with exasperation. "I've spent my whole life around people with money, Cameron. Rich people who spend every waking moment complaining about the price of everything, drinking cocktails out of jelly jars because they claim they can't afford fine crystal. All of them pretending they're poor, spending every waking moment acting like they aren't ruled by money, even when they're totally enslaved by it. Using it to gain entry, to deny others entry, to stay in their tiny little cluster, clinging to what someone else built for them like a lifebuoy," he said. "I'm done being ruled by it."

As was I, though in truth, having never had any, I had never let it rule me. My wish was still for me, the colonel, and our baby to move back to West Virginia and live the simple life in a cabin along the New River, with a wood-burning stove and a screened-in porch to protect us from the bugs. If he wanted us to stay in Charlottesville and be rich, that was okay, but as for me, all I cared about was having a daddy for my baby and breaking the curse of single-motherhood that had plagued our family for five centuries.

31.

The sun hovered over the mountains as me, Colonel Bland, Governor Corter, Senior Trooper Prewitt, and Master Trooper Turpin walked towards the lake.

"I think you're about five million dollars short on your estimate," I overheard Master Trooper Turpin say to Senior Trooper Prewitt. "That donor in Appomattox County, his farm was worth fifteen million dollars. And he had less acreage than this."

The governor spun around and gave the members of his security detail a hard look. They stopped talking.

"Sorry that Bitsy and Lucy were no-shows, Cleet. They're still a little squeamish after the bee incident at the Fox Hunt Fundraiser."

"No hard feelings, Bingham. Besides, we wanted this as small as possible." The colonel chuckled. "I suppose you can't get any smaller than a governor and his two bodyguards as witnesses."

"Well, either way, I'll be sure to tell them about the effort you made to bee-proof the ceremony. Bitsy would have been impressed by all this mosquito netting."

"I'm sad to say we've drastically reduced their numbers,

but not eliminated them altogether. Better safe than sorry," the colonel said.

Governor Corter's eyes tracked a squadron of yellowjackets zigzagging at the western perimeter of the property. "Indeed."

We walked to the center of the gazebo.

Since we had no guests, the governor didn't bother with a lot of official welcomes and small talk. He took out his script and handed us ours. When ready to begin the ceremony he stomped his foot and said, "Let's get crackin'," repeating his favorite catchphrase, one displayed on half the bumper stickers in Virginia. "Do you, Cletus Esmond Bland III, take Tamsin Euphemia Venables to be your wife?"

"I do."

"Do you promise to love, honor, cherish, and protect her, forsaking all others and holding only unto her?"

"I do."

"Okay, Tamsin, over to you: do you, Tamsin Euphemia Venables, take Cletus Esmond Bland III to be your husband?"

"I do."

"Do you promise to love, honor, cherish, and protect him, forsaking all others and holding only unto him?"

"I—"

"—what the . . . ?" The governor made a face.

Everybody turned towards the source of the racket. It wasn't so much a siren as much as a distress call of some sort, the vehicular equivalent of a yelp. Within seconds it appeared: a Brink's armored truck, coated in dust and soot rattled up the Blands' long driveway.

"The dowry?" the governor asked.

The colonel looked over at me and I shook my head in equal wonder.

The armored truck stopped momentarily at the crest of the hill, its engine gunning in neutral. Then it angled its wheels in our direction, nudging forward and facing us, staring down its nose at us from on high. Then it jerked forward, rolling down the ravine towards the gazebo, its jumbo-sized, double-axle rear wheels bouncing in the grass like a five-ton mountain bike. *"Boom, boom, boom!"* The armored vehicle rolled up the knoll to the gazebo. Air brakes hissed. The driver idled the engine.

"Look at that, Cleet," the governor said, pointing to the side of the truck. Finger-painted in the dust were pictures of dogs, horses, oxen, birds, lions, griffins, flowers, and vines. "It's like the ceiling of the Sistine Chapel."

The engine died. The Brink's truck stood still and soundless.

"I can't see the driver," Senior Trooper Prewitt said to Master Trooper Turpin.

"Me neither. It's like there's a fog machine inside," Master Trooper Turpin said, cupping his hand over his holster.

"I can make out figures moving," said Senior Trooper Prewitt.

"Two?"

"No. Three."

The troopers unsnapped their holsters and stood at the ready.

Finally, the driver's side door opened. A gigantic plume of smoke burst out, like from a cannon, and I felt my stomach sink down to my ankles. My mama was yelling: "You never even bothered to learn to drive. Always expecting your gentlemen friends to drive you everywhere. But they ain't around no more to give you rides now, are they? So you turn me into your chauffeur." Mama squished a cigarette on the ground.

Grandmama Marlene exited from her side of the truck. A

big cloud of smoke followed her, too. "It's my money from the settlement that paid for this truck, so I got some say in how you treat my property, Velvet!"

"Shut up and get Charlene down," my mama said to her mama.

"What on God's green earth is *that*?" Governor Corter asked.

"A vardo," I mumbled.

He turned and faced me. "A what?"

"A horse-drawn wagon used by Romani people. It doesn't matter."

"It does to me."

There was no way on God's green earth she could have tracked me. I hadn't exchanged a word with her since exiting Thurmond, empty-handed, weeks before.

Grandmama Marlene pulled Great-grandmama Charlene down. Outside the truck, Great-grandmama Charlene inserted a cigarette in her mouth and rolled the wheel on her Bic lighter a few times, but it kicked out only sparks. She threw the lighter on the ground. "Piece of shit."

The colonel clasped his hands behind him and stood at parade rest. "May I help you, ladies?" he belted.

Mama approached the wedding party. I cast my eyes downward and pretended to be checking my manicure, praying fiercely to the Lord Sweet Jesus she wouldn't recognize me. Luckily, she paid me no mind whatsoever. "Which of you is Cleet Bland?" she said, hands on hips.

"Who are you and what do you want?" the colonel barked.

"I'm Velvet Vaduva. I'm looking for my daughter, Tami, who come here looking for you."

The colonel looked at my mother disapprovingly. "She's

not here," he said. "This is private property. Kindly leave before I ask these gentlemen with the guns to escort you off it."

Mama stepped forward, an unlit Eve 120 cigarette dangling from her lip. "You knocked up my girl when you was in the Army and she come here to find you."

"She's not here and I don't know where she is," he said, shrugging his shoulders. "Nor did I impregnate her."

"Liar," mama said.

The colonel spread his arms wide. "I don't know where she is. Look around – do you see her anywhere?"

Mama chewed on the filter of her cigarette, making the business end of the Eve 120 bob up and down. "That woman down at the post office—nasty piece of work, that one, but that don't scare me none—she said she sent Tami here more than two months ago. That means you seen her. Because my Tami, she don't give up and retreat. *NEVER.* Now, where is she?"

I pretended to be looking for something in my purse while the colonel begged mine and the governor's pardon and spoke to my mama. He approached her and, in a low voice, said, "Yes, your daughter, Master Sergeant Vaduva, visited Derbyshire Farm," the colonel said. "*Once.* But it was months ago – as you said. She was a highly decorated combat veteran, a great solider, and a great American who served under my command," the colonel continued. "However, she's suffering from PTSD. I'm very sorry to tell you, ma'am, but she's gone A.W.O.L. Your daughter was, in fact, hysterical on the night she visited. Unhinged, I would say. Check with Walter Reed Hospital in D.C." The colonel finished his spiel, but was quick to add, "She has never been seen nor heard from again by me or anyone else, as far as I'm aware, in Albemarle County."

"Bullshit. Tami would never let you or nobody else put her

in no mental asylum." Then she directed her eagle eyes to me, looking me up and down. She started at my feet, beginning with my burgundy satin peep-toe pumps . . . then scanned upward, landing her gaze on my ivory wedding dress. She studied the necklace, the pearls the colonel loves. Her face was a mixture of skepticism, envy and hostility. She reached out and traced her fingers along a strand of my ash-blonde hair. "You're a fancy one, ain't you, princess?" she snarled.

"If you say so," I said, terrified that mama would be able to detect her Tami in my voice—despite that I was speaking in my Anglo-Swiss-Hungarian accent with a dash of Bombay.

Mama cocked her head and scrutinized my face. My tinted eyes, my corrected jawline, my new aristocratic nose and silicone-injected lips. "If a stranger saw you and my Tami walking down the street, he'd reckon you was cousins—her rich, stuck-up cousin."

"I'm not so sure about that," I said. Then, for good measure, I flipped my hair.

Mama fished around in her jeans for a packet of matches, found one, and lit the Eve. She blew a puff of smoke and sneered at the colonel. "Guess you have a type."

"Guess I do. Now kindly leave, all of you!" the colonel barked.

The governor jumped in: "As Colonel Bland has explained to you, ma'am, your daughter isn't here. I believe your next stop should be Walter Reed. A member of my security detail would be happy to escort you there."

"I need $9,285 for an operation."

I gasped, looking mama up and down and trying to see what could be wrong with her.

Mama lurched forward towards the colonel and the governor.

"Stand back, ma'am!" Senior Trooper Prewitt ordered.

My mama was a coarse woman, but she was still my mama. I felt a pang in my heart. "What's wrong,"—I almost said "mama" but caught myself at the last second—"ma'am?"

My mama inhaled her cigarette. "I got vagina prolapse."

The men's eyes popped.

Mama looked straight at me. "You don't know what that is, do you, princess?"

I didn't. "No."

"Course not. You're all young and tight. But it don't stay that way forever, I can tell you. They get loose and jiggly over time, a lady's private parts do."

All the men grimaced.

"Her intimate relations with her gentleman friends is now painful," Grandmama Marlene said, offering up information the wedding party was not keen to have shared with them. "You should hear her when she's on the sofa. Howling like a dog that caught his paw in a bear trap."

"Urinary tract infections come with the ailment," Mama griped.

"I'm very sorry to hear that," the governor said, "but—"

"—she's wet all the time," Great-grand-mama Charlene added "But too proud to wear Depends."

"I ain't wearing no diapers, Charlene. And I ain't ready to close up shop down there neither."

Mama looked at the colonel. "My daughter was supposed to pay for my operation, but you run her out of town. Which means *you* now got an obligation to pay."

The colonel snorted. "You're out of your mind, lady."

Mama ran her hand through her electrified-looking hair. "It's $9,285 to fix my honey pot."

The men winced again.

"You'll never see a penny from me."

The governor stepped forward. "I don't want to make presumptions about your income or employment status, Ms., uh, Velvet, is it? I suspect, however, you may be eligible for coverage under the Affordable Care Act. Did you sign up at www.HealthCare.gov?"

"I ain't in the system. I ain't never gonna be in the system, neither. They can track your whereabouts with HIPPO."

"HIPAA—the Health Insurance Portability and Accountability Act of 1996—is not a surveillance program, ma'am. It's about protecting your privacy, access to care, pretax medical—"

"—whatever."

"She pays cash for everything," Great-grandmama Charlene said. "I get $1,164 in Social Security every month. Not that I ever see any of it. Velvet blows it all on cigarettes and beer."

"And the riverboat casino in South Charleston," Grandmama Marlene chimed in.

The governor made a coughing sound and pulled the colonel aside. "Cleet, I'm supposed to be back in Richmond for a TV interview in eighty minutes. We've got to get this woman out of here so I can complete this ceremony. Unless you'd like me to come back another time. Do you and Tamsin have something you need to discuss?"

The colonel looked over at me. "There's nothing to discuss. Let's get this done." The colonel turned to my relatives: "It's time for you ladies to leave," the colonel said, firmly.

Mama planted her feed wide in the ground and jutted out her breasts. "We ain't going nowhere."

The governor looked at his watch.

"Ladies," he said, "we have about sixty seconds' worth of business to complete, then Colonel Bland will be happy to discuss the matter of your missing relative and your access to healthcare. If you'll just indulge me for a moment . . ." The governor pursed his lips and found his place in the script. He looked to me and the colonel for the go-ahead, and we both nodded.

"Do you, Tamsin Euphemia Venables, take Cletus Esmond Bland III to be your husband?"

"I do," I said, proud as a pigeon, even under the circumstances.

"Do you promise to love, honor, cherish and protect him, forsaking all others and holding only unto him?"

"I do."

It was time for the rings and the colonel dug into his pant pocket. "I, Cletus Esmond Bland III, take Tamsin Euphemia Venables to be my wife," the colonel said, sliding the gold band down my finger. "To have and to hold, in sickness and in health, for richer or for poorer, and I promise my love to you. With this ring, I thee wed."

I slid the wedding band Shelby Nash gave me down the colonel's finger and said, "I, Tamsin Euphemia Venables, take Cletus Esmond Bland III to be my husband. To have and to hold, in sickness and in health, for richer or for poorer, and I promise my love to you. With this ring, I thee wed."

Governor Corter rushed through the remainder of the script. "If anyone gathered here today can show just cause why this couple cannot lawfully be joined together in matrimony, let them speak now or forever hold their peace. By the authority vested in me by the—"

"I object!" mama said. I just about screamed.

"On what grounds?" the governor demanded.

She pointed at the colonel. "I object to you not marrying my daughter. I object to you not supporting my grandchild." She spread her arms out, as though to scoop up the estate around her. "I object to you not sharing any of this wealth with me, because, technically, I'm your mother in law."

Governor Corter snarled. He pulled the colonel aside. "I'm sorry, old buddy," he said. "But I'm out of here."

The colonel clenched his teeth and looked over at me all helpless.

I grabbed the governor by the hand. "Wait."

I leaned over to my fiancé and whispered in his ear. "You know what I want for my wedding gift?"

"What?"

"Buy this crazy lady her operation."

Colonel Cletus Bland looked at me like I was crazy. "I'll do no such thing."

"Take the money you were going to spend on Rome and buy her the operation. I'll take you fishing instead. It'll be just as much fun. Even more so. I hate Italian food."

A confused look came over the colonel's face. "You're serious?" he said. "You'd give your honeymoon to . . . *a stranger*?" He looked over at mama, who was glaring at him like an angry raccoon.

"If it means we can consummate our marriage fifteen minutes from now, and fifteen minutes after that, and fifteen minutes after that, yes."

The colonel clutched my wrists. "God, I love you," he said.

The governor huffed. "Now or never, Cleet."

"Stay, Bingham!" the colonel said as he turned quickly to my mama: "Okay, lady. I'll buy you your operation."

"No checks. Only cash."

"Agreed!"

"The whole $9,285?"

"Every cent," the colonel said. "Now kindly stop talking so I can marry my bride."

Mama put on her poker face, mindful that she had a bird in hand and better not let it fly away.

The governor spoke rapidly: "By the authority vested in me by the Commonwealth of Virginia, I, Bingham Corter, now pronounce you husband and wife. The bride and groom may kiss."

The colonel leaned in and gave me the best kiss of my life.

"It's official," the governor declared.

Great-grandmama Charlene and Grandmama Marlene both burst into tears. "Us Vaduva girls ain't never been to a wedding before," Great-grandmama Charlene sniffled.

Colonel Bland escorted the Governor and his security detail to their car. The two men shook hands.

I was dizzy, wobbling. I'd just become the first Vaduva woman in twenty-five generations to get legally married. The first to break a spell that dated all the way back to Petrești, Romania. I wanted so much to hug and squeeze Mama, and Grandmama Marlene, and Great-grandmama Charlene. They'd have been so proud of me if they knew. Yet I was forced to treat them like strangers, and not say a word. I fought back the tears but failed. Just a drop in the eyes at first. Then the waterworks came flooding out of both eyes.

Mama pulled a handkerchief out of the back pocket of her jeans. It was dingy and wrinkled, smeared with what looked like a decade's worth of lipstick. She waded it up and tossed it to me. "I don't know what you're so sad about, princess. From the looks of this place, you just bagged the biggest prize in Virginia."

Colonel Bland, who approached from behind, gently wrapped his arms around my waist. "It's me who won the prize."

32.

I was sitting backwards in the canoe, facing my husband. I knew every inch of the river: every turn, every patch of rapids, every shallow point, though I could not reveal my mastery of my surroundings to my new husband. We were supposed to be discovering this place together.

"I can't believe I grew up three hours from here and am discovering this place for the first time," the colonel said. "How did *you* of all people discover it?"

Above us, the pale blue sky was the exact same shade of Great-grandmama Charlene's eyeshadow.

"Are you familiar with Gonarezhou National Park?"

"No," my new husband said.

"It's in Zimbabwe's lowlands. In the local language, the word 'Gonarezhou' translates into 'Place of many Elephants.' For the two years we were living in Harare, when my father was at the embassy, we went on several weekend trips to the park." I had read about that park while I was still in the Army in an old *National Geographic* Magazine I found in the latrine. Always wanted to go there, as it reminded me of the terrain along my beloved New River.

The sun was warm, beaming with optimism. I untied the strings of my bikini at the neck and my breasts spilled out.

The colonel licked his lips. "They get juicier, riper, and more luscious every day."

The swelling was really starting to accelerate now that I was entering my fifth month of pregnancy. My belly finally pooched. The time was coming—sooner rather than later—when the colonel was going to figure out I was pregnant. He could also do the math, and would want to know how any baby conceived on our honeymoon managed to arrive, full-term, four months later. I began war-gaming communications scenarios in my mind as the colonel kissed my right breast. If I remained in Tamsin undercover mode for the duration of our union, which I had no objection to doing so long as our destiny was fulfilled, he'd conclude that the child was another man's. If I told him the truth—that the baby was his and was conceived not with aristocratic Tamsin Venables on our West Virginia honeymoon but inside a tent in the sandbox, with soldier-under-his-command Tami Vaduva, he'd go nuclear after discovering he'd been tricked. In a military situation, when you're presented with two bad choices, you don't accept the less bad one; you find a third way. Problem was, I had not yet figured that third way out. And it was getting harder and harder to formulate my strategy, as I was getting heated up.

After we had our go, I opened the lid of the cooler, fished out a can of Vienna Lager and handed it to my husband. I plucked out a can of non-alcoholic beer for myself.

"What were we talking about before we got distracted?"

"Zimbabwe."

"There were three major rivers—the Save, Runde, and Mwenezi—that ran through Gonarezhou National Park. I was raving to one of the people in our group about how the beauty along those rivers was unrivaled. And this gentleman seated next to me—someone from the U.S. State Department—told me there was indeed an even more spectacular river for me to see, an ancient river in West Virginia that flows backwards, from south to north."

"I believe him."

"I've wanted to see the New River for years. And now I am here, sharing it with the love of my life. The man I am destined to be with."

The colonel twirled the paddle in his lap.

"Getting hungry?"

He nodded. "We'll tie up soon and I'll get a fire going."

"After we've finished our *aperitifs,*" I said, clinking the cans.

"What's on the menu?"

"What do you think, my handsome husband?"

"Channel cats, I presume?"

"Fresh and local."

He sat up and faced me. "Where'd a British girl who grew up in exotic third world hellholes learn how to cook Southern-style catfish?"

I learned from my Great-grandma Charlene. But I wasn't about to tell the colonel that. "I watch cooking shows on TV. The secret ingredient is cream cheese," I said. "I coat my catfish in a thick plaster of cream cheese instead of buttermilk, then dredge it through the cornmeal, which has so much paprika it turns the cornmeal red."

I likewise omitted the detail about how and why cream cheese became the secret ingredient: when she went to the IGA, Great-grandma Charlene was less likely to get caught stealing a four-ounce packet of Philadelphia cream cheese than a half-gallon of buttermilk.

The colonel stuck the paddle in the water and rowed. "I could eat it every night."

"And get fat as a house," I teased.

"I notice you're getting a bit of tummy yourself, Mrs. Bland. Just the tiniest little bit. Which I find adorable, by the way. After two-plus decades with a human toothpick, I've longed for a woman with some meat on her bones. Now I've got one."

He pulled the paddle out of the water and laid it perpendicular across his lap. He stretched out on his back across the canoe's stern and gazed up at the blue sky; I did the same at the opposite end of the canoe. The valley sides had long ago fallen away; we were now in the heart of a three-hundred-and-twenty--million-year-old gorge, staring nine hundred feet upward. An eagle circled above. One gracious loop after another before gliding back to its nest. Cleet smiled. "God, I love my new life!"

We floated in silence for another half hour or so. When the night's campground was selected, Cleet jumped out and towed us in. Then he scooped me up and in both arms. "Let me carry my bride to shore so her delicate little limbs stay dry." He set me gently on the sandy bank.

The next morning, after we'd had our morning go, Cleet said, "I have never slept so well as on this trip. Not since I was a kid."

"Me neither."

"Is it all the, uh . . . ?"

"Yes."

When we weren't having a go, the colonel loved to talk about military matters. At breakfast, we discussed the Battle of al-Faw. During cleanup, when we were washing the skillet in the river, the topic was the First Battle of Fallujah and Operation Law and Order. He had not seen combat in any of those theatres, but had read about them, and held strong opinions about how the battles were or should have been prosecuted.

I let the colonel do the talking. I chimed in on occasion, of course, though mostly to let him know I was paying attention and taking an active interest in his passions.

"For someone with no military training, your observations are spot on, Tamsin," he said later, when we were both on the banks of the river, shaving. He sharpened the blade on a leather strap and lathered my legs. "Stay still," he commanded as he swiped the blade from calf up to thigh. "I've never said a word to anybody about what happened over there. Not to Dabney, my so-called best friend. Certainly not to Ginny." He dipped the razor in the river and rinsed off the soap. "There were things that happened in the moment . . . things I'm not proud of. I cracked up once." He told me about surrendering when we were sent to take out Mehdi Hashmi in Karz. "I never thought I'd tell anyone that," he said as we packed our gear into the canoe and prepared to shove off for the day. "I was raised not to show weakness. Ever. When you come from wealth, like we do, people are always watching. Gloating when you stumble. It's not just me. It's all of us in what Ginny used to call 'our set.' Everyone I went to school with, golf with. Ginny and all her friends. And their husbands. And ex-husbands. And their kids. And estranged kids. Everybody's got their game face on. And everybody's got a different dark, nasty secret they're terrified will be discovered by the others, whom they're convinced are perfect, or at least more perfect than they are." The colonel pushed us out and hopped into the canoe.

I knew the colonel loved Albemarle County, Virginia. He was born there – everyone he ever knew was born there. Except for his time in the Army, which seemed almost like a dream to him, he'd really never left central Virginia. Sure, he'd gone on fancy vacations, but it was always to the same places, with the same people– most of them from Charlottesville, too. I wondered if he might actually like being someplace else. The way he liked being with a woman like me. "Maybe your destiny is to build a cabin over where those cows are grazing. A wood stove to keep us warm in winter. A screened-in porch to protect our children from the mosquitos when summer comes."

The colonel stroked his chin. "I've never met anyone who so clearly doesn't give a damn what others think of her," he said. "How did you manage to be so supremely indifferent to public opinion? Especially given *your* background?"

"I focus on getting things done, that's all. I see only the target before me. I am uninterested in the periphery, unless there's something there that can shoot back at me. Anything that blocks the target, I take it out."

The colonel eyed me curiously. "Now it's *you* who sounds like a combat veteran."

33.

When the late afternoon sun began to sink, I pitched a tent beneath the canopy of a weeping willow tree. The colonel collected firewood. We cooked the days' catch.

"The idea of building a cabin here is sounding increasingly attractive," my husband said after dinner, when we were next to the fire, eating peaches straight out of a can. "With each nip of Horsebit, the idea becomes more plausible. There's not much keeping me in Charlottesville these days, is there? Got a new wife. Augusta will soon be settled in Switzerland—not far from her mother. Hell, it's not like I have a job that's keeping me in Charlottesville." He sighed and took a big sip of peach syrup. "I would miss Worthington, though."

We laid on our backs, staring at the stars, and hammered out all the details of our fantasy cabin: an iron stove with nickel plating, rag rugs, a plot of land on the east side of the river so we could view sunsets from the porch at cocktail hour, perched in rockers, and a cabin close to the rail line so we could hear train whistles blowing at night. We could even drive up to Charlottesville on weekends, so that the colonel could play golf at his country club.

In the tent, before we got down to business, we were snuggling beneath the blankets. "Cleet," I said to the colonel.

"What about having Augusta live over here, with us and the baby—when we have one? She could go to the high school in Beckley?"

"She wouldn't thrive over here."

"In America?"

"In West Virginia."

"What makes you say so?"

The colonel folded his hands behind his head. A troubled look came across his face. "Let me explain something to you about West Virginia, Tamsin? Meth labs. Hillbillies. Incest. White trash. Living here would be out of the question for people like us." He took another sip of whiskey and became somber. "Leaving Charlottesville wouldn't be easy. Making hot chocolate on Christmas morning, sneaking out for lobster rolls during summer holidays in Maine, watching Fourth of July fireworks at Worthington. This is what I always have done. These are my rituals."

"If you say so."

I rolled over and picked up the vintage Louis Vuitton hat box Shelby gave me as a wedding present, shaking it like I was ringing a dinner bell. Unfastening the lid, I invited my husband to gaze inside.

He sat up. "Sex toys? I've got to be honest with you, babe, with the exception of a one-off encounter in Afghanistan, just before I cycled out of the military, I had never seen any of this junk. Now, it appears, they're part of *everybody's* sexual repertoire."

I giggled and flashed a naughty smile. "I'm not interested in everybody else, only us." I presented the box as though it were a box of chocolates. "Pick your poison, colonel."

"Riding crop . . . leather paddle. What the hell are these? They look like jumper cables."

"Nipple clamps."

He rummaged through the box. "These fleshlights I've seen before, under every nineteen-year-old G.I.'s pillow. What's in the Tiffany's box?"

"A silver ring."

"From Tiffany's?"

"Teething ring. Why let it sit in a box and tarnish when it can be put to good use on a honeymoon?"

The colonel reached inside. "Why, may I ask, are there electrical wires doing sprouting out of this, this . . . *contraption*?"

"It's an electro-prostate massager. These settings dial up vibrations, heat, pulsing, numbing, and so on."

He dropped it like he was just told he was handling toxic waste.

"I don't want to sound like a bossy wife, but I'd recommend a combination of the mechanical and the manual."

"I vote for a combination of neither," the colonel said. "I don't know what it is about me that makes women think I'm into toys, but at the end of the day I'm pretty square—and proudly so."

His eyes squinted up as he watched me undress.

I watched him as he undressed, too. When we were naked, I reached down and cupped his bean bag in my hand. "Time to fire up those proud, even-hangin' balls of yours."

I smiled lovingly at my husband.

But all he did was scowl.

On every morning of our honeymoon, I awakened to the colonel's gentle snoring, which kept time with the rhythms of the flowing water.

But not today. On this, our fourth morning, he was not beside me. I unzipped the tent flap and peered out into the gray pre-dawn. No sign of him: not at the riverbank washing, shaving or peeing, nor brewing the coffee.

I grabbed the roll of toilet paper and headed over to the bank and voided what felt like a gallon of water as I watched a ten-pound spotted bass jump every five seconds or so, as though convinced it was a dolphin.

I slid my hand down to dab the toilet paper over my privates and knew upon feeling the baby-smooth patch of skin that my week-old marriage was in serious jeopardy. I gazed down at my pelvis, shorn of its dyed ash-blonde hair at some point during the middle of the night, and discovered—or, rather, *re-discovered*—my zipper tattoo.

34.

It was close to 1 p.m. and still no sign of the colonel.

I occupied myself with cooking and cleaning the pots, pans, and cutlery during the morning. My stomach was in knots. I was sick with worry and fear. I P.T.-ed to burn off the stress, then disassembled the tent. Fished. Lunched. Swam. I read a few more chapters of *The Glass Castle*. It'd been hard to keep my mind focused on these tasks, but I was determined to stay busy rather than wonder if he was ever coming back.

The nose of the canoe became visible around 3:30 p.m. When he tied up and stepped ashore, he looked rough, like he hadn't slept. His eyes were bleary, his hair sticking up at the back in full-on bedhead mode, though it was late afternoon. Each step he took seemed an effort. "I left in the middle of the night. About six hours downstream, I turned around." He picked up a twig and snapped it in half. Then snapped the half in half. "Despite what you've pulled off—or *think* you've pulled off—you're never going to get away with it. I'm only back here because my honor code as a U.S. Army soldier prohibits me from abandoning a woman in the middle of the New River Gorge. Of course, the joke's on me, as always, because you are doubly capable of surviving alone in the wilderness." The colonel paced. "Alas, the honeymoon is over, Tamsin . . . or Tami . . . or whatever the hell your name is."

He stopped and put his hands to his side, clenching and unclenching his fists. "I'm only going to ask you once to get in the canoe," he said.

He must have done a lot of thinking on his twelve-hour float, because as we paddled, the accusations poured out of him, fully formed. "Every great con artist knows that the mark is always *anxious to believe*. In my case, ladies and gentlemen of the jury, I am guilty as charged. That first time I saw you outside the clubhouse at Worthington, in that vintage Rover, I thought, 'Christ, if only I'd met a woman like that before . . .' Oh, forget it. Who cares what I thought. The point is, you delivered: the international pedigree, the heroics at Ginny's party with the rattlesnake, the mystery and intrigue over drinks at Worthington. You played me like a fiddle, darlin.' And no matter how fantastical the tale, I *wanted* it to be true. I *willed* it to be true."

He suspended prosecution while we navigated a series of Class III rapids, then resumed when the waters calmed. "I'm not beating myself up too hard," he said. "You're trained at deception. How many terrorist cells did you infiltrate when we were over there, four? Five?"

"Nine."

"But you made some big tactical errors. The biggest of course was inviting all your relatives to our wedding."

"I didn't invite them. They came looking for *you*—not me."

"Yeah, right." He looked stared at a cluster of trees swaying in the breeze. "Then you defined the word 'vardo' for Governor Corter. Nobody would know what that word means."

The canoe veered towards the bank. We were about to get

tangled in a cluster of prickly bushes. I knew this part of the river like the back of my hand and it was treacherous. I took charge of navigation.

"It's plausible that someone raised in the UK would know about a Gypsy wagon," I said, even though I knew it would make no difference. "There are a ton of Gypsies in the UK and Ireland."

He tossed his paddle into the canoe and threw his hands up. "You're not really going to try to keep this ruse going, are you . . . Master Sergeant Vaduva?"

"No, I'm not. Now I'm the one guilty as charged: I am who you say I am."

"Tami Vaduva."

"And I'm Tamsin Venables. I'm whoever you want me to be."

"When you cried at the end of the wedding ceremony, I didn't have the heart to tell you that, when you wiped the tears away, I noticed one of your contact lenses folded onto your eyelid. You thought you slyly wedged it back into place without my noticing, but the contrast between the seafoam green right eye and the coal-black left one had me wondering if I wasn't marrying David Bowie. Get me a beer, will you?"

I got him a beer. "It's called envy green."

"What?"

"The color of the contact lens."

He shook his head in disgust. "And then there was your big slipup when we were discussing Mehdi Hashmi and Karz. You asked me if I had considered shooting at the chandelier over Mehdi Hashmi's head, which would have been a brilliant maneuver. The only problem is I'd never told you there was a chandelier over his head. How could you have known that was there unless you'd been in the room? Which, of course . . . you were!" He took a long, angry swig of beer and swallowed hard. "All of those revelations were plausibly deniable—except for one. Know which?"

"No."

"Your praise of my 'even-hangin' balls.'"

"I regretted it the moment the words came out of my mouth."

"Were you *trying* to get caught?"

"No. I was excited. Overwhelmed with joy. Joy I have never known in my life—and will probably never know again. Our destiny, to be together forever, was coming true."

He stood up, making the canoe rock back and forth like a cradle.

"You're wrong about 'our' destiny," he said, pointing his finger at me like a gun. "I promise you that."

I shook my head, slow and sure. "No, I'm not."

We exited the river and loaded our gear and canoe into Harlan's truck, doing so in complete silence. The colonel jerked the truck into gear and we bounced along the backroads.

"You were behind all the PSYOPs attacks on Ginny, weren't you? Her being an illegitimate Slovak girl from Chicago adopted by the Stiths? Exposing her affair with Dabney?"

"I had a mission to complete and a destiny to fulfill."

He white-knuckle gripped the steering wheel and floored the gas pedal. Once we were able to get cellphone reception, the colonel called his lawyer. "Congratulations, Cameron, you get to gloat and say 'I told you so.'"

Colonel Bland instructed his lawyer to draw up divorce papers. "My soon-to-be-ex-wife and I will be at your office at noon tomorrow to sign." He touched the button on his phone, ending the call. He looked at me. A cruel stare scarier than anything a terrorist ever directed at me. "And you *will* sign."

"You'd do that to our son?"

"Nice try," he said. "You aren't pregnant, Master Sergeant Vaduva. You were never pregnant."

"That's not true, colonel. I'm very much pregnant." I pulled up my t-shirt and showed him the lump. And it's yours."

He looked ahead and called the owner of the Inn at Judiciary Circle, a classmate from his boarding school days, and booked a room for himself. "Wait a minute. I don't know why I booked a room for me—it should be for you! You're the one who's getting kicked out of my house!"

I retrieved from my purse the folded paper and tossed it in his lap.

"What's this, an invoice?"

"It's destiny."

He unfolded the ultrasound photo, gave it the once over, then crumpled it up and threw it on the floor. "There are five million pictures like this on the internet. I'm done with your PSYOPs."

"You're the father."

The colonel flared his nostrils. "You're wasting your time, Tami. When we get back, you've got some papers to sign. And you *will* sign them. And you *will* forfeit any claim to a settlement. Aside from the fact that you defrauded me and my case is airtight, you are even further incentivized to pack your gear and get the hell out of town before the ink on the divorce papers is dry because, if you don't, I'm reporting you A.W.O.L. and you'll be spending the next five years in a federal prison."

I pointed to the crumpled up ultrasound photo at my feet. "That's Cletus Esmond Bland IV. And he's coming in four months. Didn't you see him? Those big, strong bones, and that faint trace of a Bland smile? I want to raise this beautiful boy with you, colonel. Together. I can be whoever you want me to be. Tami, Tamsin, Judy, Trudy—I don't care. All I want is to be with you. It's all I ever wanted. We can move to West Virginia and you can retire and I will get work as an auto mechanic. Or we can stay in Charlottesville and you can teach me to play golf. I'm learning French right now and am almost fluent. We can move to France, maybe. Can't you see it's our destiny to be together? You, me, and Cletus Esmond Bland IV. And Augusta, who I will raise as my own if her mother doesn't want her."

The colonel started taking the curves on the road a little too fast and I suggested he ease up on the gas, which he did. "You're never seeing a penny of my fortune. Not a penny."

"I never wanted a penny of your fortune. I still don't. Just tell me what to sign and I'll sign it. I just want to live in happiness with you and Cleet IV."

"Quit calling him 'Cleet IV'!"

The colonel said nothing for the next thirty minutes.

When we pulled off to get gas in Covington, Virginia, his face reddened, which meant he was about to berate me again. "What really gets me," he said, isn't just your gaslighting of me and my now ex-wife, but the way you breezed into my town, infiltrated my friend group, and joined my club. You don't have a penny to donate to that club."

I nodded my head, affirming his suspicion.

After the gas was pumped, I asked permission to be excused, as me and the baby were starving again. When we were back on the interstate, I said while unwrapping a package of pink Snoballs, "When I told you I loved you – when I tell you now – it's the truth!"

"I thought I was marrying international millionaire socialite Tamsin Venables only to discover I'd been duped by . . ."

"What?"

"West Virginia white trash!"

"Well, you seemed to enjoy Tami Vaduva in the tent and in the truck in Afghanistan."

"I wasn't the only one!"

Another woman would have slapped him. But I am not another woman. I always enjoyed the company of men, a variety of men. Until I met Cleet—and lost interest in other men. "You are the only one who matters to me!" I told him. "And you seemed to like my company just fine at the Framers bar, in your barn, and this whole week on the river."

"When I thought you were someone else! When—"

"—when what? When you thought I was a fancy, educated woman with breeding and money?"

"When I thought you were telling the truth!"

The people passing us on the highway took a notice of our yelling.

"So what's the difference between Tami and Tamsin now? You didn't like the way I talked redneck, so I fixed that. You didn't like my nose, so I fixed that. You didn't like my taste in clothes or cars, so I fixed that. Shouldn't that make you happy? With the new me, you've got somebody you can be seen having drinks with at the bar at Worthington. Someone who knows good furniture and can pick out a picture to put over your fireplace. Someone who will make love to you until your eyes roll backwards in your head. What's the problem?"

"You committed fraud. That's the problem!"

"Didn't you say you loved the easy, stimulating conversation we had together? That you had more of that with me in a week than you did over almost twenty years with your ex-wife? Isn't that what you told me yesterday?"

The colonel shrugged and looked out the window. I saw the reflection of his face in the glass.

"I believe in destiny, colonel. My people always have. *Always.* And I'll do anything I need to do to make sure destiny is fulfilled. You want me to come up with some money to give your fancy club that squandered its treasury? I'll do that. Can it be harder than what I already done? You want me to sign a piece of paper that says I have no claim on your money? Fine. You want me to be Tamsin Venables for the rest of my life? I'll do that, too. No problem."

The colonel pushed his bangs aside, giving a big sigh like when a waitress thinks she's done for the night and that last couple wanders in and sits down at one of her tables. "There's the matter of my reputation," he said. "I'm from a family with a three-hundred-fifty-year legacy in Virginia. Four months from now, when you give birth to a full-term baby, folks in town will know you were pregnant on our wedding day—even if I did not. Which means they will know that I was knowing you – and awfully well – even before you landed in Charlottesville."

It was the first time Colonel Bland acknowledged that I was, in fact, truly carrying our baby.

"I don't approve of cursing," I said. "When my mama, grandmama and great-grandmama do it, it makes me bristle. Ever since I was a little girl. So, kindly excuse me when I say *fuck you* and *fuck* your reputation, too, Cletus Esmond Bland III. Is my company really so awful? Will standing next to me compromise your reputation so much?"

"I didn't say that."

"It's exactly what you said. You're about to start a new family.

With a woman who has the best pedigree in Charlottesville. Yes, it's made up. So what? So are half of your friends who claimed to come here on the *Mayflower*."

"*Discovery* and *Godspeed*. The *Mayflower* landed at Plymouth, Mass."

"I don't care. Who will know other than you and me?"

He took a cigar out his pack and chewed on it unlit, saying nothing, until we were on the other side of Lexington. An hour later, when he dropped me off at the hotel, the colonel said, "Our appointment with Cameron is at noon tomorrow. I'll pick you up from your hotel at 11:45. Don't be late. And don't even *think* about leaving town. One phone call from me to Bingham Corter and we'll have state troopers and military police in five states looking for you twenty-four-seven. And then it'll be: 'Hello, Leavenworth!'"

35.

In my quest to not look as crushed as I felt, I said to the colonel when he greeted me in the lobby of the inn, "You're dressed fancy for someone about to get a divorce." I pinched the bows and evened out his lopsided bowtie.

He backed away.

"When southerners have official business to conduct, we dress appropriately."

The floor creaked as we walked across the wide, uneven planks of the lobby.

"I see you felt no similar obligation," he said.

I buttoned the pocket flap on my desert camo uniform, the only outfit I've felt normal wearing in months. "There's nobody at the lawyer's office I'm keen to impress."

The colonel eyed me up and down. "Takes me back to Afghanistan," he muttered. "I see you've got your munitions box with you."

"I use it the way civilian women carry a purse. A place to store my gear."

"Which, I assure you, isn't the same gear Ginny and her friends carry in *their* purses."

We stepped outside onto the cobblestone streets, into the

historic district. We headed towards the square, where his attorney's office was located.

"How'd you sleep?" he asked.

"Badly."

"Me too."

We walked in silence. Then he said, "Something wrong with the room?"

"No. All the furnishings were period. I slept in an antique cannonball rope bed, circa 1830. Great mattress." I shrugged.

"Listen to you: 'antique cannonball rope bed, circa 1830.'"

"I learned a few things since Afghanistan. Not that they're of much use or, frankly, interest to me. Just missed sleeping next to you, I guess."

The colonel cleared his throat and gave me one of his loud and hard swallows. "Worried about your new life?"

"I don't worry."

The colonel pretended to study a Civil War memorial plaque in front of an old brick building.

"How'd *you* sleep?"

"I didn't. Until I did, with the help of three-quarters a bottle of Horsebit."

"Your head must be pounding." I flipped open the munitions box. There was a bottle of aspirin in there somewhere.

"Cobwebby, but no pain. Still, these'll help," he said with gratitude as I shook two pills into the colonel's palm. He popped the pills in his mouth and swallowed saliva to wash it down as we crossed High Street. A brass placard outside the front door of the restored federal-period house read: "LAW OFFICES OF CAMERON J. SMALLWOOD, PLLC."

"Ready?" the colonel asked me.

I reached for the door knob. “Always.”

The colonel intercepted my hand. “You seem to be in a very different place since yesterday.”

“I don’t re-fight yesterday’s battles. Let’s go.”

The colonel didn’t budge. Instead, he looked down. His eyes rolled over my belly.

“What are you staring at?”

The colonel kicked the tip of his suede loafers at the ground like a little boy. “You know.”

I did.

“Can we talk some more?” he said. He plunged his hands into his pockets. “I did a lot of thinking last night.”

“And drinking.”

The colonel finally met my eyes. He inclined his head, signaling me to follow him, and we crossed the street into City Square Park. There, we sat down on an old iron bench. The colonel plopped his elbows on his knees and rested his chin between his palms. He fidgeted. Then he sat up and combed his fine hair with his fingers before looking up and out over the park. “I reached a conclusion last night,” he said.

“About what?”

“About you.”

“Oh.”

The colonel pulled out his phone and began texting. I couldn’t see what about. He finished and put the phone back in his pocket. Right away his phone began dinging like crazy.

“Turn around and wave to Cameron. That’s him, up there in that second floor window, looking like he’s about to explode.”

I waved at the red-faced man standing in the window.

“Now, where were we?”

“Something about thinking.”

"Right," the colonel said. "Specifically, I was thinking about our honeymoon."

Considering how it ended, I reckoned they were not happy thoughts.

"How maybe we should extend it," he said quietly.

"Extend it?"

A couple of older ladies walked by and the colonel gave them a polite nod, which they returned. He waited until they were far down the footpath before speaking again. "I'm not making any promises, and I've still got Cameron drawing up the documents regarding my assets, but I've been wondering if perhaps we shouldn't be quite so hasty in finalizing any kind of divorce situation."

I took a deep breath and remained stone-faced. "I'm confused."

"I'm saying let's give it a try. To be perfectly honest, I'm not confident it will work. But I have this nagging feeling that five, or ten, or fifty years from now, I'll hate myself if I don't at least give it a try."

"I see."

The colonel next waved to a man dressed like him in a bow tie.

"What made you change your mind?"

"As I sat there drinking last night, I kept thinking about you, all the joy you bring me. You know cars, Cavaliers football, quail-hunting, whisky-distilling . . ."

"To be truthful, colonel, I only learned about those things because they're things you like."

"That's more than Ginny ever did."

"Except for the cars. I do like cars."

"Speaking of which. Where'd you get the Rover?"

"I have been told I am 'resourceful.'"

The colonel laughed. Then he pulled me a little closer. "You understand my interests—and me—better than anyone else I've ever known. And military strategy. And you fish. You can catch and kill a rattlesnake. You don't panic in the rapids. You can take out a terrorist at two thousand yards."

"Twenty-two hundred, sir."

"Stop calling me 'sir.'"

"You're flushing your life down the toilet!" boomed the voice from across the street. A big-bottomed man in khaki slacks and a pastel bow tie similar to the colonel's was waddling towards us. "Don't be an idiot, Cleet. Or at least, if you're going to be an idiot, come back to my office and do it the right way."

"We're coming, Cameron. Just give us a minute."

Cameron Smallwood halted, crossed his arms and watched us from a distance.

"But for this to work," my husband continued, "we need to try it out somewhere else, not here. Let's go overseas for a while. Someplace where we can clear our heads, start fresh, get to know each other, and . . ." He lowered his voice. ". . . have the baby."

"You mean it, colonel?"

He blotted the tear under my eye with his thumb. "I just said it."

"Where do you want to go?"

The colonel stretched out his legs and peered up at the sky. "Pick a place."

"Maybe that national park with the three rivers in Zimbabwe?"

"I'm not having my first son delivered by some witch doctor," the colonel said.

"Maybe some of those places I put in my made-up biography: Indonesia, Dubai, or Singapore."

"No Arabs. No Asians. Europe."

"England sounds nice, as I am now an expert on all things English: tapestry, china, diction, military, and diplomatic history. There's a castle in Wiltshire I did a lot of research on. It's for rent. They have cottages in the village, too, which would be gentler on the pocketbook. Lots of countryside—like you're used to here in Virginia."

"That sounds good. Two conditions."

"Name them."

"First, revert back to 'Tamsin mode': blonde, green-eyed, classy. That's the woman I fell in love with."

"Easy. Second?"

The colonel put his hand on my thigh. "And sex. Lots of sex. I've got a two decades' worth to catch up on."

"I'm happy to comply with your terms, colonel."

36.

Fifteen Months Later . . .

"Skinny vanilla latte?"

"Me!" Lemon-Colored Kiawah Hat replied.

"Nonfat cap?"

Bronwyn tapped a lacquered fingernail on the table.

"Nonfat caramel macchiato?"

"You're an angel," Tangerine-Colored Pinehurst Hat said to the café owner.

"Soy chai tea latte?"

"Right here," said Lime-Colored Bay Creek Hat.

"And a Kale Koncoction for the lovely Mrs. Bland," he said, placing the beverage before me with a flourish.

"Thanks, Clifford," I said.

"Congratulations, Tam. We've been coming here for a decade and he's never bothered to learn any of *our* names," said Lemon-Colored Kiawah Hat.

I wanted to tell her it's because I bothered to learn his, but I refrained.

"How's it feel to be back?" Tangerine-Colored Pinehurst Hat asked.

"Nothing appears to have changed during my absence," I said, before adding, in the spirit of *Always,* "I *love* that!" I told the yoga ladies I appreciated the venerability of my adopted hometown. "The continuity here, the reverence for ritual and tradition. It's a great source of comfort."

"Oh, there's been change aplenty," Lime-Colored Bay Creek Hat smirked. As coffees were sipped, the yoga ladies caught me up on a year and a half's worth of malicious gossip: The student cheating scandal at Digby Day, which cost the headmaster his job, the eighty-mile-per-hour windstorm that took down trees that fell on Dabney Hines's farmhouse, the uproar created by the general manager's decision to change the lunch menu at Bounty, the friends' children who got into Washington and Lee, Davidson, UVA, Vanderbilt, Sewanee, Sweet Briar, and Hampden-Sydney despite being unqualified—and, with relish, reports of the disappointed parents whose kids *did not*. Mostly, though, the ladies complained about the dismal social scene in Charlottesville before demanding details of our time away: the food and weather, the places we saw, our trips beyond Wiltshire to London and the Continent, our getaways down south, to Corfu, after Cletus IV was born.

"I love that you call him 'the Fourth.' That's so cute," Lemon-Colored Kiawah Hat said. "My dad is called Quint, because he was the Fifth. His real name, of course, is Lawson."

"Cleet III calls him 'the Fourth;' I prefer 'Cleet IV.'

"I saw Cleet III and IV yesterday at the Worthington pool. He's so gorgeous!" Tangerine-Colored Pinehurst Hat said.

"Which one?" Bronwyn teased.

Tangerine-Colored Pinehurst Hat purred: "Okay, let me just state this for the record: I don't know *what* you're doing to him, Tamsin—well, I have an inkling—but Cleet looks ten years younger."

"Of course, we're friends with Ginny and always will be,"

clarified Lime-Colored Bay Creek Hat. “That said, it’s amazing how an unhappy union ages you.”

“And that child!” Tangerine-Colored Pinehurst Hat said. “Those gigantic, jet-black eyes. That silky black hair. When you and Cleet are both green-eyed and fair-haired!” She nudged me with a finger. “Are you sure you didn’t meet some handsome Italian on your extended honeymoon?”

“If anybody’s bloodline is dodgy, I’m sure it’s mine,” I said with a giggle and self-deprecating wave of the hand. “Have I told you ladies about my grandfather’s grandfather’s job under the Raj? He was chief of staff to the Viceroy and Governor-General of India in the 1880s. For all I know, one of his wives or daughters—someone in my line—secretly mated with a dashing Maharaja.”

The ladies giggled.

“The Maharaja must have been a giant. Cleet IV is *huge* for his age!” Lemon-Colored Kiawah Hat said.

“That shouldn’t surprise anybody,” Bronwyn chimed in. “Cleet’s tall. His mother was a Viking. Stand up and let me get a look at you, Tamsin.”

I obeyed. She sized me up with an envious eye. “None of us ever looked so good after childbirth. Bitch!”

When the laughter died down, I told the ladies about Prakash, our yoga instructor, a man just shy of eighty, from Bombay, whom we installed him in one of the carriage houses in Wiltshire. “Cleet can touch his toes now,” I reported.

“No!” Lime-Colored Bay Creek Hat said. “He always hated yoga and made fun of men who practiced.”

“Not anymore. He’s a convert,” I told the girls. “He noticed that Prakash, an old man, had more strength and muscle definition than himself—and half the body fat! That sold Cleet.”

"Does this mean he's going to start coming to our yoga class?" Bronwyn asked hopefully.

"Cleet wouldn't be caught *dead* at our yoga class. But Augusta said she wants to try it."

"You and Cleet are saints to have brought her back here after Ginny's . . . *breakdown*," Bronwyn said. "Now she can be with everyone she's always known at Digby Day."

"Parenthood is about duty," I said.

Lime-Colored Bay Creek Hat adopted a confidential tone and whispered, "I'm told she's having a rough time at Digby Day. If you don't mind my saying."

"It's no secret."

"My Huntington is two years ahead of her," she added, unhelpfully; I knew what was coming. "He's heard stories about Augusta. Disruptive behavior in class. Apparently very highly sexualized. Drugs—not just pot, but harder stuff, too. I'm not bringing it up to embarrass you, Tam."

No, of course not.

"She just wants to make sure you're aware that she's struggling," said Tangerine-Colored Pinehurst Hat.

"Cleet and I are well aware of the situation."

"It'd be abnormal if she wasn't struggling, what with all the adjustments. Especially her mom refusing to see her when they were both in Switzerland at the same time," lamented Lime-Colored Bay Creek Hat.

"Dare I ask? Where's Ginny and Dabney?" Lemon-Colored Kiawah Hat asked.

"Dabney's apparently in Asheville with his new girlfriend," Bronwyn gleefully reported. "*Nobody* has heard a word from Ginny, but the girl who cuts my hair is the roommate of a girl who works at Galaxy Travel and, apparently, Ginny has booked herself into some five-star yoga resort in Thailand, of all places."

Everyone agreed the whole situation was very, very sad.

"Socially, everything came to a grinding halt after Ginny left," Tangerine-Colored Pinehurst Hat said.

"I still don't know how she managed it all. Running that house. Staying in shape. Plus raising all that money for so many worthy causes," said Lime-Colored Bay Creek Hat.

"She was a force of nature!" Lemon-Colored Kiawah Hat added.

All of the ladies glanced over at me and Bronwyn stepped up and apologized on behalf of the group for brining Ginny up. "I'm sure it's uncomfortable."

"Not in the least."

After a brief lull in the conversation, during which everyone checked texts, emails and social media accounts, Bronwyn asked, "Who's going to organize all the charity fundraisers now that Ginny's gone?" She sipped her nonfat cap. "I know it's not going to be me. I ran the Digby Day auction and I'm still exhausted from it!"

Exhausted or unindicted? I thought to myself.

"I can't host a party until the guest house renovations are done," said Lemon-Colored Kiawah Hat.

Tangerine-Colored Pinehurst Hat and Lime-Colored Bay Creek Hat tendered their excuses, too.

"Well, Tamsin, ready to step up and host your first fundraiser?" Bronwyn chided.

"Me?"

"After Worthington received that $1.1 million check from Colonel and Mrs. Cletus Bland III, you two pretty much announced yourselves as *the* power-social couple of Charlottesville."

"I'm not so sure about that," I told them. "Cleet Three and Four are keeping me busy as a bee. I'm cleaning the house and doing all the cooking now that Peaches retired and moved to Roanoke to live with her daughter. Harlan's still around, of course, but he's been diagnosed with Type 2 diabetes. He's slowed down quite a bit. So I'm doing a lot of the yardwork."

"*You?* It's a two-thousand--acre farm!" Tangerine-Colored Pinehurst Hat said.

"I love being outside. Fresh air. And I know my way around a John Deere tractor. I do the mowing and baling; Cleet's only job is to get rid of those blasted yellowjackets. You should see the west side of the property: it looks like a combat zone. He's out there daily, at dawn and dusk, soaking rags in gasoline, stuffing them into underground nests, tossing Molotov cocktails at the enemy. It's like he's back in Afghanistan!"

"Well, he'd better get rid of them," Lime-Colored Bay Creek Hat said. "Or else Governor and Bitsy Corter will never come back."

"You've just *got* to host a fundraiser, Tamsin," Bronwyn said. "Ginny's focus was on youth issues. Peanut-allergy research, campaigns to reduce added sugar levels in kids' foods, eating disorders. Of course, you don't have to adopt Ginny's agenda, but there really are some emerging youth issues capturing a lot of attention. Before he was fired, the headmaster at Digby Day brought in a child psychologist to talk to parents about boys who take pictures of their genitals on iPhones and text them to girls. Aside from the fact that this can get our sons expelled and derail the college admissions process, it's an actual psychological disorder—called narcissistic exhibitionism—that's brought on by stress and anxiety. And get this: the incidence of this disorder among affluent boys who attend elite private schools is almost *three times* the national average."

There was a collective gasp.

"Given the pressure to be perfect these kids are under, is it any wonder so many of them are acting out?" Lime-Colored Bay Creek Hat lamented.

"Tamsin, you could really make a difference by hosting a party," Tangerine-Colored Pinehurst Hat agreed.

I finished my Kale Koncoction, folded my hands in my lap, and smiled pleasantly. "I'll think about it." Standing, I slung my leather tote over my shoulder and grabbed the key to my new Chevy Suburban off the table. "You will have to excuse me, ladies. But I'm late for an appointment. *Ciao!*"

37.

"I've never seen so many monster trucks," observed an awestruck Cleet. "There must be a thousand of them out there."

"Or Johnnies-on-the-Spot," I added.

"If my mother were alive, she'd be appalled."

We were at Derbyshire Farm, off to the side of the concert stage, on the VIP deck. The elevated concert stage erected for our fundraiser was the size of an Olympic swimming pool. The band was set up on an industrial-sized Lazy Susan, rotating slowly so audience members on all sides could see them.

"How many people you think?"

"Every bit of twenty-five thousand," Cleet said. "The handicapped section alone has what looks like a thousand wheelchairs. I'd guess another five thousand on the bleachers. And all those families and kids milling about."

"Good thing we have two thousand acres."

"Where did you find all these people, Tam?"

"We posted signs at gas stations, in bars, on factory floors, at 4H Clubs, post offices, truck stops, government services buildings, beauty parlors, VFW halls, hospitals, and doctors' offices." My eyes scanned the property: food trucks, pie-eating contests, caricature artists, and face-painters, bingo tables, and vintage car clubs. I saw a row of fully restored El Caminos: gleaming black ones with white racing stripes on the hood, menacing red ones with black racing stripes on the hood, ice blue ones, orange ones, silver ones, white ones. The vintage car club's members were gathered around a keg of beer that stood in the bed of a gold '67 SS396.

"I wish I still had my El Camino."

"That ship has sailed," Cleet said. "You're Tamsin Venables Bland now." He looked down at his watch. "You know we've got to talk to these people at some point."

"I can't wait to."

Cletus IV stood on a chair in front of me, surveying the crowd. He wobbled as he pointed at a six-foot-high Plexiglas booth, filled halfway with water. Dr. Davis Warren was sitting in a collapsible chair, just above the water line. "It's called a dunk tank," I told my son. "You throw a ball at the target and if you hit it, Dr. Davis Warren will fall in the water."

"I still can't believe he and Shelby Nash are on this property."

"It's for a good cause, Cleet. And your hundred-year-old Hatfield and McCoy feud was long overdue for a resolution."

Cleet IV giggled and tried to jump out of my arms. The chance to watch an adult plunge into a tank of cold water was too much temptation to resist.

"Look over there," Cleet said. One of the beer tents was collapsed. "Second one today. Too many people storming the kegs at once," my husband lamented.

I radioed security and instructed them to check in on beer tent No. 137.

When Cletus IV saw the aircraft swoop down from the top of the mountain, he gasped.

The chopper lowered, wind whipping the grass and tree

branches nearly in half. Hands clutched hats as revelers dispersed in every direction, beer splashing out of cups as they ran.

"The governor is already here. Who else were we expecting to arrive by chopper?" I asked.

Cleet III grinned slyly. "You'll see."

The chopper doors opened and out stepped General Loehr, followed by Major Psotka and Private Second Class McKim. General Loehr and his entourage were ushered to the VIP area. Cletus and the men had a sentimental reunion while I stood quietly to the side, pretending not to know them at all, as I was still, technically, A.W.O.L. from my post in Afghanistan.

"And you must be Mrs. Bland," General Loehr said, sizing me up. The general looked over at my husband and nodded approvingly. "You have chosen well, colonel."

"Believe me, general, when I tell you that Tamsin chose me." Cleet looked at me and winked.

Fearing they might recognize me, I decided not to chat up Major Psotka and Private Second Class McKim, despite my curiosity about their new assignments in Washington.

The general pulled Cleet off to the side. "I honor you for hosting this fundraiser, Cleet. You've invited the salt of the earth into your home, and that's a generous thing to do," he said as the men lit their cigars. The general drew in three deep puffs and inspected the tip. When satisfied with its glow, he continued: "But whatever you do, keep your wife and child up here in the VIP area. That's one hell of a motley crew out there. Ex-soldiers, yes. But a lot of rough stock out there, too, from the looks of them." The general leaned in to Cleet and lowered his voice. "Walking up here from my chopper and I saw this lunatic woman. She's leaning against the side of this Brink's armored car like it's a streetlamp in the red-light district of New

Orleans, blowing smoke rings. My eye must have lingered for a half second too long, because all of a sudden she starts cat-calling me. Me! A fifty-two-year-old one-star! Stuff about men in uniforms and launching missiles. Then—get this!—she starts shouting this gibberish about her new 'honey pot' and how it's tighter than a drunk cheerleader's on prom night because of some surgery she had. Then she asked me do I want to climb into the back of her armored car and have a 'go?'" The general shook his head. "We're talking bat-shit crazy."

"Would you believe me if I told you that woman who cat-called you was my new mother-in-law?"

The general roared and slapped his thigh. "I miss having you under my command, colonel. You're the only officer in that wretched place who could ever make me laugh."

I interrupted Cleet and the general's reunion. "Time to get out there and face the music," I said.

When the band stopped playing, we collected Cleet IV from the arms of Da'Shajay, Warren Davis's and Shelby Nash's daughter, who was feeding him way too much peach ice cream, and headed to center stage. The American flags along the perimeter of the stage billowed in the breeze as we walked out. Cleet III hoisted Cleet IV onto his shoulders and the boy squealed with excitement. A tech handed Cleet III a microphone.

"GOOD AFTERNOON, MY FRIENDS, AND WELCOME!" Cleet's voice boomed from the speaker towers, which were wrapped in yellow ribbons. "We're your hosts, the Bland Family."

The audience applauded.

"What do y'all think of the entertainment?"

The crowd roared.

"What do you say I introduce the band?"

Fans hooted and howled.

"On lead vocals we've got a three-time Grammy winner—one for Best Country Solo Performance, one for Best Country Song and one for Best Country Album. Ladies and gentlemen, give it up for the one, the only, Ed Earl Turner."

The crowd cheered as Ed Earl Turner waved and hollered, "God bless y'all!"

"On lead guitar and co-lead vocals is a young man who has placed more than a dozen songs in the Top Forty over his short career, including the number one song in the country this week, the triple-platinum-selling hit single "Merica'. A big round of applause for Cody Codder."

Cody bowed and the women in the audience began to chant, "CO-DEEEE! CO-DEEEE! CO-DEEEE!" Cody picked up a bunch of roses from one of the urns and threw them out into a big herd of ladies. They scrambled for stems.

"On rhythm guitar, and sharing vocal duties, is a Grammy Living Legend Award-winner who needs no introduction. Y'all better show Dusty McGhee the respect he's due!"

The crowd raised their paper cups when eighty-year-old Dusty McGhee tipped his ten-gallon hat.

"Who wants to hear some country music!?" Cleet asked. Applause thundered. "Well, if you want them to play, then y'all got to pay! Here's my gorgeous wife, Tamsin, with more."

Cleet stepped aside and the crowd went as quiet as a possum as I explained why the Wounded Warrior Project deserved the generous support of everyone attending. "We know most folks in our live audience and watching this broadcast via satellite on military bases and in two hundred countries and territories worldwide aren't rich. But you don't have to be a millionaire to make a difference in a veteran's life. Give five dollars, if you can. Or twenty-five dollars. Pledge five hundred dollars if you can pay your bills and don't live in fear that the electricity's about to be turned off." I directed the audience's attention to the fifty-foot-tall fundraiser "thermometer" center stage, which displayed, in real time, charitable donations received from around the world. "We're up to $2,748,263 and if you want to hear Dusty McGhee sing, you've got to get us up to three million. Download the app if you haven't already. You can donate with the push of a button. You've got ten minutes to make it happen!" I cued the tech guy to start the "Profiles in Courage" videos. Every few seconds the thermometer jumped in increments of ten thousand dollars.

When the thermometer topped three million dollars the crowd went absolutely wild. The decibel level rivaled an F-18 at takeoff when Dusty McGhee's booze-and-cigarette-burned voice growled its way through the first verse of "Old Women and Young Whiskey."

Once we were off stage, Cleet and I returned to our duties as hosts, providing refreshments and making introductions up on the VIP deck. We connected General Loehr and his staff with Governor and Mrs. Corter and their daughter, Lucy. The Worthington Country Club yoga brigade, smitten with Senior Trooper Prewitt's and Master Trooper Turpin's physiques, quizzed the governor's security detail about their respective exercise regimens. Our family attorney, Cameron Smallwood, warned Dr. Bernie Goulb, owner of the Scandinavian Skin Spa, about his liability exposure. The yoga ladies' respective husbands, clad as always in creased khaki trousers, gingham shirts, and blue blazers, tried unsuccessfully to make small talk with my two best friends from childhood, Ricky Ray Jeeter and Scooter Skinner, who, visibly smashed, had no idea who invited them to this party, or why, but nonetheless enjoyed mightily the free beer.

Between managing food and beverages logistics with the caterers, getting Dusty McGhee offstage periodically for vitamin shots, and working with the crew to ensure the other musicians remained hydrated, I felt like I was back in the Army.

But as the beer flowed, the crowd got rowdier, and raunchier, by the minute. Security was under strict orders to arrest no one, unless a violent crime was committed. In lieu of arrests and expulsions, a makeshift "drunk tank" was established in the barn, where misting machines cooled hot heads.

We were about six hours into the concert, which began at noon, when I made the call to clandestinely swap out all the kegs with nonalcoholic beer.

The media wanted a piece of me, too.

I was grabbing a slider off the grill when Bronwyn approached and introduced me to a reporter from *Hound & Hammock* magazine, an old friend of hers from Sweet Briar. I set my burger down on a paper plate and shook the reporter's hand. "The terms of the commission were that I would not disclose the designer's name," I told her as she swooned over my dress. "If you print his name in your magazine, he's convinced he'll never work again."

"Just answer me this: did you have it made here in Charlottesville?"

"God, no," Bronwyn chimed in. "Tamsin got it in New York."

"It's just . . . *genius.*" The reporter inspected the stitching and ran her fingers along the hem. "I love that all the flora has been recast in military camouflage. The netting, the fake vegetation, the dust and sand. It's just flawless. Couture Camo: Lilly Pulitzer meets Rambo."

"I told you the detail work was exquisite," Bronwyn added. "And to pair it with the triple strand of pearls. So whimsical."

The reporter requested a tour of the house and a sit-down with me and Cleet for her profile, which I half-heartedly committed to as I watched Cleet, encircled by General Loehr, Major Psotka, and Private Second Class McKim, become absorbed in war stories.

"I hope you'll excuse me," I said, "But I need to check on my son."

I walked over to Cleet. "I need to put Cleet IV down for his nap."

"Ok," Cleet said, half-attentively.

"Where is he?"

"With Shelby and Davis's kids, isn't he?"

I went looking for Da'Shajay, who I found backstage, along with her brother, Malik, Augusta, Brandi, the receptionist at Scandinavian Skin Spa, and Misti, the postmaster's daughter. The kids were having their t-shirts autographed by Cody Codder.

"Where's Cleet IV?"

"With my dads," Da'Shajay said.

But when I finally found Shelby Nash and Dr. Davis Warren, they said they were convinced my son was with me.

I scoured every inch of backstage and the VIP tent. "He's not with anyone," I told Cleet upon my return, trying to sound unworried.

"I'm sure he's running around here somewhere." Cleet was eager to return to his conversation about a recent terrorist attack on a U.S. Army base in Germany, but I wouldn't have it. I pulled him aside. "Do you recall anybody saying they were going to take him up to the house?"

Cleet put his beer down. "No. I just assumed you had him."

"When's the last time you saw him?"

"About an hour ago."

We discreetly assembled a search team—our soldier friends, the governor's security detail, the yoga ladies, and headed out into the crowd. While the band played and the crowd cheered, more security men and women and volunteers were conscripted. We split up into groups, fanning out across the property, combing through the mob in search of a black-haired toddler in a miniature army uniform.

The afternoon sun soon turned into the early evening sun and sunk behind the Blue Ridge Mountains. Cleet radioed me from his side of the property. "We've got about a half hour until dark," he said.

"If he gets sucked into that crowd, we'll never see him until morning. He doesn't come up to the guests' knees."

"I know," Cleet said, worry seeping into his voice for the first time.

The stage lights went on, as did the searchlights mounted on the scaffolding. Their rotating white rays beamed out across the property. No sign of Cleet IV.

I was inside the stables when Major Psotka appeared. "We found him!"

"Praise Jesus," I said, reflexively, despite not having stepped foot in a house of worship since attending the Pentecostal Tabernacle of the Holy Ghost's Testimony church during my girlhood.

"There's only one problem," he said, extricating himself from my embrace and looking me straight in the eye. "He's trapped."

"Like, in a well?"

"Not exactly. Follow me."

We ran towards the foot of the mountain, near the property line, far from the crowd. Major Psotka pointed towards the horizon. "He's out in that pasture, the one that's all fenced off."

"Why hasn't anybody got him?"

We came over the hill and I immediately surmised why: My son stood in the middle of the field, shivering. Above him was a squadron of yellowjackets the size of a cumulous cloud. The wasps swayed and zig-zagged, occasionally dive-bombing in formation.

Senior Trooper Prewitt estimated the colony's number at one hundred thousand.

Master Trooper Turpin said, "If we run out there, they'll go into full-on attack mode. So far, they've left the boy alone."

"Don't move! Stay perfectly still! Do you understand?" Cleet yelled to our son through a bullhorn. He turned to the other men. "We need smoke. A lot of it. If we smoke them out, I can go in and get him."

I evaluated the situation. "We don't have any wind and the fans aren't powerful enough. There are three firetrucks on standby out on 32 Curves. Get them in here. Water will work better than smoke."

"It'll agitate them," Cleet III insisted.

"Bees fly up when sprayed, not down. Trust me, I know this."

"Yes, ma'am," one of the security guys replied.

I ordered the searchlights mounted on the scaffolding be aimed at the yellowjackets.

Cleet IV saw me and cried out.

"Help is coming, baby. Stay still."

The cloud of wasps ascended vertically, in a pillar formation, before dive-bombing, kamikaze-style, at Cleet IV, zipping past his ears and nose, and swooping back upward just as fast.

My boy shrieked.

"I'm going in there!" I screamed.

"No!" General Loehr and Major Psotka each grabbed me by the arm and held me back as I struggled.

"Damn, she's strong," I heard the general say.

The music onstage stopped. We heard the sirens and saw the lights on the trucks as they rolled up the driveway.

"Stay still another thirty seconds and this will be over!" I yelled to my son.

The yellowjackets regrouped, preparing to dive again. Cleet IV started flailing his arms, attracting their attention.

"Stay still!" I hollered.

"Wait for the truck, Cleet!" Governor Corter shouted, but my husband leapt over the fence and ran towards our baby.

The squadron detected motion from a large, moving target and put Cleet III in their sights. Cleet wasted no time and dove atop our son, like a linebacker sacking a quarterback one-tenth his size. Cleet spread himself across the boy, enveloping him fully under his chest and torso, wrapping his forearms and hands over Cleet IV's head.

Within seconds, the entire yellowjacket colony swarmed my husband.

Cleet swatted the wasps at the nape of his neck as they maneuvered their way below collar, between flesh and fabric, and burrowed downward to the small of his back before re-ascending and re-grouping.

The fire trucks were rolling up. "Get those hoses going!" I screamed. The firefighters unspooled the hoses and ran towards the fencing as the swarm commenced its next dive-bombing sortie, this time swarming Cleet's ankles, calves and legs, eventually spiraling upwards into the leg openings of his cargo shorts. He sustained yet another punishing round of stings just as the fire trucks unleashed their first torrent of spray.

The yellowjackets dispersed, flying off to the foot of the mountain.

I leapt over the fence and rushed out to the center of the pasture, where Cleet lay inert, atop Cleet IV, whom we could hear beneath his father, whimpering.

I flipped Cleet over onto his back and my son jumped into my arms, ducking his head below my armpit for cover.

One of the paramedics signaled his comrades on the fire truck. "He's in anaphylactic shock!" The paramedics ran into the pasture with their first aid kits and began stabbing him repeatedly with EpiPens as the few remaining wasps, a dull buzz droning out of them, entered and exited my husband's ears, nostrils and mouth, which was agape, his purple-black tongue swollen with bites.

Three minutes later we were in the general's chopper, swirling above the concert stage, on our way to hospital. Our son nestled in my lap, his face buried in my dress. We were above Worthington Country Club when one of the paramedics shouted, "We're losing him!"

Outside the window I saw the hospital's illuminated helipad, a big cross in its center. "Stay with me, Cleet! Just two minutes to go!"

But as I looked into the blank stare on my husband's face, I knew better. I'd seen that face so many times in combat. The man on the stretcher, on the ground, next to you in the transport. When the strain gives way and the facial muscles go slack. Before the landing skids hit the helipad, he was gone.

"It's over," I said to the paramedics. I stroked my son's head as the chopper powered down.

"We need to get him inside, Mrs. Bland."

"Check his vitals. He's gone."

The paramedic checked, looked at his partner, and shook his head no.

"Can we have a few moments with him, just me and our boy?"

The paramedics and pilots stepped out somberly.

Our boy stared at his father for a moment, and nuzzled deeper into my breast. "Your mama's cursed, child," I said to my son. "Just like her mama—and her mama before her. I thought I could break the spell with you and your daddy. But it's true: We Vaduva women can't keep a man."

"Daddy sleepy," said Cleet IV.

"Yes. Sleeping peacefully, my dark-haired prince. Rub your hand on his cheeks like this." Cleet IV and I laid beside my fallen husband and stroked his still-red, swollen cheeks. I whispered to my deceased husband: "Remember when we were in that food and medical relief convoy in Afghanistan? I told you I saw a prince. A dark-haired prince who'd come out of the desert. The gentlest, kindest, handsomest prince there ever was. And he came."

I pulled the hem of my dress up to my eyes and wiped them. "Until today, my focus had been on our destiny, yours and mine. On true love, on our union." I stroked my husband's hair. "I had not given thought to the second half of my prediction: that our dark prince would also bring despair. My heart is truly broken." I kissed Cleet III's cool, swollen lips. "You were the love of my life. And now you are gone. But I—*we*—must accept that this was our destiny, Cletus Esmond Bland III, father of my child, love of my life, husband of my dreams, for it was, alas, in the cards."

EPILOGUE

"It's so odd to see a beautiful young woman's face under a black veil. Incongruous. The young skin and bright eyes concealed by the black lace," lamented Cameron Smallwood.

We were seated at a burled-oak conference table above High Street, in his law offices. He stirred a packet of sugar into his coffee. "For people with backgrounds like ours, the worth of a life isn't measured by how one occupied him- or herself with daily duties of careers. And certainly not by the pursuit of mundane pleasures like golf or billiards or shooting. The measure of a life is how one coped with, and overcame, ordeals. Cleet had his share. At school, in battle, in nature. He faced, and overcame, each ordeal with grace, culminating in the most profound display of courage and self-sacrifice I have witnessed in my lifetime."

"Cletus IV has big shoes to fill."

"You bet he does, Tamsin." The lawyer ran his short, thick fingers through my son's silky hair. "And I'm sure you will nurture in this young man the values and traditions that have distinguished the Bland family in this community for centuries."

The lawyer next turned to Augusta. "Values and traditions

displayed by the lovely young Miss Bland, whom we are thrilled is back in Charlottesville, where she belongs.

Augusta, on her phone, did not look up.

"Which is why it saddens me deeply," he continued, "that we won't be able to watch either of these young Blands as they transition from childhood to adolescence to adulthood and root themselves firmly in this community." He rolled back in his antique wooden chair. It popped a slight wheelie. "Which brings us to business . . . "

On the table were five rows of documents, original and file copies, all neatly paper-clipped and collated.

"This document establishes the Cletus Bland III Scholarship at the Endicott-Woodland School for Boys." Cameron indicated where I was to initial, sign, and date. I did the same for the funds earmarked for low-income, high-potential students who aspired to attend the University of Virginia and the Virginia Military Institute.

I signed the document establishing scholarships for deceased warriors' children and the cash transfer to the conservation groups Cleet supported.

The lawyer looked anxiously over at Augusta, who was in one of her "moods." "And this," he continued after clearing his throat, "will establish you as the adoptive parent and legal guardian of Augusta."

I looked down at the document. Above my signature line was Ginny Bland's elegant scrawl. I signed, looking over at Augusta, who was photographing her freshly-painted sparkly fingernails and posting the image in social media.

"Next up we have the matter of the transfer of the house." Cameron exhaled heavily and lowered his head, pinching his temples with the thumb and middle finger of his hand. "As your attorney, Tamsin, I must, for the one hundredth time, advise you that what you're doing is beyond—"

"—I'm selling the house to Shelby. It's settled."

"But, Tamsin. This is a property valued at $19 million dollars! You realize of course that more than a dozen Bland relatives are already lining up to sue you. And I'm confident a judge will very seriously entertain their claims that you are mentally unfit when he learns you are selling it to Mr. Nash for one dollar."

"It's settled, Cameron. Show me where to sign."

Cameron shook his head slowly.

After I signed and initialed, Cameron rose and asked to be excused. "I've never witnessed $19 million vaporize purposely with the stroke of a pen. Give me a minute, won't you, Tamsin?"

Augusta, head buried in her iPhone, was now swiping through photos. Cleet IV resumed his play, arranging his Army Ranger action figures around the plastic tanks, Humvees, and aircraft on the conference table. He whisked the Humvee across the table and it went airborne before it crashed into a credenza.

"You idiot!" Augusta shouted without looking up from her phone.

"Don't talk to your brother that way!"

"You always take his side!"

"Quiet, both of you!"

Cameron returned. I could smell liquor on him.

"After giving the house away, liquidating all assets, and paying your tax obligations, that leaves you with an estate valued at approximately $51 million."

Augusta looked up, her mouth agape. *"Whoa!"*

"This is none of your business, young lady. Get back on your phone and forget you heard that."

"Initial here . . . here . . . and here. And kindly sign and date here." He opened a manila folder. "A cashier's check in the full amount, Tamsin. Don't lose it." He handed it to me.

I folded the check and tucked in my purse.

"So where you going?" Cameron asked.

"I'm going to build a cabin on the New River in West Virginia. Live the simple life."

Augusta looked up at me for the first time and rolled her eyes. "Over my dead body."

"We'll talk about that later, Augusta," I said.

Cameron leaned over the conference table, palms down, looking straight into my eyes. "How will you occupy your time?"

"Get a job. I don't like being idle."

Cameron winced. "A job?"

"I'm good at fixing cars."

"My friends will be impressed," sniffed Augusta.

"Oh," is all Cameron said before he added, "I see."

He glanced over at Augusta and Cleet IV, then back to me. "To be perfectly honest, I wasn't so sure about you when you and Cleet first married. Nothing personal, of course, it was just you, um, not being from here and all." He fiddled with the cap on his fancy lacquered fountain pen. "But I've come to respect and admire you deeply, Tamsin—more than the other women I've met in this town."

"Are we *done* yet?" Augusta asked.

"May I have a word with you in private?" my attorney asked.

"You and Cleet IV go outside, Augusta. I'll meet you in a few minutes in the park across the street."

Augusta huffed towards the door.

"Aren't you forgetting something?" I said.

"What?"

"Your brother."

Augusta grabbed Cleet IV by the wrist and yanked him out the door.

After the kids exited, Cameron said, "I hope you don't mind my saying, but I don't think West Virginia—the slow lane, the simple life, call it what you will—is going to suit you. Cleet was always cagy when he discussed you, but he said you are a woman of action. A woman with about three times as much adrenaline as the average person. Whenever we were golfing he was always using words like 'fierce' and 'unstoppable.' He actually called you 'a force unrivaled in nature.' In the short time I've known you and witnessed how you operate under the most extreme stress imaginable, I'm prone to agree. Forgive me if I'm over-stepping my bounds, Tamsin, but I just don't see you fixing cars or reading books on your front porch rocker."

Remorse and regret, which I had kept at bay, began to sweep over me as I contemplated the life that might have been with my now-deceased husband. I was bracing for the burden of new life as a single mother—like my mother and all the women in my bloodline before her. I rose and walked over to the window, presenting my back to him. I felt the tears coming. "I've had enough excitement to last several lifetimes, Cameron. I'm due for a rest," I mumbled as I gazed down on the park bench where the colonel first told me he loved me. Cleet IV and Augusta were fighting over who got to sit where. "Can we wrap things up, Cameron? I want to collect the kids. Leave this office, leave this town, and start a new . . ."

And then I noticed the car idling below me, on High Street. "Come over here, Cameron."

The attorney stood beside me.

"See that Chevy Tahoe?"

"The green one?"

"That's the one. When I leave here, the men in that vehicle will call on you."

"Oh?"

"Is it true that, as my attorney, you're under no obligation to answer their questions?"

"Are you in some kind of trouble, Tamsin?"

"Please, Cameron, just answer the question."

Cameron explained something called "attorney-client privilege," and assured me the day's proceedings would remain *strictly* confidential.

"You're to tell them one thing, and one thing only. Are you listening?"

"Yes, Tamsin," Cameron said as he plucked a handkerchief from his pocket and dabbed his forehead.

"Tell them me and the kids are off to Gstaad."

"Gess-*what*?"

"Gstaad," I enunciated. "It's a town in southwestern Switzerland. Where will you tell them I'm going?"

"Gstaad."

I swept Cleet IV's toys into the Gucci tote bag Cleet insisted on buying me in Corfu. And headed for the exit.

The last thing I was going to do was pretend I didn't see them, a sure admission of guilt.

On High Street, I was applying a coat of lipstick as I breezed past the windshield of the Tahoe, cocked my head in its direction for a nanosecond, then, freezing in my footsteps, executed a dramatic double take. I dropped the lipstick tube in my tote, smiled broadly and approached the vehicle's passenger side. The window lowered. "General Loehr," I said, "what a pleasant surprise!"

"Hello, Mrs. Bland. May I call you … *Tamsin*?"

"Of course."

"I believe you and I have met before, too," I said to the general's driver. "You were at our Wounded Warrior benefit if I recall. You are *Major…*?"

"Psotka." The major smiled. "I remember you, too … *ma'am*."

"How'd you know he was a major, Mrs. Bland?"

The general's tone was playful, but it was clearly a trick question intended to flush me out as a soldier. I giggled. "I was married to a United States Army colonel, general. And my father served in the British calvary. He rode in Earl Herriman's Light Dragoons. I was taught at a very young age that if a soldier expected to survive in *any* army, he needed first to know how to deploy his weapon—and second, how to identify a soldier of higher rank."

"Are we, like, *ever* going home?" said Augusta as she stomped towards the vehicle. "Or are we supposed to stay in this stupid park forever, like homeless people?"

"Both of you say hello to your father's friends."

After the general and the major, who did not communicate naturally with children, struggled to engage Cleet IV and Augusta in small talk, I said, "It was so nice seeing you both. "But, sadly, you'll have to excuse me now, as I'm late for an appointment. I do, however, hope we'll soon meet again."

"Oh, something tells me we will," the general said flatly. Then he repeated himself: "Something tells me we will."

As I ushered the children away, a bit too hastily, I worried, I merely waved, refusing to utter my customary *"Ciao!"*—the stupidest word I had ever been forced to learn.

A Humble Request

V.J. Fitz-Howard would be grateful if you'd publish an honest review of *On the Hunt*—even if it's just a sentence or two—on one or more of your favorite platforms.

Tami's Next Stop:

CHARLESTON!

The most highly decorated female combat soldier in U.S. Army history has a new mission!

After she infiltrated high society in Charlottesville, Virginia, the formidable master sergeant reckoned she had retired from military life. But in *Shrimp & Grit*, our heroine is called back to active duty. Her mission: Rescue Augusta, her snooty 18-year-old step-daughter, from the clutches of Charleston, South Carolina, socialites who turn to sex-trafficking to fund their extravagant lifestyles.

Accompanied on her mission by a tall, dark and handsome FBI agent, Tami hunts down her daughter's captors, and applies an outrageous array of "enhanced interrogation techniques" to acquire the intel required to locate Augusta—before the girl's virginity is stolen.

In the process, Tami's heart will be stolen, too. Will she finally break the romantic curse that has bedeviled the women in her family for generations?

Order your copy of *Shrimp & Grit* today!

Made in the USA
Monee, IL
04 December 2022

19555100R00171